THE PRINCE

THE PRINCE OF WALES

JOHN WILLIAMS

BLOOMSBURY

Acknowledgements

Thanks to my agent, Abner Stein, my editor, Mike Jones, and copy-editor, Sarah-Jane Forder. Thanks also to Phil John, Des Barry, Jim Hawes, Anna Davis, Niall Griffiths, Boro Radakovic, Colin Midson, Rosemarie Buckman, Sean Burke, Peter Finch, Richard Thomas, Jon Gower and Pete Ayrton. Thanks always to Charlotte. Special thanks to Mike Hart, without whose guidance and encouragement I would not be writing the books I am, and who will be greatly missed.

Note

This novel is set in a city called Cardiff that broadly resembles the real one, but it isn't a guidebook; now and again history and geography are played around with for fictional purposes. For instance the demolition of the Custom House pub has been delayed by a couple of years. And of course the people who inhabit this fictional Cardiff should not be confused with the fine upstanding citizens of the real one. All the events depicted herein are entirely fictional.

First published 2003
This paperback edition published 2004

Bloomsbury Publishing Plc, 38 Soho Square, London W1D 3HB

A CIP catalogue record for this book
is available from the British Library

ISBN 0 7475 6829 4

10 9 8 7 6 5 4 3 2 1

All papers used by Bloomsbury Publishing are natural, recyclable products made from wood grown in well-managed forests. The manufacturing processes conform to the environmental regulations of the country of origin.

Typeset by Hewer Text Ltd, Edinburgh
Printed in Great Britain by Clays Ltd, St Ives plc
www.bloomsbury.com/johnwilliams

For Abner

Bobby Ranger was sat in the back of the cab waiting for her girl, Maria, to get the chicken and chips from the Red Onion. She looked out at Caroline Street, a sixty-yard stretch of chippies and shops selling army surplus or dirty mags, populated this time of night by very drunk people trying to get a little ballast into their stomachs and even drunker people busy unloading their stomachs into the gutter. Still and all, Bobby felt at home on Caroline Street. It was a single defiant blast of seediness in a city that was getting slicker by the month.

What was happening to the city was rubbing out Bobby Ranger's life. Five years back she had a routine. It was simple. Get up in the morning, sort out your domestic business: shopping, whatever. Midday you'd hit the Custom House, get your girl out there on the street, working the lunchtime beat, while you sat inside having a laugh, game of pool. Back to the pub again in the evening. Then, soon as your girl had made her corn, you'd head off, get something to eat – Red Onion, Taurus Steak House – then down the docks to the North Star, little club full of ship guys, lesbians, prostitutes and queers. Stay there chilling out, dance, fight, whatever. Maybe your girl'd do a couple of the ship guys, she was still sober enough. Chuck you out at three thirty and then it was home to bed or down the Cabbies Club if you was in the mood.

It wasn't much of a life, Bobby knew that. It was a bunch of places any respectable person would have run a mile from, fair enough, but they didn't need to go there. It was Bobby's world, one that had accepted her, one she'd been at home in, one where people let her be.

But step by step all the nice respectable people were taking it away from her. First they took the North Star, knocked it down so they could build a shopping mall. Right down there in the docks. She couldn't believe it when she'd first heard about it, thought they were taking the piss, but now there it was – Mermaid Quay – and all of a sudden it wasn't the docks, it was somewhere called 'the Bay' – rebranding was the word – like Opal Fruits changing to Starburst.

And now they were going to demolish the Custom House. Three more days and it was closing its doors for good. Jesus, how much of her life had been spent in there, listening to the jukebox, playing pool, drinking cans of Breaker cause everybody knew you didn't want to drink anything on draught, watching the girls and the punters, watching your back when the other pimps were about. It had been her workplace for nearly twenty years and now they were tearing it down to build something called Bute Square, a nice big roundabout with a bunch of bloody office blocks around it.

All her life the city had left the docks alone. Whatever went on down under the bridge, people turned a blind eye. Then all of a sudden someone somewhere decided there was money to be made out of tarting up the docks and they were just going to flush the Custom House out of existence.

So what was she going to do? To be honest, she hadn't a clue. One thing you didn't find a lot of in the pimping and prostitution business was career planning. You lived for the night. Never saved, never thought about tomorrow if you could avoid it. Once or twice it struck her that she was making a fair bit of money by anybody's standards: hundred quid a night, two hundred even. What was that a year? Plenty. Tax free and all, but where had it gone? Up her nose, up her girl's nose, cabs and drinks and takeaways. Any time there was anything left over there would always be fines and payoffs to take care of that.

So what now? Most probably she'd do what she always did – wait till the worst happened and take it from there. For tonight, though, she knew what she was going to do. Forget about it. Have a good time.

Maria got back in the cab, one hand already raising the chicken to her lips.

'You want some chips, Bob?'

Bobby shook her head. 'Where you fancy going then?'

Maria shrugged, kept on stuffing the chicken into her mouth.

'Hippo?' said Bobby.

Maria nodded, kept on eating. Two minutes later the driver, Len, dropped them off outside the club. Maria dumped the remains of her takeaway in the bin and Bobby led the way inside. Karl was on the door as usual so he didn't charge them and they headed upstairs towards the rhythm. Half two in the morning and the place was rammed. Big black room full of all sorts; plenty of students and kids, of course, but a lot of older faces too, people Bobby had known for ever: docks boys, city boys. Didn't take a moment to get sorted; everyone knew the Hippo was the place to go for that. Maria was off on to the middle of the dance floor straight away. Bobby stood by the bar letting the music wash over her, letting the E take the edge off, gazed around her, saw Mikey Thompson all over some girl looked like she'd come out in her underwear, smiled to herself and wondered why the night ever had to end.

2

Pete Duke was trying hard to have a good time. After all, that's why he'd done it, wasn't it? That's why he'd walked out on his whole life, so he could have a good time. Well, here was his chance.

Pete was stood at the bar on the second floor of Clwb Ifor Bach listening to what might or might not have been deep house, he wasn't sure. House was about where Pete had lost track of dance music, somewhere in the mid-Eighties. Back then house seemed to be fast gay disco music from Chicago; now it seemed to be more a lifestyle choice than a kind of music and there were about three hundred different varieties of it. Still, he was pretty sure that this was deep house, that's what it had said on the poster outside, and it had a lot of bass and nothing whatsoever that approached a song so he figured he was probably right. Deep house. Fine. Cool even.

The people he'd come with were having a good time. Dan, Guto, Liz, Angie and Angie's friend who he supposed he was probably meant to be checking out but so far he hadn't said a word to and couldn't even remember her name. They were all dancing and laughing and generally acting like this was the finest time you could possibly have. Course that almost certainly had something to do with the pills they'd all taken in the pub beforehand. He was starting to regret not joining in now, standing there drinking a bottle of Budvar watching all the young people having a good time. Not that they were that young really, you looked closely. Lot of them past thirty. It was just he couldn't help feeling like sad dad at the disco. Hardly surprising really, seeing as he had two teenage kids. Actually that had been his big dread, running into Becky and her boyfriend – whatever he was called. Like 'Hi, Dad, what on earth are you doing here?'

'You all right?'

It was the girl, Angie's friend, yelling in his ear. Obviously he wasn't doing much of a job of looking like he was having fun.

'Yeah,' he said and then, for want of anything else to say, 'you want a drink?'

'Thanks. Bottle of mineral water.'

Pete ordered it along with another beer for himself, staring at his reflection in the mirror behind the bar, seeing a tall fresh-faced bloke with short wavy brown hair, good-looking he supposed, though he'd never really made much of it. The drinks came and he turned round, aware that he was getting drunk in a decidedly unpleasurable, already-feeling-the-headache-and-anticipating-the-hangover kind of way.

'Ta,' she said, then, 'I'm boiling, let's go out by the stairs.'

Pete shrugged and followed the girl out to the relative quiet of the stairwell, still racking his brains for her name. She was nice enough looking: late twenties, mid-length black hair looked like she was growing out a short haircut heading for long, little bit on the heavy side maybe but better than being a stick insect, a strong face, looked like the kind of girl knew what she wanted and mostly got it, and what the hell was her name? Angie came into the pub with her, said hello to Pete and then, 'This is my friend . . . Kim.' That was it.

'So, Kim,' he says, standing at the top of the stairs watching a couple on the next landing down get seriously intimate with each other, 'how d'you know Angie then?' Christ, smooth line or what.

'Ange?' she says, flicking her hair back out of her eyes. 'We were in college together, though I didn't really know her then, but her boyfriend used to go out with my flatmate and then when I started at the BBC I saw her about a bit cause she was working for the Assembly before she started with you lot,' she paused briefly to take a breath, 'but anyway really I know her cause we both joined the same gym on the same day and it was like oh God it's you, yeah?'

'Yeah,' said Pete, wondering if it was just the E or she always talked like that.

'So how about you?'

'Well,' said Pete, 'I work at the *Post*, you know, with Angie.'

'Yeah,' said Kim, 'Ange said. Are you new?'

'No,' said Pete, 'I've been there fifteen years.'

'Christ,' said Kim, 'so how come I haven't seen you before?'

'Well,' said Pete, 'I was married.'

'Yeah,' said Kim, 'so?'

So indeed. How to explain it? Seventeen years of marriage, and after the first year, once Becky was born, he'd been out at night on his own maybe twice, and both times there'd been hell to pay. Viv, his ex-wife, had done her nut. And he had decided that it wasn't worth it, seeing his old mates, if it pissed Viv off that much, plus none of them had kids, they didn't know what it was like. So sixteen years and the only times they went out was to see Viv's parents, Viv's sister, Pete's parents, Pete's sister. And it wasn't like they were unusual. None of the people in the close did anything much different. Julie and Duncan next door, they literally never went out. Sixteen years.

'So,' said Pete, aiming for light, 'so I've stopped being married.'

Which was about as good a way of putting it as any. That was all it was really; it wasn't like he and Viv had had a big bust-up or anything, it was just he woke up one morning and thought there's no need for this any more, this marriage thing. The kids are fine, not even kids any more, Viv's fine, the house is paid for, more or less, and I'm bored out of my mind and if I don't want to become a complete bloody vegetable I am going to have to stop being married.

'Oh yeah,' she said, 'well, good for you . . . Sorry, I can't remember your name.'

'Pete.'

'Yeah, good for you, Pete,' she said and tipped the remains of her water over her head. 'You going back in?'

'No,' said Pete, 'I think I'd better get going.'

'Oh for Christ's sake, mun,' said Kim, 'I thought you said you stopped being married,' and with that she grabbed him by the arm and practically dragged him on to the dance floor. And once he was there and stopped thinking about how much he hated this music, it was actually kind of OK, you just had to surrender to it. So he did and after a while even loosened up enough to try a few little moves, things his feet remembered from twenty years ago. Probably he looked like an idiot but no one seemed to mind, and then it was later and he was back at the bar ordering another beer and a water and he was telling Kim about his job, how he was the features editor, oh and motoring editor every Thursday afternoon, and then all of a sudden Kim was saying c'mon, this place is closing now, you want to come to the next club and Pete just laughed, no way was he going anywhere else, he was suddenly somewhere beyond tired, and told Kim he really really did have to go this time and she said good to meet you like she really meant it and told him to give her a ring at the BBC and Pete smiled and said sure and walked down the stairs on a bit of a high.

Which lasted all the way out the door and on to Womanby Street before the night air seemed to chill not just his bones but his soul and a wave of sadness swept over him. What the hell had he done? Where was the excitement in being alone at night in the city heading back to nothing but an empty bed?

Pete was woken up at six by the sound of Randall coughing in the next room. Not just any old coughing, mind, but the kind of coughing fit that sounded terminal. Par for the course if you'd been smoking God knows how many fags a day for the past fifty years. But still, Jesus, the sound of it. Not that Pete could complain. Robert Randall, the *Post*'s senior reporter, had done Pete one substantial favour, letting him stay here.

He'd certainly landed on his feet. Westgate Mansions was a grand old Thirties mansion block made you feel like you were in some pre-war movie every time you walked in there. Great views of the city and not the sort of place Pete would ever have imagined living in if Robert Randall hadn't extended the hand of friendship those first couple of days after Pete moved out and was staying in a guest house on Newport Road.

So, yeah, if Randall's coughing woke him up Pete was hardly going to complain. Instead he buried his face in the pillow, tried to get back to sleep. Wasn't easy; this was always the time he missed Viv, waking up next to her in the morning, a warm sleeping body next to you, it was just an inexpressible comfort. Just another heart beating close to yours. He missed that. That and the sex of course. Funny, really: the sex had carried on regardless. God knows who she was thinking of when they were doing it but it had never been a problem and now he missed it.

Been a month now and he hadn't had the glimmer of any action. His mates on the paper had all been joking about how he was going to have the time of his life now he was single again, girls all like older fellers, blah blah. Well, maybe it was just he was out of practice. Truth of it was he'd never been much in practice. He'd hardly been Mr Loverman before he'd got together with Viv. Like she always said, if she hadn't come up to him and asked him out the first time he'd still be living with his mam. Jesus.

Still, there was that girl last night. Kim. He had her number and he would ring her, definitely. Just a question of when, really. Was it too keen if he rang her today? Almost certainly. Anyway she'd probably be in a right old state today. Probably hadn't even got to bed yet. Just the thought made Pete groan involuntarily and wrap himself tighter in the duvet, glad to have had at least some sleep and a hangover that already felt manageable.

That was another thing he'd had to get used to all over again – drinking. After years of a bottle of wine lasting a week and having a headache after a couple of beers with Viv's dad, all of a sudden he was hanging out with Robert Randall who was firmly established in the pro drinking leagues. But unlike womanising, he'd managed to adjust to the drinking easily enough; rather ominously so, in fact. Sitting in the Old Arcade with Randall at lunchtime or in the Cottage of an evening, he could see a rather scary vision of his future – a geriatric hack with an Irish tan and an outsize beer gut whose only sexual encounters were strictly commercial.

Not that Randall was like that. Randall at sixty-two was a cove with sparkling blue eyes, a shock of white hair and lines that looked mysteriously distinguished, given that he'd spent the last twenty-odd years doing nothing more arduous than the occasional vox-pop interview on international days. He also had twice the stamina of most people half his age, let alone someone two-thirds his age like Pete. He never went to sleep before four. He'd roll in from the pub around midnight then closet himself with his ancient typewriter and a bottle of Bell's and Pete would hear him furiously banging away. He never told Pete what he was working on and Pete didn't like to ask; it certainly wasn't his journalism as that was always knocked off in a couple of hours in the morning before the pubs opened. Maybe it was a novel; it was amazing how many journalists had a secret novel in them. All the girls at the *Post* were busy attempting to do *Bridget Jones Comes to Cardiff*, and the younger blokes would always brag on about how they were going to do *Trainspotting Comes to Cardiff*, except right now they were like living the life, man. Pete had even had a go himself – not a *Trainspotting* clone of course, he was hardly qualified to write one of those, but a thriller set in the world of rally driving. He'd really enjoyed working on it for a bit, but Viv would always go on at him to do stuff around the house and he ended up shelving it.

Looking back now, he could see she was jealous of anything took up his time, but then he'd just thought it was normal. But enough of that it-was-all-Viv's-fault crap. Pete knew it had suited him, all that domesticity, all that predictability. The strange thing, and the thing Viv would never forgive him for, was the way it had suddenly stopped suiting him. Strange . . . he thought, then early-morning tiredness swept over him and he gratefully submitted to it.

When he woke up again, just before eight, he could hear Randall coughing once more but this time from further away and the smell of bacon was in the air. Soon he was sat at the table across from Randall, a mound of newspapers between them. Randall was smoking, of course, and drinking coffee, of course. Pete was finishing off two eggs and two rashers of bacon, mopping up the egg with a chunk of stale baguette. Randall had obviously been much impressed by France some time in his youth, as its products seemed to make up most of his staple diet: French cigarettes, bread, cheese, coffee, red wine.

Randall waited till Pete had finished eating, then looked over the top of the *Telegraph*. 'How was your night out?'

'All right,' said Pete, never a great one for breakfast conversation. But Randall wasn't going to leave it there.

'Welsh club, was it?'

'Yeah,' said Pete, 'you know.'

'Bunch of you go, did you?'

'Yeah,' said Pete, 'Dan, Guto, Liz, Ange and a mate of hers.'

'Oh yes, she's a nice girl, Ange.'

'Leave me alone,' said Pete, 'you're sounding like my mother. Anyway, she's going out with Guto.'

Randall shook his head. 'Not yet she isn't.'

Pete's turn to shake his head. 'Oh. Right.'

'Oh right indeed. You could do a hell of a lot worse, I can tell you, Pete boy.'

Pete laughed, looked down at his copy of the *Post*. Here he was being told how the land lies by a bloke who was only a year or two younger than his dad. But then again, when it came to romantic entanglements Robert Randall reputedly wrote the book. How many times had he been married? Five? Six? Whatever, the trouble Pete was finding at the moment was that in a lot of ways he felt like this old pipe-and-slipper geezer – kids practically grown up, about as wild and crazy as a cagoule – and that was the way most people related to him, reliable old Pete. But then there was another side to him coming out now which felt like he was still twenty-three and had been in cryogenic suspension for years.

He leafed through the paper, checked his pages were in order. It all looked OK, the photos had the right names under them, his interview with the ex-rugby player turned TV presenter was present and correct. Fashion page, recipe, token book review, check check check. Sometimes he looked at this stuff of a morning and couldn't remember ever having written or commissioned any of it. It was as though he actually was doing it in his sleep. Maybe his job wasn't challenging enough. He smiled. Of course it wasn't challenging; that was the whole point, the whole way he'd run his life. You could put it on his tombstone –

Pete Duke: he ducked life's challenges. He put the paper down. Time to start another day of it.

'You ready to go?' he asked Randall. Like he always did. And Randall shook his head like he always did. 'Be along a little bit later,' he said.

3

Bobby Ranger was in Asda's thinking bad thoughts about Maria. Like how come it was always Bobby got up in the morning, got Jamal his breakfast, took him to school? How come Lady Muck got to lie in bed snoring like a bloody heifer cause she's drunk God knows how many Moscow Mules the night before? Come to that, how come it was Bobby in Asda's checking out the two-for-one offers on oven chips and remembering to get some more bubble bath?

It was a joke was what it was. There was her, meant to be this evil mean bloody pimp, and yet she spent all her bloody time running round for a lazy cow, only ended up being a hustler cause she was too bone bloody idle to do a proper job. It was time Bobby got a few things sorted out.

She left the trolley where it was, next to the frozen-foods aisle, and wandered over to have a look at the clothes. Clothes in Asda weren't too bad. Coming to a bit of a pass, mind, when you started looking at the clothes in supermarkets thinking they're not too bad, but that was getting older for you. Anyway mostly she just ended up buying stuff for Jamal. But Bobby didn't begrudge that; she loved Jamal, loved buying him things, liked to see him look smart when she took him into school.

So there she is looking at these kids' jean jackets and thinking they're actually pretty nice and they've got them right up to teenager's sizes, so she tries one on herself, then looks in the mirror and sees herself there – a short but stocky 38-year-old woman, light brown skin and freckles, her hair still in the same short locks she's been wearing since the dawn of time, and she knows she really does still look like a teenage boy, but today she kind of wished she didn't, wished she looked her age. So she takes the jacket off and hunts for one in a little-kid's size, thinking Jamal'd look nice in one of them even if wasn't that practical if it rained or whatever, when someone taps her on the shoulder and she turns round and there's Mikey Thompson.

'Mikey,' she says, 'hell are you doing here?'

'Easy, Bob. You like that jacket?'

Bobby shrugged.

Mikey looked at the price tag. £19.99.

'Tenner, Bob?'

Bobby did her best to suppress a smile. 'Nah,' she said, 's'not that nice. Fiver maybe.'

'Fiver? What are you talking about, girl? You think it's worth risking getting nicked for a bloody fiver? Fuck off.'

Bobby paused; she still had a hundred quid left over from last night. What the hell. 'All right,' she said, 'tenner.'

'Sweet,' said Mikey. 'So how's your girl Maria?'

'Same as,' said Bobby, 'and you keep your hands off, right.' Mikey'd had a go at pimping once or twice over the years, always ended up with some girl giving him a good slap.

'Christ, Bob,' said Mikey, acting all injured, 'what d'you take me for?'

Bobby was just about to reply when she noticed that sometime in the last thirty seconds Mikey had made the jacket vanish. Calmly he led the way over towards the lingerie. 'Anything else you fancy, Bob?'

Bobby laughed; she wasn't a lingerie kind of girl. 'Later, Mikey,' she said, 'got to finish my shopping.'

'Sure,' said Mikey, 'you catch me in the Custom House later on, yeah, I've just got a couple more orders to fill.' He paused.

'Yeah, Bob,' he said, 'last day this week, isn't it? Where you going to go?'

'Search me, Mikey,' said Bobby, 'search me.'

'Yeah well,' said Mikey, 'long as they don't search me.'

Bobby laughed and walked back over to the food section shaking her head. Mikey Thompson was one of those people, no matter what they did – and he was always trying to pull shit – you just had to laugh. Partly it was his size, hardly any bigger than her five two, partly it was just the way any time you saw him didn't matter how pissed off with life you were you couldn't help smiling. Anyway, that was Mikey. And he was a damn good shoplifter, no question about that.

She was looking forward to giving Jamal the jacket. He was just at the age now, five, that he'd started to notice what he was wearing. She loved buying him stuff, seeing his face light up, all that. Suddenly, as she was reaching around in a giant box of potatoes, trying to find some weren't already going green, there were tears rolling down her face. What was the matter with her? Ever since she'd had the hysterectomy, two years ago now, she'd been like this, crying over nothing. Crying over milk that was so long spilt, it was practically fossilised.

Yeah, sure it was hard when your mum doesn't want you, dumps you in a home. Yeah, it was hard not even knowing who your dad was. Well roll over Beethoven, tell him the fucking news.

Bobby wiped her face. Bobby Ranger was damned if anyone was going to see her crying. But what dried her tears from the inside was letting herself say it. Something she'd been brooding on for months now. She was going to look for him. She was going to find her bastard dad. Living or dead, Bobby Ranger was going to find him.

4

Pete was sat at his desk, ten to eleven, just waiting to go in for his regular eleven o'clock with Graham the editor. In front of him he had a shortlist of today's features plus a longer list of possible stories for the future. Central to this was an ever-present wish list of the three or four A-list Welsh celebs that the *Welsh Post* would gladly interview any time they hoved into view. Catherine Zeta-Jones, Sir Anthony Hopkins, Tom Jones. Charlotte Church. Below that was the list of names you actually landed on a good day: Ioan Gruffudd and/or Matthew Rhys, Cerys from Catatonia, Julien MacDonald. Underneath that was the list of people you'd settle for on a quiet news day and to be honest most days on the *Welsh Post* were quiet news days – soap stars, weather girls, sportsmen, TV chefs and all the rest of them. Pete hardly ever did these. He hated doing interviews and Graham was convinced that women made the best interviewers anyway. So he had a couple of girls took care of those, while Pete himself would do most of the think pieces – should the Assembly building go ahead, where to now for Welsh rugby, that kind of stuff. Which more often than not meant simply dusting off last year's article and sticking in a couple of references to something that had been on the TV in the past week.

Was that cynical? Pete didn't think he was a cynical kind of person, just a realist really. The point was that he wasn't dissatisfied; he didn't think he ought to be writing leaders for *The Times*. Far as Pete was concerned he'd done pretty well to get where he was and, if he could do the job in his sleep these days, well so what, better than not being up to it. Plus there were some decent perks; just now, for instance, he was on the phone to the Audi people trying to get them to let him review the new TT over the weekend. That was a little gig he'd secured for himself, motoring correspondent, and he really enjoyed it – every weekend another new motor to try out. It was the one part of the job Viv had been impressed by and all. She liked to see a flash motor parked in their drive, liked to wave at Julie and Duncan next door when they'd head up to the Brecon Beacons for a tryout of a Sunday. Damn, he didn't want to think about that. It was amazing how it was the little things that made you miss being married, just those bloody boring familiar little rituals you never thought twice about at the time.

The Audi PR came back to his left ear, said the car would be fine. Pete said thanks, put his phone down, wondered if he'd be driving it alone.

'Pete.'

Graham calling him in. Pete gathered up his papers, walked into Graham's office overlooking St Mary Street, sat himself down.

'So what've you got for me today?'

Pete handed Graham the piece of paper. Graham scanned it quickly, said, 'Who's Owain Meredudd?'

'Young Welsh artist, Catherine Zeta-Jones bought one of his paintings.'

'Got a picture of them together?'

'Yeah.'

'Good man.'

Graham put the piece of paper down. Editorial discussions didn't take long. They'd both been doing their jobs for what seemed like for ever and Pete knew exactly what Graham was looking for. Pictures of CZJ mostly.

'Anything good in the pipeline?'

Pete shrugged, ran through the list of usual suspects.

Graham sat back, rubbed his chin a bit and generally acted like the great thinker rather than the efficient sub-editor and good man with a budget that he was. Pete braced himself for a suggestion.

'How about a feature on Leslie St Clair?'

Pete raised his eyebrows. This was actually a perfectly solid idea. Leslie St Clair was an interesting man, from what Pete knew about him. Came from the Cardiff docks, been a pop singer in the early Sixties, now he was a publisher and entre-preneur – computer mags and dirty mags. There was repeated talk about him being in the market to buy Cardiff City football club. He was based in London, though, which was why Pete had never got round to covering him before.

'Sure,' he said, 'good idea. I'll put Cherri on to it.' Cherri was Pete's star interviewer; he was sure he was going to lose her to one of the London tabloids before long.

'Great,' said Graham, 'I was thinking for Saturday week, yes?'

'Fine,' said Pete, 'I'll get her on it right away.'

He called St Clair's company, Rival Publications, got on to St Clair's PA and in no time was passed on to the man himself, who seemed bizarrely pleased to be talking to Pete, and would you believe it he was going to be in Cardiff tomorrow so why didn't they meet for lunch, and before he knew it Pete had said yes. Oh well, looked like he'd be doing the story himself. Never mind, he'd been thinking he should get out of the office more. Time to live a little, you know. He laughed at himself but even as he did so he was digging into his wallet till he found Kim, the girl from last night's number. Was it a bit pushy calling her next day? Maybe, but then again Pete figured he wasn't that interesting a guy that you'd remember him for weeks, might as well strike while the iron was warm. He picked up the phone.

5

Half six Bobby and Maria were ready to go to work. At least Bobby was; Maria was still pissing about with her make-up. Little Jamal was running round in circles shouting while *The Flintstones* was on full volume on the Cartoon Network and Maria had some garage nonsense blasting out in the bedroom and Donna the babysitter was chopsing on about her new boyfriend and what a fucking great car he had and if he didn't she'd dump him cause he didn't show her half enough respect, like, and Bobby was thinking she didn't shut up she'd show some real disrespect, right in the gob, and the same went for Maria she didn't get her arse in gear, and oh fucking hell Jamal love could you stop doing that.

'Fuck!' she shouted at no one in particular and stomped into the bathroom where she dug out a couple of Ibuprofens and chased them down with a swig of mouthwash, half of which spilt on the floor, her hands were shaking so much. She sat on the edge of the bath, amazed. She was nervous. Just cause she'd got a little date lined up for this evening, soon as she'd got Maria safely on the beat. She was shaking like a bloody teenager. Actually, cancel that: when Bobby was a teenager she'd had no nerves at all. Balls of bloody steel she'd had back then, little sixteen-year-old black girl going down those hardcore lesbian clubs, Barrells and that, walk straight up to the sharpest girl in the room, ask her how's about it. No, it was getting old fucks you up. Here she was, thirty-eight and shaking cause some pissy little piece worked for the TV had asked her for a drink. Hell was wrong with her? Next thing she'd be feeling guilty. Like she should be sitting at home with her legs crossed while Maria did it with half Cardiff. Bollocks. Still, it had been a while. Four, five years they'd been seeing each other now. On-off, like, at first, but most of the time it had been good. Not so much lately, though. Maria was letting herself go a bit, truth be told. Couldn't blame her, really, what she had to do, but still you didn't keep your standards up in this game you went downhill fast. Bobby knew that all right, seen it happen enough times with other girls.

'Christ,' she said, back out in the living room, 'get your arse in gear, girl. We got a job to do.'

Maria sighed extravagantly but then caught one of Bobby's coldest looks and swiftly got to her feet, went over to Jamal and gave him a big hug and kiss. Bobby followed suit while Maria gave Donna instructions as to what programmes Jamal was allowed to watch before bed, like Donna didn't know from the five nights a week she was usually here, but still Maria liked to feel she was doing the proper mum business.

They parked up round the back of the Custom House, had a quick spliff and Bobby came in with Maria. They had a drink together then Maria went out on the beat and before Bobby had got back to her car she saw a newish Escort pull over and the window wound down next to Maria.

Five minutes later Bobby was at the bar of the Dome in the Atlantic Wharf UCI. Bobby loved the UCI – twelve-screen cinema, bowling alley, restaurants, bars, the worst nightclub she'd ever been in – of course she did. Cardiff loved the UCI; you went there any time day or night it was packed. There it was parked in a bit of old docks wasteland no one had bothered with for decades, like a giant spaceship come to land, and from the start Cardiff loved it. Course Bobby and Maria were some of the few people who could walk there and they'd do that a lot in the afternoon, take Jamal over there after school, let him have a look at the video-game machines and take him to a film there was anything on. Bobby'd buy him loads of sweets from the pick-'n'-mix – most expensive pick-'n'-mix in the known world by the way, don't say she didn't warn you – and it was nice. You know, an improvement of the area, like.

But Bobby wasn't stupid and she could see what it was as well. Another death-knell for the kind of life she knew down there. The street prostitution – how long were they going to let that last down here? And now they had the Assembly. No way all the politicians were going to want to see all that. Not that they weren't regular customers, a few of them, but they liked it all out of sight and out of mind the way the docks used to be. Now, well Christ only knew.

'Hiya,' said a voice beyond Bobby. It was Kim, the girl from the BBC, standing there in all black; trousers and shirt buttoned up to the neck.

'Hiya, darlin',' said Bobby, smiling. 'What're you drinking?'

'Gin and tonic,' said Kim and Bobby waved to Roger the French guy behind the bar and ordered the drink along with another bottle of cider for herself. She didn't usually drink much these days, but she'd got the feeling tonight might be a bit of an exception.

'So,' said Kim, once they'd got their drinks and found a little table right at the back of the bar, 'you want to go and see a film then?'

'No,' said Bobby. 'It's you I was wanting to see.'

Kim giggled and blushed a bit and said, 'Oh yeah, I just thought meeting here . . .'

'No,' said Bobby. 'This is where I live down here, innit.'

'Oh yeah, of course,' said Kim, blushing again.

Bobby could see she was on a winner here already so she didn't say anything, just moved her chair round so she was right next to Kim and put her hand on Kim's thigh.

Kim didn't bat an eyelid, just smiled and waved her hand towards the waiter to order up another gin and tonic – more, Bobby suspected, so she would have an excuse for what she was about to do than because she needed it.

'So,' said Kim once her drink showed up, 'I suppose you'd like to know a bit more about the documentary.'

'Um, yeah,' said Bobby, who to tell the truth had completely forgotten that that was Kim's pretext for setting up this drink. Kim was this girl from the BBC, a researcher. She'd done some story before down the docks, and got to know a few of the people. Anyway Bobby had met her down the Hippo the night before, and Kim was chatting to Maria who she knew from God knows where and Bobby barged in thinking the snotty bitch wasn't stealing her girlfriend and then Maria told her not to be stupid, which normally she'd have given her a slap for but this once she could see she had a point, so Bobby'd got to motor-mouthing away about this and that and the life and Maria'd got bored and gone off for a dance and Bobby got into one about what a great pimp she was and this Kim had got horny for it you could see but she, like, covered it up with all this horse-shit about what a great subject for a documentary – the secret world of the lesbian pimps or something. Course Bobby knew a chat-up when she heard one but now here they were and this Kim wanted to carry on pretending – well, fine. So 'Yeah,' she said, 'what about it?'

'Well,' said Kim, 'are you up for it?'

She was leaning into Bobby now, their cheeks almost touching, and Bobby could feel her squeezing her thighs closer together. Christ, she thought, time to get on out of here and into some private place soonest.

'Yeah,' she said again, 'well maybe. Tell you what, this isn't the best place to discuss that kind of business, you know. How about we go back to mine?'

'Your place?' Kim looked almost shocked for a moment. Bobby wondered what she'd been expecting. A quick one in the Ladies'?

'Or yours, darlin', I don't mind.'

Kim looked suddenly relieved. 'Yeah,' she said, 'that's fine. You want a lift?'

'No,' said Bobby, 'got my car out the front too. I'll follow you like.'

They had just made it out to the car park and Kim had half turned to Bobby, ready to snog her Bobby was sure, when a mobile went off. Bobby and Kim both reached into their pockets but it was Bobby's that was ringing. Maria.

'Quick,' she said, 'I got trouble. Back of Aspro's.'

It took Bobby three and a half minutes to make it down Bute Street to the front of Aspro's Travel Agency – three minutes' driving and half a minute to put Kim off – 'Sorry, love, emergency come up, call me, yeah?' Kim had nodded quickly and Bobby was sure she was in there. Driving down Bute Street, though, she couldn't help feeling like a total bitch.

As she got out of the car she pulled her lock knife out from where she kept it hidden, taped in place under the gear-stick cover. She walked round the back of the boarded-up old travel agency till she came to the alley.

'Ri,' she called. No answer. Bobby kept on walking down the alley. It was pitch dark; there was a street lamp at one end but someone had smashed the bulb out of it ages back. Mostly the girls liked it dark; kept you from having to focus too much on the punter. Personally Bobby liked to keep as far away as possible from the business end of things. You went out with a hustler, you didn't want to know all the details and you sure as hell didn't actually want to see them on the job.

There was still no sign of life in the alley. She came to the point where it dog-legged round to the right and dead-ended in a warehouse. Christ, she was scared now, she had to admit. She turned the corner and called out 'Ri' again. Still nothing. She waited for a moment, letting her eyes adjust to what little moonlight there was. Still nothing, just a few horrible little noises she was sure were rats. Christ, she didn't know how the girls did it, coming down here with some bloke they'd met thirty seconds previous, opening themselves up to the bloke up against the wall. She was almost at the end of the alley now and there was definitely nothing and nobody there. No crazed punter, no Maria lying bloody on the ground. Nothing. Just a door flapping open on the side of the warehouse.

Bobby freaked when she saw that door swing open and she just ran back out the alley, almost falling as she skidded round the corner. As she made it back on to the street she was at the point of hyperventilating. No way was she going in the warehouse. No way no way no way. She'd seen enough movies, shouted enough times at the screen telling the stupid girl not to go in the haunted house on Friday the thirteenth to meet Freddie. She was going to do the sensible thing, get help, ring the police. No way was she a coward, no way no way. She was doing the right thing.

She got out her mobile, cursed One 2 One to hell and back when she couldn't get a signal, then crossed over the road to the Custom House, knowing the payphone wouldn't work but it was an emergency, like, and Peter the landlord would let her use the phone behind the bar.

First person she saw when she walked in the door was Maria standing with a can of Breaker in her hand, arm round Big Lesley.

Bobby walked straight up to her and smacked her one full in the face.

6

Pete was sat at a table in a place called the Cambrian Club along with Robert Randall and a bloke called Gary or possibly Geraint who was a playwright and a girl called Natalie who worked for a film company.

The Cambrian was the place you ran into these kinds of people. Up till three weeks ago Pete had never been there in his life; since he'd been staying with Randall he'd practically become a regular. Not that Randall was particularly bothered about drinking with micro celebs from the Welsh media, but he was certainly fond of somewhere you could get a late drink.

So, round about eleven, they'd decamp from whichever pub Randall had chosen for the evening and walk down leafy Cathedral Road away from the city centre till they got to the short strip of shops that made up the heart of Pontcanna – or 'Cardiff's media village' as it was obligatory to refer to it in the *Post*. Past the shops and you came to the Cambrian which looked like your average wine bar but being a members' club could stay open till all-hours.

Randall wasn't a member, of course, he was just one of those blokes that everyone knew and no one could say no to, so they'd be waved in and Pete would get the drinks in while Randall glad-handed and then they'd end up at a table talking to techies or directors, writers or editors or, as in tonight's case, dodgy playwrights.

Pete had drifted away from the conversation, some typically bloody Welsh argument about Arts Council funding – you took the subsidy out of the arts in Wales you'd have a big fat zero far as Pete could see – but, hey, meanwhile good luck to them. Pete wasn't in the mood for an argument. He was feeling pleased with himself. He'd called up Kim at the BBC, nervous as all get out, and she'd sounded pleased to hear from him and didn't even wait for him to ask, just went, 'You fancy meeting up, then?' and just about gave him time to grunt a yes before telling him she couldn't do tonight as she was on a top story but how about Friday, meet in Ha Ha's about eight, see you, and put the phone down, leaving Pete gazing out the window thinking how simple was that? How different to when he was twenty or so, last time he'd been in this position, when he'd spend for ever faffing about chasing after some girl who most likely didn't want to know. Which sort of explained why he'd ended up with Viv, who clearly hadn't cared what the rules were and had just walked up to him at a barbecue on a Sunday afternoon in 1980 something and kissed him and taken the whole thing out of his hands for which he had clearly been so bloody grateful that he'd married her and spent umpteen years with her.

And then, just to prove that Pete Duke was now the kind of guy made things happen, didn't hang around scratching his arse while the world whistled by, Kim walked into the Cambrian Club.

She didn't see him at first, just walked in by herself, frowning a bit till someone waved at her and she plastered on a smile. She didn't notice Pete till she'd gone up to the bar, ordered a drink then turned round to survey the room. As soon as she spotted him, though, she waved, and moments later she was pecking him on the cheek and squeezing in next to him.

'All right, darlin'?'

'Yeah,' said Pete, 'you know,' and smiled at her and she smiled back and hey, just like that, he thought of something else to say. 'How did your interview go?' Easy.

Kim made a face. 'Started off all right, but went a bit pear-shaped after that.' She picked up her drink that looked like a vodka tonic, took a big gulp. 'Christ, needed that.'

'Yeah,' said Pete, 'so who was it with, what's the story?'

'Christ,' said Kim, laughing, 'I've only known you ten minutes and you're already trying to nick my stories.'

'No, no,' said Pete, immediately embarrassed, 'I didn't mean . . .'

Kim nudged him in the ribs. 'No, only teasing. I don't mind telling you what it is, just don't tell anyone else, specially not anyone in here. Anyway, right, the story is, well basically I met this amazing woman the other night. She's this really tough black woman, right, and I asked what she did and you know what she said?'

Pete shook his head.

'She goes, "I'm a pimp. Top pimp." You believe that? People think of pimps, it's always some big guy with gold teeth and a Rottweiler, not a girl. So I can see it straight away, the documentary title *The Secret World of the Lesbian Pimps* – great, yeah? – and I ask her right out if she'll do it and she just says yeah, sure, and I'm like I don't believe it, what a great story.'

'Christ,' said Pete. 'So was that who you just went to see? Did she do the interview?'

'No,' said Kim, 'that's why I'm in here drinking vodka. I met up with her at the UCI, had a good chat. We were all just ready to go back and do the interview when her bloody mobile goes and she has to charge off somewhere, so I don't know if I pushed too hard and pissed her off or what.'

'Doubt it,' said Pete. 'Probably just had to get back to work.'

Kim frowned. 'Yeah, I guess.'

'So who else are you going to talk to?' asked Pete, getting into this now, thinking how he'd handle a story like this, not that the

Post would be seen dead with something this seedy. 'Are you going to talk to the hookers?'

'Hustlers,' said Kim.

'Oh, right. Anyway, d'you think this woman will let you talk to her girls?'

'I dunno,' said Kim, looking worried, 'it's early days.'

'What about the punters?' said Pete. 'It might be interesting to talk to the punters if you can.'

'Who cares about the bloody punters? This is about women, it's not about some sad old perves.'

'Hmm,' said Pete, not wanting to say that it was the punters that interested him, that he had often wondered what depths of loneliness, what desperate need for human comfort, sent men down to the Custom House, not wanting to say there were four-a.m. times lately when he'd seen this vision of himself in years to come, a grey man in a grey car paying some lost young girl to make him feel joined to humanity for half an hour. Not thoughts you wanted to share with a girl you'd just met, really, and anyway it probably wasn't like that, probably all the punters were married blokes with Vauxhall Vectras and nasty little desires. Except he knew they weren't all like that. Hadn't he been driving past the Custom House years ago, seen a familiar car pull up, seen a girl get in, checked the car's number plate to be double sure it was his cousin Carl, lived with his mam in upper Bargoed, went to chapel every single bastard day of the year. Cousin Carl with his stupid moon face and clothes his mam put out for him. Hadn't he seen cousin Carl take a girl in his car and hadn't he driven round the corner, pulled up his own car to the kerb and put his head in his hands and cried, overcome by the sadness of the world? Of course he had, but it still wasn't anything you wanted to say to this girl you'd just met, so he just smiled and shrugged, and said, 'Still, might be an interesting angle, though.'

'Yeah, maybe,' said Kim, but he could see she'd lost focus on him now; her gaze was wandering past him, checking out who else was in the club. 'Shit,' she said then, her eyes finally resettling on Pete's face, 'you know what I could do with right now?'

'No,' said Pete, his heart suddenly beating faster.

'A nice fat line of Charlie. You don't have any on you, do you?'

'No,' said Pete, feeling an involuntary wave of repulsion, telling himself not to be such a bloody puritan, didn't he read his own bloody newspaper, didn't he know that the young, free and single used drugs with casual ease? 'Sorry.'

'Oh God, your face,' said Kim, and laughed and grabbed his cheek, gave it a quick squeeze. 'Course you don't. Ange told me you were Mr Straight and Narrow.'

Pete started to protest, 'I'm not . . .' but Kim cut him off.

'Course you are. But don't worry, it's all right, makes a change from most of the people you get in here, all – what's the opposite of straight and narrow?'

'Bent and wide?' offered Pete.

Kim laughed. 'Yeah, bent and wide, that's about right. Thing is, though, I'm feeling like getting a bit bent and wide myself tonight, so if you'll excuse me . . .' She stood up then, picked up her drink. And started to move off then thought of something and turned and bent down to Pete. 'I tell you what, though. Friday night, how about instead of Ha Ha's you come down to the Custom House with me? It's the last night before they close it down, be good for my story and should be interesting.'

'All right,' said Pete, thinking that was one weird place for a date but what the hell.

'Cool,' said Kim and pecked him on the cheek, 'see you Friday,' and walked off towards the bar and started chatting animatedly to a tall bloke in a leather jacket, goatee and an earring. Pete saw her whisper conspiratorially in his ear, saw them head off, one a few seconds after the other, up the stairs towards the toilets, then felt an acrid mix of jealousy and disgust – or was it desire? – knot up his stomach.

7

Bobby was thinking. Jamal had woken them up at six and Bobby couldn't get back to sleep, still pissed off with Maria, and she'd got up and made a cup of coffee and was sitting in the living room watching the sun come up from behind the UCI and thinking through her options.

Something had to change. She just couldn't handle things like last night any more. Thinking your girl's been killed in some alleyway. And now with the Custom House on its way out the girls were already looking around, finding a patch here or a patch there, but without the pub as a base it was going to be hopeless.

So what were the options? Well, a lot of girls worked in the massage parlours now, three or four of them around town. And from the girls' point of view it had its advantages. You were inside, for one thing, and you had a bit of back-up any punters started getting funny. On the other hand, though, a lot of the girls didn't like it cause it was a bit too much like having a job, clocking in clocking out, and they'd always be complaining about how the management wouldn't let them have a little smoke on the job, or a little drink, wasn't the laugh you could have in the Custom House.

Other problem, from Bobby's point of view, was Maria went to work in one of them places, what would Bobby's role be? Maria's handing over half her earnings to the management in Dawn's Sauna or wherever, she's not going to be wanting to cut Bobby in after. Unless . . . unless Bobby was the management.

Why didn't she open up her own place? Bobby shook her head. Could she take a step up?

Maria came out of the bedroom then, rubbing her eyes, looking rougher than rough, heading straight for the bathroom. Bobby waited for her to come out then grabbed her.

'Sit down, girl, I got an idea.'

'Not now, Bob, I'm sleeping.'

Bobby grabbed her by the wrist. 'No, you're not. Sit here and listen.'

Maria shook Bobby's hand off. 'Give us a cup of coffee at least.'

Bobby sighed and turned round to the kettle, busied herself making a couple of mugs of coffee while Maria slumped down at the table and lit a fag.

'I've been thinking,' said Bobby, once she'd put the coffee down on the table, her voice a little nervous, 'maybe I could open us up a little sauna–massage place.'

'Where's the money?' said Maria.

'What?'

'Where's the money, you going to buy a place, put the saunas and shit in it. Where's the money?'

Bobby frowned. 'You got to have all that stuff?'

'Course you have,' said Maria. 'You don't have the sauna, the massage tables and that, you think they're going to let you stay open? You don't have that stuff, you might as well hang a red light outside, call it Bobby's Knocking Shop.'

'Yeah,' said Bobby, frowning, 'I suppose.'

Maria sipped her coffee, then brightened. 'Tell you what I've been thinking.'

'What?'

'Lap-dancing. You know up town they got a couple of nights. Was talking to one of the girls in the Cross the other night, said she's making a packet doing it.'

'She shag the blokes afterwards or what?'

Maria shrugged. 'Just dancing. Least that's what she said she did. Said some of the other girls do some extras, like. But they kick you out, they catch you setting something up.'

Maria jumped up, pulled a dancing pose, then bent herself right over and looked back at Bobby from between her legs. 'What d'you reckon? Think I'd be good at it?'

Bobby looked at her, trying to imagine, if she'd never seen Maria before, what she'd reckon. She saw a tallish girl – five seven or so – dark brown hair with a dodgy henna job scraped back in a ponytail, good body, tits a bit small maybe, dunno if the blokes expected the girls to have boob jobs. Still, she had a nice rose tattoo on her left one. Had a couple of piercings too – nothing kinky, just nose and navel. Worst thing was her skin; dead pasty, though what d'you expect you live on chips and Red Bull and vodka and speed? Hurt Bob to acknowledge it but there it was: two years of street prostitution were starting to leave their mark on Maria. She didn't make some changes soon she'd be on the fast track down. And try as Bobby might to tell herself it was none of her business, she knew it was crap. She wanted Maria to come off the streets, it was up to her to make it happen.

'Dunno, girl,' she said eventually. 'Clean yourself up a bit you might have a chance.'

Maria flicked a V-sign at her from between her legs then stood back up and walked huffily into the bedroom. But ten minutes later, much to Bobby's amazement, she was running a bath. Stayed in there for hours too and by the time she came out – after Bobby'd given Jamal his breakfast and was just about to walk him to school – she was really looking dead good – something like the way Bobby remembered her, first time she ever saw her come in the Custom House, back when doing the odd punter was still a bit of a laugh, little top-up for the giro, and not the life.

'What d'you reckon then?' said Maria. 'Think I should give it a go?'

Bobby patted her on the bum, a for-real smile coming unbidden to her lips. 'I'd pay you, girl, I'll tell you that much.'

Bobby headed into town around lunchtime, drove in even though it was less than a mile and probably quicker to walk by the time you'd parked and all, but she couldn't face all the dumb conversations she'd have to have on the way if she walked down Bute Street. She left the motor in the car park next to Toys 'R' Us and started walking up through the Hayes, her head still crowded with thoughts.

One moment she had her mind on business, checking out the new lap-dancing club in town, finding out what the deal was for the girls, next minute she was lost in the past, walking past Halfords looking down the Oxford Arcade and remembering the club they used to have down there – Hunters. First nice-looking gay club they'd had in Cardiff. Before that all the girls used to go to Barrells, just over by the bridge, but they knocked that down and opened up Hunters. Nineteen years old she was then and already queen of the scene. Old before her time, she thought about it now. Nineteen: she'd been running with the City Boys for years, only girl in the soul crew. She'd been in the band too, had the hit record. Thought she was ace. And she was. Had she felt higher than that – nineteen years old in Hunters, Evelyn King singing 'Love Come Down' on the sound system, any new girl walked in the room Bobby knew she could have her.

Eighteen more years past and gone and where was she now? A bastard pimp. Top pimp, though, she'd say that for herself and all the girls would agree. Top pimp with the gold teeth to prove it. Top pimp with two hundred and fifty quid in the building society, a girlfriend who was right on the edge of the skids, right on the edge of a decline Bobby had seen too many times with too many other girls. Top pimp with a hysterectomy two years ago. Top pimp who was tired of the life. Top pimp who felt like sitting down in the Hayes Island Café with a cup of tea and never moving again, letting them roll her into the gutter when the night came down. Let her be, leave her in peace.

Christ, snap out of it. She was Bobby Ranger and she was going to get it together.

Her mobile went off. Disorientated, it took Bobby a moment to remember which pocket she had it in. Finally she snapped it open just before the call got redirected to her voicemail.

'Whassup?' she said.

'Is that Bobby?' said a voice. Female, Cardiff but educated. Kim.

'How you doing, darlin'?'

'I'm fine,' Kim giggled. 'You sort out your problem last night? I was sorry you had to go.'

'Me too,' said Bobby, 'me too.'

'Where are you now?'

'In town, going round Cupid's Lounge.'

'The lap-dancing club? Really? I was thinking of doing a story about that place.'

'Yeah?' said Bobby. 'Why don't you come down, meet me there?'

'Now?'

'No, next week.'

'Well, I don't know . . . yeah, why not? Will there be anyone there?'

'Manager should be there. I knows him a bit.'

'Yeah?' Kim sounded really interested now. 'D'you think he'd mind me coming along?'

'Don't see why, pretty girl like you.'

Kim giggled again. 'No, you know, me being from the TV.'

'Don't tell him,' said Bobby. 'Say you're looking for a job there. Go undercover, like.'

'Oh,' said Kim, and paused. 'Well I'm hardly dressed for it.'

'It's not exactly about what clothes you're wearing, darlin', is it?'

Kim laughed. 'I suppose not. OK, you're on. I'll see you in Ha Ha's in fifteen minutes, all right?'

'Fine,' said Bobby, and smiled to herself. This ought to be a laugh, she reckoned.

Half an hour later and Kim was taking Bobby's arm as they came out of Ha Ha's, Kim's face flushed by the two gin and tonics she'd downed in the fifteen minutes they'd been in there.

Bobby squeezed her arm briefly then removed it. Bobby wasn't one for public displays of affection. Girls from the beat saw her walking arm in arm with an up-herself piece like Kim they'd piss themselves. Any suggestion she wasn't tougher than the rest, she'd have a mutiny on her hands.

The club was in Crockherbtown Lane down the side of the New Theatre. One of those buildings must have been there for ever but you never noticed it before. There was a lorry pulled up outside and a feller lugging beer kegs over the pavement. Bobby and Kim stepped round him and walked into Cupid's Lounge.

Inside it was a typical nightclub by day; all rips in the velvet banquettes and a pervasive stink of beer, fags and cleaning solvents. Marco was stood behind the bar reading the racing page of the *Mirror*.

'All right, bra?' said Bobby.

Marco looked up, then did a comedy double-take. 'Looking for a job then, Bob? Bob a job?' He started laughing at his own joke.

'No,' said Bobby, rolling her eyes, 'but my friend here is. Marco, this is K . . . Kelly.'

'Hi, Kelly,' said Marco, looking Kim up and down. 'You a dancer then?'

'Not really,' said Kim, then paused for a moment before carrying on, 'but I'm good at taking my clothes off.' She burst out in a peal of laughter.

Marco looked at Bobby and raised his eyebrows. Bobby shrugged.

'You done it before then?' asked Marco.

Kim shook her head, said, 'Well, not in public,' and laughed again.

'So you haven't got an agent then?'

Kim frowned. 'What, you need an agent to take your clothes off, do you?'

Marco nodded.

'All right then, Bobby here's my agent, how about that?'

Marco shook his head. 'Sorry, love. Thing is, all the professional dancers we use come from one agency; it's like a contractual thing. Tell you what, though, we're running an amateur night Tuesdays, hundred-quid prize for the best dancer. Why don't you come along to that, love? Feller from the agency'll be along too. You want to do some more, maybe he'll sign you up.'

Kim pouted. 'Don't you think I look good? Why don't I do a dance here for you now?'

Marco put his hands up in fake horror. 'Save it for Tuesday, darling. It's not what I think, it's what Bernie thinks that counts.'

Kim looked all hurt, like she couldn't believe the whole world wasn't dying to see her take her clothes off, but Bobby didn't have time for that.

'Bernie?' she said.

'Yeah, Bernie Walters,' said Marco. 'He's the agent books all my dancers.'

'Fuck,' said Bobby.

'Don't tell me you got a problem with Bernie,' said Marco, grinning. 'Everybody loves old Bernie.'

'Yeah,' said Bobby. 'They don't all love Kenny Ibadulla, though, do they?'

'Bobby,' said Kim, 'what are you talking about?'

'Nothing,' said Bobby, grimacing. 'C'mon, girl, let's get out of here.'

Marco smiled, went back to his paper. 'Tuesday night, Kelly, if you fancy it.'

'Yeah, maybe,' said Kim, then saw that Bobby was already out the door, gave Marco a quick wave and followed after her.

'What was that all about?' asked Kim, catching up with Bobby as she turned down towards Queen Street.

'Old business, old bullshit.'

'Anything I can help with?'

Bobby looked at her, started to scowl then managed a weary smile. How to explain it? Kenny Ibadulla, Bernie Walters – all these fellers had her world wrapped up, left her to feed on the crumbs. Christ, was she tired of it.

'No,' she said eventually, 'I don't think so, doll. Listen, I better go, got business to attend to. You give me a ring, yeah?'

'Yeah, sure,' said Kim, looking a little crestfallen, then brightening. 'Oh, and I'll see you tomorrow, won't I?'

'You what?'

'Last night of the Custom House, remember? I'm going to be doing some filming.'

'Oh right,' said Bobby, 'later then,' and walked off fast before she could say any of the things she felt like saying, like sod your film. Is that all my life adds up to? A couple of minutes' lowlife entertainment for Mr and Mrs Normal at home in front of their TV? Look, love, there's a lesbian pimp, last one left in the wild.

8

Leslie St Clair was a laugh.

Randall had said he would be. Pete had asked him about St Clair the night before, while Randall's memory was still more or less functioning.

'I remember him when he was plain Les Sinclair, before they canonised him!' Randall had said, laughing at his own joke then carrying on. 'Started out as a boxer, mean little lightweight. Didn't like getting his pretty face messed up, though, so he moved into singing. Followed in Shirl's footsteps up to London. Used to do a lot of calypso stuff – watered-down Harry Belafonte, if you can imagine anything more horrible. Your parents probably inflicted it on you as a baby. They'd have the social services round in an instant, you tried anything like that these days. But he was a smart one, all right, old Les, always knew just when to change horses.

'I remember interviewing him years ago when I first started on the paper, must have been 1961, and he'd just done the Royal Variety Performance. And I just asked him so how long d'you think the calypso craze will carry on, just a standard little pat-ball question and I'm expecting him to say the usual shit, I'll be singing calypso till I die, and he just looks at me and says, casual as anything, "Six months, maybe nine. I'm getting out at six, though." And he did.'

'Yeah?' Pete had said. 'So what did he do next?'

'Sort of a Sammy Davis Junior thing, 'cept Les couldn't dance for toffee. Then the Beatles came along and he was at a bit of a loss for a while. Came back a bit with *The Leslie St Clair Rock and Soul Revue* but I don't know many people took him seriously. Course by then he was already diversifying, had his own theatre and everything. Lost touch with him after that. But he's still a good laugh, by all accounts, so you make sure and send him my best.'

It was fast becoming clear why Randall had liked St Clair. For starters, they weren't doing the interview in the Hilton or the St David's or any of the shiny new Cardiff landmarks the celebs usually confined themselves to, but in the Red House, a pub stuck out on the spur between the Rivers Ely and Taff, the last unmanicured bit of the bay, home to a bunch of scrapyards, a down-at-heel yacht club and a boozer that looked a bit posh about thirty years ago but had roughened up considerably in the interim while the rest of the world got smooth.

St Clair was a funny mixture of the two. He was smooth, all right, glad-handed everyone in the pub, but he was rough too in a you-can-take-the-boy-out-of-the-docks-but-you-can't-take-the-docks-out-of-the-boy kind of way.

Anyway, Pete had got there at two, expecting he'd have half an hour tops, and he'd been there for two hours now, on their third round – Pete buying them all, of course; one thing Pete had noticed about the rich was they didn't get that way by putting their hands in their pockets to buy the drinks – and Pete had had to phone Graham twice to say he was going to be late back to the office but not to worry cause he was getting some great stuff. And he was.

God knows how much of it the lawyers would let him use, of course. The stories about Dame Shirley back in the day were definitely not going to be running. Nor the stuff about Tom Jones. Wales didn't have so many cultural heroes that it was ready to see their reputations besmirched. Plus of course Pete was far from sure St Clair was telling the truth. He was the kind of feller liked a bit of mischief-making for its own sake.

Finally St Clair switched the subject to the present. He moved quickly past his computer-magazine business ('Doing fine, course it's a difficult market at the moment, but it's a lean, mean operation') and his often-stated ambition to buy Cardiff City ('Still interested, obviously, but of course Sam's doing a great job') before getting on to what was evidently his current passion.

'The Castle Market,' he said to Pete, 'that's what I'm going to call it. You know where the old Sophia Gardens exhibition centre was? Well, that's where we're going to build it. Assuming our bid's accepted, of course.'

'So what's it going to be?' asked Pete. 'Another shopping mall?'

'No,' said St Clair, 'what it is, and don't laugh, cause in my old age I've acquired a bit of a philosophy – what I call community capitalism.'

'Oh yes?' said Pete, wondering if St Clair was putting him on. 'So what's that then?'

'Let's just step outside a minute,' said St Clair, 'and I'll show you what I mean.'

'OK,' said Pete and they walked out of the pub, leaving their drinks on the table. Outside St Clair led the way to a vantage point where they could look across the bay. He pointed over towards the new development.

'What d'you reckon?' he asked.

Pete looked across the water. He could see the St David's Hotel, Techniquest and the Sports Café, hidden behind which he knew there was Mermaid Quay, with its half-dozen restaurants, bank and comedy club and so-called designer clothes shop. He didn't think anything much about it. He used to go down there with Viv and the kids now and again, for a walk on dead

Sunday afternoons, the girls complaining at being dragged away from the TV, or occasionally a family dinner at Harry Ramsden's or the Sports Café. It was OK.

'It's OK,' he said.

'Yeah,' said St Clair, 'that's exactly what it is. Nice. Nice like OK. Nice like it'll do for a place to go and eat in the evening if you can't face going into town. Yeah, it's nice. How about individual, though? Would you say it was individual?'

Pete thought about it, visualised the Mermaid Quay restaurants, the Bar 38 and the Via Fossa, the flash Italian and the flash Chinese.

'No,' he said, 'I suppose not.'

'No,' said St Clair, 'you're dead right it's not. What it is is off-the-peg bloody global capitalism. It's the kit version of a water-front development. Half the restaurants here you could find the same place in any decent-size city in the UK: same menu, same gormless eighteen-year-olds pretending to be waiters on four quid an hour. You know what I mean?'

Pete nodded.

'Well, is that what you want for Cardiff, you want to see a whole identikit city? Cause that's what'll happen if people like you and me don't make a stand. You take the young politicians over there in the Assembly – ' St Clair gestured in the direction of the office block that still housed the Welsh Assembly while they argued about whether to build a proper one. 'That's what they think is progress – inward investment, new leisure-themed industrial park, McDonald's and Starbucks opening ten new branches a month, more jobs – bet it's the same with the young journalists on your paper.'

'Not just the young ones,' said Pete, involuntarily going along with St Clair's line of argument.

'No,' said St Clair, 'you're right there. I'm just showing what an old fart I am; it isn't just the young ones over at the Assembly or City Hall either. But what I think a city needs is a bit of soul and with this little plan I've put together – well, we might just preserve a little bit of that.'

'Oh, come on,' said Pete. 'You build a shopping mall, that's what happens, isn't it? You end up with a Starbucks in there and all?'

'Over my dead bastard body we will, son. No, what we're planning is something different – affordable units for real people to open bars, shops, restaurants – no chains, no franchises, just a place where people like you and me can be at home and a place that'll still be there when your kids grow up and they'll say oh yeah that's Cardiff that is. You see what I'm getting at?'

'Mmm,' said Pete, 'I guess.'

'Course you do, son,' said St Clair. 'So you want to mention that in your piece, I'd be very grateful. The Welsh Development Authority are making their minds up at the moment which bid to accept; won't be announced for another month but meanwhile any little nudges they get from your paper, be much appreciated.'

'Well,' said Pete, a little stiffly, 'we're not in the business of taking sides in these kinds of matters.'

'Course you're not, son, course you're not. All I'm asking is you report what I have to say. Give me a fair hearing, like. Now,' he checked his watch, 'time we were all getting back to work, I suppose. Good to meet you, Pete.' He stuck his hand out and Pete shook. 'Anything else you need to know, call any time; I'll give you my personal mobile number. And anything else I can do – you want tickets for Big Tom, private box, the works – you just give me a call. Leslie St Clair looks after his friends.'

'Great,' said Pete, 'thanks,' and shook St Clair's hand again and walked back through the pub to his car, unable to repress a smile. He liked guys like St Clair, old-school hustlers. Be a nice story too, they dug around in the archives and got some photos of the Fifties and that. He was just working on composing the opening paragraph in his head when his phone rang, told him he'd got a message.

He picked it up expecting some voicemail from Graham yelling at him to get back to the office but instead it was a text message. 'Custom Hse 9pm Fri OK? xx Kim.'

Pete paused, thought keep it simple, texted back with OK x. Then he headed back to the office with a smile on his face.

9

Bobby Ranger couldn't sleep, was getting to be a habit. The day the Custom House was due to close she woke up around six. She was wondering where her future was headed. Lap-dancing was out. She should have known the whole lap-dancing thing would be sewn up by that old cunt Bernie Walters. Him and Kenny, chances of them giving Maria work were slight, and chances of there being anything left over for Bobby were less than zero. Back-to-the-drawing-board time.

Then there was the massage-parlour plan. Thing was you had to have some premises. No way was Bobby conducting the business round her flat, have Maria fucking God knows who on her nice bed. Neither was Maria's place a possibility, not with Jamal running around asking for his tea. No, somewhere else.

Well, there were always the kind of horrible bloody rooms the girls used, places with no leccy and no light, just one step up from doing it in the car park, but that wasn't what Bobby was after; she was looking for something classier. A place you could treat the punters properly and charge them properly too. Question was where could she find a place where the neighbours and/or landlord wouldn't freak out they saw a procession of men turning up at all hours? She was standing in the kitchen making herself a coffee when a possible answer came to her. Something one of the girls, a part-timer from Llantrisant way, had said, how she'd been using a nice pad over Atlantic Wharf, the new flats there.

Perfect, that would be. They'd built them about ten years ago, before the whole bay-development thing got going, a whole load of new flats along this big old disused wharf, half a mile or so east of Butetown. Ahead of its time, probably, but when it was built it just seemed stupid; no way were lawyers and that going to live down the docks and there was no need for anyone from Butetown to move over there – one thing Butetown didn't have was a housing shortage: the council was forever moving people out of Butetown, never moved anyone in except the odd Somali refugee. Bobby reckoned it was a deliberate policy: another twenty years or so there'd be hardly anyone left in Butetown at all and the council would be able to knock the whole place down, build a whole lot more posh flats and Tiger Bay would have vanished from history, replaced once and for all by Cardiff Bay.

Anyway, thing was, no one rich wanted to live by the side of a derelict canal in the docks so most of the flats were just sitting there empty. All of which was why it was the perfect place for a girl to do some business. Bobby didn't know why she hadn't thought of it before. Plenty of parking space, hardly any nosy neighbours, nice and private for the punters too, no chance of being spotted. Yeah, perfect.

Nine o'clock she'd got on the phone, checking out who rented out flats in Atlantic Wharf. Now she was going to see a man named Malcolm Hopkin and she was nervous. He'd told her to come to the Wharf pub; just ask behind the bar, love, he'd said, they'll point me out.

In fact there was no need for that as he was practically the only person in there and even if he hadn't been she'd have known him at once: one of those times when the voice on the phone and the real-life feller go right together. Funny thing – don't know why she thought of this – was that seemed to happen more often with blokes; with women quite often the ones with the sexy voice on the phone were some fat old sort with glasses

50

in real life, and the pretty ones sounded like Kate Moss does in that advert – Obsession – dumb plain little voices.

But anyway, like she said, Malcolm Hopkin matched his voice. Dodgy. Well dodgy. Fiftyish feller with bit of a bouffant and a drinker's face sat over a pint at a little table by the window, bunch of newspapers on the table in front of him, talking on his mobile.

As she walked over he snapped the phone off, looked up at her and asked, 'You the young lady interested in the flat?' Little bit of a Valleys accent in there.

'Yeah,' she said, sitting down opposite him, 'that's me.'

'Hmm,' he said, looking her up and down and frowning a little, 'well, I'll just finish my drink and we'll walk round to the flats. You care for one yourself?'

'Coke, ta,' said Bobby.

Hopkin came back with Bobby's coke and a whisky for himself.

'I've seen you before,' he said after taking a swallow of his pint.

Bobby shrugged. 'Probably, I've lived here all my life,' she said, wondering too if she'd seen him before. Only place she mostly saw blokes like that was out on the beat pulling up next to Maria and winding their windows down. Was he a punter?

'Definitely seen you around,' said Hopkin again, nodding to himself. Then he fixed her with a look. 'Now, would you be planning on actually living in the flat yourself?'

'Yeah, well,' started Bobby but Hopkin cut her short.

'Or would you be thinking of using it as a business base? A lot of entrepreneurial types favour these flats.'

Bobby's turn to look at the bloke closely. Was he saying what she thought he was saying?

'Well, perhaps,' she began tentatively but he cut her off again, big smile on his face this time.

'No, no, no need to go into the detail of your business, up to you entirely. It's just that were there to be business use then of course a special business rate will apply. You understand, I'm sure.'

Bobby understood all right: this Malcolm Hopkin was a pimp just like her, only a layer further up, kept his hands nice and clean.

'Course,' she said. 'I understand but it depends what it is, this special business rate, doesn't it?'

'Does indeed,' said Hopkin, draining off his pint and chasing it with the last of his whisky. 'Tell you what, let's go round to the flat and if you like it then we can talk about the financial side.'

Bobby did like the flat. You could see why it hadn't appealed to any regular person. The only reason you might want to live in these flats was to get the view over the water and this one looked straight out on to the car park. But that suited Bobby fine; meant you could get a good look at the punters before they came in the front door. Then you had an entryphone system, so if you didn't like the look of them close up, you could just tell them to fuck off over the intercom. Otherwise the place was just what you'd expect: boxy little rooms halfway between a hotel and a home. Soulless as anything. The layout was fine, though. You walked into the living room – that's where Bobby could base herself and the girls could sit around – then there were two bedrooms opening off, neither of them much bigger than a cupboard but big enough for them to do the business. Nice kitchen, which would come in handy, and a decent-size bathroom, which would be a definite plus. Yeah, Bobby liked it a lot; big step up from the Custom House beat this would be for all concerned.

'Bit bloody small,' she said to Hopkin after he'd finished showing her round.'

He shrugged. 'Compact, love, that's the word they like to use – the developers,' and he laughed.

'Can't even see the water,' said Bobby.

Hopkin laughed again. 'Good view of the car park, though,' he said. 'Some of the other . . . entrepreneurs appreciate that.' Then he smiled and waited.

Bobby's turn to shrug; no point in carrying the charade on any longer. 'Yeah, suppose it's OK,' she said. 'How much?'

'Five hundred.'

'What?' said Bobby. 'A month?'

Hopkin chuckled, no mirth in it at all. 'No, love, a week. Payable Friday morning. On the dot. Two late payments and you're out.'

Bobby walked over to the window, looked at the car park, thought about it. Five hundred a week. Bloody hell. Any way you looked at it, that was a lot of money for a flat. Specially one you weren't even going to live in. Five hundred quid: what was that? Seventy-odd quid a day. Meant Maria doing three guys a day just to pay the rent. Except those were street rates. Working inside like this she could charge more. Fifty a time, say, basic. And then it didn't have to be just Maria working here; say she had three or four girls working, all charging fifty a go, well it was nothing really. If if if. Thing was she barely had five hundred quid to put down for the first week. Nah, this was crazy, out of her league. And a rip-off too.

It was like Hopkin was reading her mind.

'You get more than the flat for five hundred, mind, love, you also get a bit of protection. Say, for instance, your business might be the kind of thing gets the law interested, gets coppers coming round with their hands out asking for little contributions to keep it all running smoothly, you know what I'm talking about? Well, all that's covered, I guarantee you. Any copper comes round with their hands out, you send them straight to me.'

'Hmm,' said Bobby, thinking that made a difference.

'All right,' said Hopkin then, 'don't know why I'm offering

you this, but I like you. First two weeks you can buy one get one free, just till you get settled in, like. Give us five hundred now and that's the first fortnight taken care of.'

Sod it, thought Bobby, why not, so she smiled and stuck her hand out. 'Deal,' she said.

10

Five o'clock Pete went to pick up the Audi TT from the dealership. Couldn't deny it was a lovely-looking motor; even just driving it back to the office you could see the envy radiating off every bloke you passed. Three hours left before it was time to meet Kim and rather than go back to the flat Pete carried on working, transcribed his St Clair interview, impressed again by the sheer chutzpah of the man. Chutzpah: could you use that in the *Post*? Pete wondered, and decided you probably could, though he still remembered the piss-taking he'd received from Graham when he tried to use schadenfreude in a piece about Anglo-Welsh rugby rivalry. It was funny it was only the Germans had a word for it; you'd have thought the Welsh would have half a dozen, like the Eskimos have a hundred different names for snow, cause if there was one thing the Welsh were good at, it was schadenfreude.

Anyway the time passed by easy enough; the quiet of the evening was always the best time for getting some serious work done in the office. And suddenly it was quarter to nine and Pete was closing down his terminal and heading out. He debated for a moment whether to take the car, weighing the practical – the fact that it would be quicker to walk – against the desire to show off. To his surprise he found himself opting for being a flash git. He walked down to the office car park, gunned the motor out of there, couldn't resist taking it for a quick spin on the feeder road from the town centre to the bay before pulling up in the Welsh National Opera car park, across the road from the Custom House.

You could hear the noise from outside the pub, Tom Jones's 'Sex Bomb' – what else? – blaring out at hideous volume accompanied by the sound of a lot of very drunk people singing along. Pete paused for a moment, wondering whether he was really up for this.

Just then there was a yell of rage from inside and the window to the lounge bulged out momentarily before giving way altogether in a shower of glass as a body smashed through it. Pete stopped moving, watched open-mouthed as the victim stood up apparently unscathed, made a vague effort at brushing some of the glass off his clothes, ignored a bloody cut on his forehead and headed back into the pub.

Looking through the hole in the window, Pete could see a bloke with a hefty, professional-looking video camera looking out at him. Then in a kind of slow motion Pete saw someone approach the cameraman, shout something in his face, snatch the camera, throw it through the broken window and rapidly follow it up with the cameraman himself.

'Fuck,' said the cameraman, 'fuck, fuck, fuck.' He was a tall bloke with a straggly beard wearing heavily padded clothing that looked to have protected him from much physical damage. The bloke didn't seem too bothered about his own welfare, though; he was much more concerned about his camera.

He picked it up tenderly as a child. 'You see that?' said the bloke. 'You see what happened?'

'Yeah,' said Pete, 'I saw it. You all right?'

Before the cameraman could answer, the pub door opened and a woman in flared jeans and a tight top emblazoned with the word Pornstar emerged. Kim.

'Christ, Dan,' she said, 'is the camera all right?'

Pete couldn't help it; he burst out laughing. Kim spun round.

'What the fuck are you laughing at?' Then she saw it was Pete. 'Oh,' she said. 'Hiya.'

'Hiya,' said Pete. 'You need some help?'

'No,' she said, 's'all right. Let me just sort this out. If it's broken it could cost me my bloody job. Dan, tell me it's all right.'

Dan was busy fiddling with the camera, still swearing under his breath. Finally he turned round, looked at Kim. 'It's OK, I think.'

'Thank Christ for that,' said Kim. 'Right, let's go back in.'

Pete laughed again. The cameraman just stared at her. 'You serious?'

'Yeah,' she said, 'we're getting some great footage in there.'

'You're out of your mind,' said the cameraman, picked up his camera and walked across the road to an MPV. He unlocked the back, put the camera in, walked round to the front and got in the driver's seat. 'You coming?'

'No,' shouted Kim, 'I'm bloody not. I'm staying here. I'll record some more stuff.'

'Fine,' said Dan the cameraman, 'your funeral,' and drove off.

'Gutless fucking hippie twat,' said Kim, obviously not impressed by this turn of events. 'So what are we waiting for, let's go in.'

This time it was Pete's turn to say, 'You serious?'

'Yeah,' said Kim, 'course. C'mon in, it's a laugh in there.' And with that she took Pete's hand and practically pulled him into the pub, Pete thinking to himself, well you wanted a bit of excitement in life, no point in complaining when some's on offer.

Inside the place was riotous but not, as far as Pete could see, especially menacing. The bloke who'd been chucked through the window in the first place was stood at the bar with his mates, all of them clearly under the impression it had been a great laugh. The overall vibe was of the party at the end of the world. One and all off their faces, looking like they'd been drinking since eleven o'clock opening time. Young hustlers, old hustlers, lesbian pimps, middle-aged black pimps, even the young hard boys cruising around the scene dealing a little bit of this, little bit of that; they were all pissed. Pete pushed towards the bar, got a couple of cans of Breaker, made his way back to Kim and they perched themselves on top of an upended fruit machine and watched the show.

They got a few looks at first. Couple of pissed-up old girls made some remarks; a bunch of hard, shaven-headed black boys swaggered into the pub, looked them over then decided whoever they were they weren't the law. At least that's what Pete assumed they figured when one of the fellers offered to sell him a couple of rocks. 'How did he know I wasn't a copper?' Pete asked Kim, outraged.

'If he'd thought you were a copper, he would have given you them,' said Kim, laughing, and Pete shook his head and wondered if she was joking. Only copper he'd had much to do with was a bloke called Simon lived four doors down in the close, and he couldn't really imagine Simon having much of an interest in crack. But then sometimes he thought he was simply naïve; maybe he really knew nothing of the life of this city he'd been chronicling for the past decade and a half.

By now talking was almost impossible; the jukebox had been turned up to total distortion level, blasting out the usual unlikely mixture of chart hits through the ages. Pete remembered coming into the Custom House years ago, in search of an errant journalist, and finding the whole place singing along to Salt'n'Pepa's 'Let's Talk about Sex' – which you might have thought would be the last thing anyone in here would want to listen to. Tonight it was anthems all the way: Rod's 'Sailing', Kool and the Gang's 'Celebration' three times in a row, TLC's 'No Scrubs' and now 'Dancing in the Streets', the grisly Jagger and Bowie version.

Pete was enjoying himself, sucking on his beer, soaking up the atmosphere of this wake for a vanishing era, wondering how he'd write it up: 'Old-time street prostitution – another great British industry goes under the cosh.' Maybe it would work on the financial pages. He looked over at Kim to see her gazing at a couple who'd just emerged from the toilets, a stocky boyish-looking black woman with short locks and a tall white girl with hennaed hair scraped back from her forehead.

'Hiya, Bobby,' shouted Kim, 'over here,' and the black woman rolled her eyes in mock amazement and headed over towards Pete and Kim.

Pete felt a momentary tinge of alarm at the prospect of actually having to engage with this world rather than simply look at it, but also an undeniable excitement.

'Hiya, darlin',' said the woman, Bobby, 'brought your boy-friend have you?'

Kim ignored the suggestion, just said, 'Pete, this is Bobby and this is . . .' Kim looked towards the hennaed girl.

'Maria,' said the girl. 'You don't remember me, do you?'

Kim stared at her and then her hand flew up to her mouth. 'Maria, Christ. How are you, girl?'

'You two know each other?' said Bobby.

'Yeah,' said Kim, 'I met Maria when I was doing a doc down here before about the drugs trade, yeah?' and with that first Kim and then Maria burst into a fit of giggles.

Bobby stared at them, shook her head wearily then turned her attention to Pete. 'Who are you, then?'

'I'm Pete,' said Pete and got halfway through sticking his hand out to shake when he decided that the Custom House wasn't a shake-hands kind of place and let the motion abort in mid-air.

'That right, you her boyfriend?'

Pete shook his head, managed a smile. 'Just friends, you know.'

Bobby rolled her eyes, seemed to find him of no further interest. Before she could move away, though, another bloke came up to them, short black guy in a big jacket, looked to be about Pete's age, big smile on his face and what Pete couldn't help thinking of as a joint in his hand, though he was sure people didn't call them joints any more.

'All right, Bob,' said the guy.

'Later, Mikey,' said Bobby and immediately moved away. Pete watched her go; maybe it was the whole world she was pissed off with.

'All right, man, what's happening?' the feller, Mikey, said to him.

'Nothing much,' said Pete, raising his can in what he hoped was an appropriate gesture of matiness.

'Yeah, man, that's the truth,' said Mikey and laughed like Pete had said something profound yet funny. Then he took a long draw on the – what the hell was the right word – spliff? Spliff would do, it was better than joint; anyway he handed the herbal cigarette to Pete, who was so busy wondering what to call it, if asked, that he took a long toke without even considering that this was the first dope he'd smoked since 1984 and he'd never smoked much even back then cause most of the time it made him paranoid.

It was only when he let the smoke out and felt the dimly familiar spread of intoxication in his brain that he had a moment of panic but it subsided at once. Maybe it was getting older, but the pleasure centres were winning over from the paranoia nodes. He took a second long drag, then handed the spliff back to Mikey. 'Thanks, man,' he said, 'nice one.' Man? Nice one? What was going on? His whole vocabulary was reverting to the early Eighties.

'Nice,' agreed Mikey and Pete was just thinking what a cool guy he must be, just making friends, hanging out like this, when the Mikey feller leant up close and shouted in his ear, 'You looking for a girl?'

For a moment Pete thought he meant had Pete lost someone then the penny dropped and it was all he could do to stop from blushing. 'No,' he shouted back and then, feeling the need to justify himself, added, 'I'm with her.' He turned to point at Kim who was out in the middle of the ad hoc dance floor, dancing suspiciously closely with Maria.

'Oh right,' said Mikey, looking genuinely contrite, 'sorry, man.'

Pete waited for Mikey to walk on, find another lonely-looking bloke who might be interested in a little commercial intimacy. But he didn't, he just passed the spliff back to Pete, waited till Pete had taken another couple of tokes, then said, 'So what sort of business you in, Pete?'

'Newspaper,' said Pete, before breaking off into a coughing fit. When he'd pulled himself together he elaborated, 'I work for the *Welsh Post*.'

'Oh yeah?' said Mikey. 'You're a journalist?'

'Yeah,' said Pete, thinking that was one of the few questions he could manage a categorical answer to right at the moment. Christ, he felt out of it. And he had the car outside; what was he thinking of?

'Oh yeah? A news reporter, is it? You doing a story on this place?'

'No,' said Pete, 'just . . .' He paused, trying to remember why he was here. 'I just came with her, Kim. I do, like, features and stuff.'

'Cool,' said Mikey, looking bored now.

'I do the motoring, though,' Pete blurted out, thinking where did that come from, and, before he can stop himself, he says, 'You want to see the motor I'm trying out?' and Mikey nods and suddenly they're draining their pints and heading over the road to pay homage to the Audi TT.

'Sweet,' said Mikey reverently as he got up close. 'They let you drive it?'

'Yeah,' said Pete, aware he was showing off but powerless to stop himself. 'Yeah, I've got it for the weekend.'

'Nice, man,' said Mikey. 'Can I have a look inside?'

'Sure,' said Pete and then they're both sat inside the car playing around with the controls like a pair of kids when Kim, Bobby and Maria emerge from the pub, Kim looking around like she's wondering where Pete has got to.

Pete leaned out of the car, shouted at Kim and waved them over. This time Bobby's first to come out with 'Nice car' and Pete can't help but reflect that there is a reason why blokes buy these kind of motors. You want to impress the girls, spend thirty grand on one of these babies. You'll see.

'So,' said Kim when she got up close, 'you going to take us for a ride then?'

Pete shook his head. 'No way. I've got a lot of sobering up to do before I'm going anywhere.'

'Aw, c'mon,' says Kim, who was obviously some way out of the vicinity of soberhood herself. 'Be a laugh, wouldn't it, Maria?'

Kim turns round to Maria who, now Pete sees her in the outdoors, is not looking well at all. She's swaying and glassy-eyed and suddenly she just turns her head to one side and throws up.

'Fucking hell, Ri,' says Bobby, 'state of you.'

Maria doesn't say anything, just finishes retching then stands up, wipes her hand across her face and says, 'I'm going back in.'

Pete, Kim, Bobby and Mikey stand there watching her.

'Kin'ell, Bob, aren't you going to see she's OK?' says Mikey.

Bobby shrugs. 'What's the point? She's like that every other bastard night. Let's have a look inside.'

Bobby's turn to admire the inside of the Audi. 'How fast does it go?' she asks.

Pete tries to remember. 'Hundred and seventy miles an hour, I think's what they said.'

'Shit,' says Bobby, 'not bad. You sure you don't want to take us for a ride?'

'I'll drive it,' says Mikey. 'I haven't been drinking and I'm a hell of a driver, aren't I, Bob?'

And then Bobby starts telling Pete some long story about Mikey being chased by the police and losing them after twenty minutes of leading them through every alley in Butetown and Pete's thinking sure you may not have been drinking but how much have you been smoking but Kim's got her mind absolutely fixed on going for a drive and her hand's on his back and clearly he isn't sober or unstoned or in his right mind but eventually he finds himself giving in – just a short ride, right – and then Mikey's at the wheel and Pete's next to him and Bobby and Kim are squeezed into the tiny back seat both giggling and suddenly they're off, and fair play Mikey takes it nice and slow out of the car park and round the roundabout but when he hits the arterial road fucking hell the acceleration's like something else and they're all laughing and Pete's caught between terror and exhilaration, feeling like he did on the back of his cousin Rog's bike up on Cwmcarn Scenic Drive when he was sixteen.

Mikey slows round the roundabout then turns right down into the underpass and floors it once again. Now he has a ten-mile straight run, dual carriageway all the way, to the motorway, and within seconds he's up to a hundred miles an hour; they fairly flash past the few other cars on the road. Mikey is indeed a good driver, not over-steering, easing the car round the bends, and Pete allows himself to relax a little; he swivels round to look at Kim, her eyes are shining, her face flushed, thrilled. Bobby next to her is casually lighting up a spliff. Pete blinks, imagining what would happen if the police stopped them now, how completely screwed he'd be, but then Kim grabs him from behind and leans over into the front and kisses him hard on the mouth and says, 'This is fucking brilliant,' and he lets go of his worries.

Three minutes later, give or take, they arrive at the motorway junction.

'You want to go to Bristol?' says Mikey and Kim goes yeah but Pete gathers his strength sufficiently to say no. So they head back to Cardiff, possibly just a tad faster than they left it, the needle touching a hundred and forty on a straight section. They're almost back, within sight of the Millennium Stadium, illuminated to their left, and Pete's just thinking that they've got away with it when he sees the police car parked up by the side of the road. They're past it in a blur of speed but behind them Pete can hear the siren start up.

Mikey just laughs, guns the car forward towards Butetown and at the last minute just before the underpass he brakes hard and swings the car up and left. The brakes do their job miraculously well and suddenly they're up by Techniquest and the siren's still off in the distance. Mikey turns and clashes fists with Pete who responds awkwardly.

They're just motoring back down Bute Street, more sedately now, Kim telling Mikey what a great driver he is, when they hear another siren and this time it's right on top of them. Just a quick blast and the cop car cuts in front of them and Mikey's got no alternative but to stop, pulling up just by the Loudoun Square shops.

Pete has his head in his hands as the copper gets out of his car and walks round to the driver's side. Mikey winds his window down and says, casual as anything, 'All right, Jimmy?'

The copper laughs. 'For Chrissakes, Mikey, who did you rob that off?'

Mikey shrugs. 'No one, Jim, it's my mate's car here.' He points at Pete.

Pete's still waiting for the breathalysers to come out or the cop to ask what the herbal–cigarette smell is, but there's none of that. Instead the feller just waves at Pete and says, 'Nice car, boss. Time you took it home, though, you know what I mean,' and Pete just nods, unable to speak, relief flooding over him.

The copper gets back in his car, drives off. Mikey claps Pete on the back. 'Welcome to Butetown, bra.' And all of them are laughing.

For the rest of the night Pete feels bulletproof. It's a blur of returning to the Custom House, drinking, dancing, snogging Kim sat together astride the fruit machine, seeing Kim snogging Bobby when he walks outside for fresh air, snogging Kim again as they all stagger out to the car when time is once and forever called.

Outside, Bobby's going, leading a comatose Maria away. Kim, Mikey and Pete are stood together, wondering what now? The car's still sat there and Pete is now not remotely in any condition to drive, but suddenly paranoid about leaving such a car in such a place. Mikey, still sober, if seriously stoned, says he'll be the taxi man and Pete's new bulletproof brain can't think of a problem with that so he gives Mikey the keys once more and sits in the front and drifts in and out of sleep and Mikey drops off Kim then delivers Pete to his door and Pete staggers out of the car and when Mikey says you mind if I bring the car back tomorrow he just nods and says sure and it's only when he wakes in the very early morning, aching and sweating, that he realises he's en-trusted a thirty-grand car that he doesn't own to a Butetown lowlife he's never met before and he can't sleep for worrying, just lies there wishing he could die.

II

The morning after the Custom House closed Bobby began trying to explain her new plan to Maria who didn't seem to get it at all, probably cause she had the hangover to end them all and was gazing fixedly at Ant and Dec while Jamal bounced around the room.

Wasn't till six in the evening, by which time Maria'd had a couple of reviving bottles of Hooch, that Bobby was able to get any sense at all out of her.

'Might as well just use this place, innit?' she said finally. 'That's what Nikki does: just gets them to bell her on the mobile and round they come.'

'Fuck's sake,' said Bobby. 'You really want that? You want him – ' she pointed at Jamal concentrating furiously on his N64 '– seeing you bring back Christ knows who? You think I'm going to sleep with you in the same bed you does it with the punters?'

Maria pouted. 'Yeah, OK, but couldn't you have found somewhere closer?'

Bobby felt like strangling her. Atlantic Wharf was all of five minutes' walk away. 'It's closer than the Custom House,' she said, doing her best to keep her temper in check.

'Yeah, but it's not going to be the same laugh, is it, not going to have our mates there?'

Bobby shrugged. 'Well, I was thinking of asking a couple of the other girls they wanted to work there too.'

'Oh yeah?' said Maria suspiciously. 'Who?'

'I dunno,' said Bobby. 'Tanya, I was thinking. Maybe Lorraine.'

'Nikki'd be good.'

Bobby frowned. Great, the two laziest cows in Cardiff together under one roof, but what the hell, she was Maria's mate, might stop her moaning. 'All right,' she said, 'Nikki.'

'Great,' said Maria, 'I'll tell her. So when do we start?'

'Feller said we could move in Monday, then we'll have to put an ad in the paper and stuff, see what happens.'

'That'll be cool,' said Maria, digging in the fridge for another Hooch. 'You want one?'

'No, ta,' said Bobby.

'So, you want me to work tonight or what?'

'No,' said Bobby, 'nowhere to work is there?' That wasn't strictly true – they could have gone over by the Embankment and tried their luck, Bobby sitting in the car, Maria out on the street – but now Bobby had got it in her head that they were taking a step up in the world and that would be a definite step down. Plus she felt like a day off. Walking past the Custom House this afternoon, seeing the boards up already, the demolition notices plastered on the walls, she felt like she'd been to a funeral or something. Needed a bit of time to mourn, like.

'Cool,' said Maria, 'cause I was thinking of going out with Nikki, have a few drinks, tell her about your idea, like, so if you don't mind looking after Jam?'

'Nah,' said Bobby, 'that'll be all right.'

In fact it sounded like an excellent idea. She couldn't face having Maria getting sloppy drunk around her, and now she could spend an hour or two playing games with Jamal, then settle down to sorting out a few things for herself.

And so by nine o'clock Maria was safely out of the way, getting pissed with Nikki in some hellhole in town, Jamal was tucked up in bed and Bobby was sat in the bedroom playing with her new computer. Neville, feller she'd known for years, sold it her, fell out the back of a warehouse no doubt. Anyway, seventy-five quid for a brand-new computer still in the box; Bobby was well pleased.

So far she hadn't done much more than play games on it, but now she'd got the flat sorted she was starting to feel a bit inspired. She'd been thinking about how to advertise for business. First thought was the obvious one: stick an ad in the evening paper like all the massage parlours had been doing for years. Well of course she'd do that, but then she thought what about the Internet? The Internet had to be the future in the sex-for-money business, everybody knew that. So Bobby decided to have a nose around, see how it all worked.

First off she checked out whether her competition was up to anything on the Net. There were half a dozen 'massage parlours' in Cardiff that Bobby knew of, either through girls who worked in them or because they advertised in the *Echo*. A couple of them had been going for ever; the rest were pretty much fly-by-night operations, waiting till the police or their rivals put them out of business.

The Internet, though, none of her rivals seemed to have got hip to it at all. All she could find was something called the Good Sex Guide where the punters actually wrote up what they thought of the services on offer and none of them were too impressed. That didn't surprise Bobby much; pride in their work wasn't something you associated with the girls of the Cardiff sauna-massage industry.

Not one of the outfits had its own website either and Bobby was getting excited at the prospect of being the first. You're a punter, what did you want to do? Take a pig in a poke out the *Echo* classifieds or d'you want to browse through a selection of beautiful girls and phone up and book the one of your choice? It was obvious really.

The main problem, of course, was the beautiful-girls bit. Maria really was pretty damn fit, Bobby said so herself. The other three girls Bobby was using, though, were a bit more a mixed bag. Tanya the half-caste wasn't too bad, nice body specially; Lorraine was frankly getting on a bit and well on the fat side, but then again she was a genuine blonde and with a lot of slap and her tits sticking out she worked all right for the punters liked a mature woman; and as for Nikki, well she'd maybe appeal to the market liked a sulky cow.

Anyway, Bobby started to get positively inspired. She was definitely going to get a website. Question was did she get someone to design it for her — and if she did find someone they might have a bit of an attitude about setting up a cyber brothel. Option two: she could have a go herself. How hard could it be? She'd seen all these magazines in the newsagent with free cover disks all said they could help you build your own site. Got to be worth a go.

Lying in bed later on, half asleep, waiting for Maria to come back pissed and aggressive, she had a vision of herself in a white room programming a computer and felt an unfamiliar calmness replace the usual jangle of her nerves. She'd always seen the future as the same but worse, the same but ageing and violent and unloved or wanted, the same plus addiction or madness or both. But now, just maybe, she thought that the closing of the Custom House might not be a death but a rebirth.

12

Pete had spent most of the morning pacing about. He'd racked his brains to work out how to find this Mikey. He'd been into work for a bit but there was hardly anyone in as it was Sunday tomorrow. He'd gone back to the flat and aggravated Randall obsessing about what to do. Randall buried himself in the papers, clock-watching for twelve when he would stroll over to the City Arms and have the first eye-opener of the day.

Half twelve and Pete was actually looking through the phone book for the police-station number wondering what on earth he was going to say when the doorbell rang. Pete answered the intercom. A voice he didn't recognise for a second, then identified with a surge of relief. Mikey.

'Got your car here for you, boss,' he said.

Pete walked downstairs and there was Mikey standing next to the car. Pete felt like kissing him, felt a wave of shame and guilt. What a bastard he was stereotyping a feller like Mikey who'd been nothing but helpful and had even – bloody hell – sprayed the car with some kind of air-freshener stuff made it smell like new and removed all traces of the dope and drink that had been consumed in it the night before. He stuck his hand out. 'Thanks, man, I owe you.'

'No problem, boss,' said Mikey. 'Pleasure to drive it, like. How long you got it for?'

'Till Monday,' said Pete.

'Oh yeah. Going to take your girlfriend out for a Sunday drive then?'

Pete just smiled and said, 'We'll see,' then dug in his wallet and found a business card, handed it to Mikey.

'And like I said, you need a favour, there's anything I can do —' even as he was talking, he couldn't imagine what kind of favour he could do for a feller like Mikey, but still '— just give me a buzz, yeah, cause you saved my life last night.'

Mikey laughed. 'C'mon, man, it was a laugh, don't take it so serious,' he said and with that he was off towards town. 'Got a little business to do, boss.' And Pete was left leaning on the Audi wondering when the last time was anyone did him a favour without expecting something back.

He thought about taking the Audi out for a test run but he was still feeling the effects of the night before and anyway what Mikey had said about taking Kim out sounded like a good idea, so he drove the car round to the *Post*, stuck it in the protected parking lot, and spent the rest of the day quietly working on the Leslie St Clair piece.

Took him till six o'clock to finish it but when he did he was well pleased. Definitely the best thing he'd written in years, made him realise how much he'd become a kind of journalistic automaton, always doing exactly what was right for the *Post*, never even letting himself think that you could try to do more than what was expected.

He'd got all the regular stuff in, the background, all the showbiz stories, even mentioned community capitalism, but he'd put his own stamp on it too. And it was a nice story. This smart kid from the docks, got nothing more than quick hands in the boxing ring and an OK singing voice, manages to make himself a name as a boxer then smoothly glides into showbiz and then, when that starts going down, moves into business. And all the time without losing touch with his roots. Just writing it down made Pete think about what a safe little life he'd had by comparison. No, it was a cracking piece by any standards and for the first time in years he was buzzing at work.

Just to prove it, he picked up the phone and, without even thinking about what he was going to say beforehand, called up Kim. She was on good form too, said she'd been working all day and all, cutting together the footage she'd got from the Custom House the night before. And yeah, she said, she'd love to go for a drive tomorrow. He knew where she lived, why didn't he pick her up about twelve? Pete put the phone down. Sorted, he thought, and grinned, realising his vocabulary was being hijacked. Better be careful before he turned into one of those forty-year-olds Cardiff seemed to be full of, all piercings, dodgy facial hair and clothes nicked off a passing teenager.

Twelve o'clock Sunday Pete had rung on Kim's bell standing outside the house on Romilly Road where she had her flat. After a couple of minutes he rang again and a couple of minutes after that the door opened and a decidedly bleary-looking, dressing-gowned Kim half opened the door, looked out at Pete in evident bewilderment, then slowly nodded and said, 'You want to come in? I'm not quite up yet.'

'Yeah,' said Pete, 'I kind of gathered that,' and laughed, and Kim half laughed back and led the way up the stairs and into her flat.

'You mind waiting in here,' she said, pointing to the living room, 'I'll just be a minute,' and disappeared into her bedroom.

Pete walked into the living room, looked out the window to check no one was taking an unhealthy interest in the car, then scanned the room. Stripped floorboards, Ikea rug, Ikea sofa, couple of Sixties-looking chairs, Matisse print, Modigliani print, framed arty photo of Kim herself, TV, video with a bunch of videos lying around it, midi system, bunch of CDs, no vinyl, and a bookcase.

He went over to the bookcase; generally it was the most reliable window to the soul. CD collections didn't tell you much, people had CDs they didn't care about, ones old boy-friends had given them, ones everybody else had – he was willing to bet he'd find Travis, Chilled Ibiza and at least one Sixties soul compilation amongst Kim's CD collection – but nobody bought books quite so casually.

Scanning the shelves, he was relieved not to be assailed by rows of self-help titles, no sign of *The Road Less Travelled* or *Men Are from Mars*; there was a copy of *The Rules* but that was probably a joke. Instead there was a surprising amount of serious fiction and poetry. She must have done English at university, he figured – hard to imagine anyone actually read George Eliot or Ezra Pound for pleasure – but the new stuff all looked pretty heavyweight too, all that Booker-prize stuff that Pete felt like he ought to have read. Well, well, and there was him expecting to find wall-to-wall primary-coloured books about girls called Jemima and their topsy-turvy love lives. Just went to show you never could tell.

Meanwhile there was a copy of yesterday's *Guardian* under the sofa so he picked that up and settled down to reading the magazine.

He was aimlessly scanning the wine column by the time Kim emerged. She was wearing jeans and a very tight T-shirt that Pete had to stop himself from staring at. She flopped down on the sofa next to him.

'Christ,' she said, 'I am absolutely fucked. I must have coffee. You want some?'

She sprang up and Pete felt a flash of irritation. If they didn't get going soon he was sure they wouldn't reach anywhere in time for Sunday lunch, but he kept it back, reminded himself that the point of the day was to see Kim, not to have roast beef and all the trimmings, though just the thought of Yorkshire pudding had him salivating. Swallowing hard, he said, 'Yeah, sure, if you're making one.'

Kim led the way into the kitchen, where she fiddled about with a flashy Italian coffee-maker and Pete propped himself up against the fridge, enjoying the domesticity.

'So, what did you do last night?'

'Oh,' she said, 'same old same old, you know. Went to the comedy club down the bay first, then we ended up in the Emporium cause Guto's mate was deejaying. How about you?'

'Oh,' said Pete, not wanting to say that he'd had a quiet night in, had begged off drinking with Randall in favour of *Match of the Day* and a takeaway, wanting to be in good shape for Sunday, 'nothing much'.

'Listen,' he said then, looking at his watch, 'maybe we should get moving if we're going to get something to eat.'

'Yeah, yeah, sure,' said Kim, 'let's just drink this,' she poured out the coffee, 'and we'll get going.'

In fact it was another half hour before they actually made it out and Pete was finding it hard to conceal his annoyance but at last they were on the move.

There wasn't the heady excitement of the Friday-night drive. In the cooler light of lunchtime the car was ultimately just a car, but even so once they got on to the motorway, and then on to the Ross Spur heading up to Monmouth, a fine empty road with sweeping scenery, there was a simple pleasure in navigating this fairly supreme product of human ingenuity through a slice of nature's finest landscaping.

Just before Monmouth Pete headed south, wound his way down Wye Valley lanes till he came to a pub called the Trekkers, which – glory be – was still serving Sunday lunch, and the sun made an appearance and they were sat in the garden and all would have been well with Pete's world if he could have shaken off the memories of coming to this same pub years ago with Viv and the kids.

Suddenly, sat there across the table from Kim, a vodka tonic in front of her, a pint of randomly selected real ale in front of him, he felt like an adulterer, a middle-ageing bloke furtively off with his cute young secretary.

Of course he knew that was unfair on him – he wasn't that old, for Christ's sake, and he was fully separated from Viv – and unfair on Kim, who wasn't that young and wasn't his secretary either and probably earned easily as much as he did.

And anyway, far as he could see, him and Kim were still some way from adultery. All he'd done was snog her once on a very drunken late night. Maybe he should have made a move when he was round her flat. Maybe that's why she was in her dressing gown when he showed up, maybe she was expecting him to . . . Maybe he was just as hopeless at reading women and their signals after seventeen years of marriage as he had been before.

'Christ, Pete, d'you always talk this much?' Kim was looking at him, shaking her head in mock despair.

'Oh God, sorry,' Pete said, 'I was miles away,' then, before he could stop himself, he added, 'Viv always goes on at me about that.' Christ, like he was still married to her.

Kim grinned, shook her head. 'She really did a number on you, didn't she? How long were you together?'

'Seventeen years.'

'Seventeen years – how old would I have been then . . . fourteen. Think you'd have liked me then? Second thoughts, don't answer that question.' She laughed.

Pete laughed too, thinking she knows I like her, thinking c'mon, man, the whole thing about this man–woman stuff, the whole thing you never managed to get into your thick head back in the day, is it's simple. You like her, she likes you – just do something about it. A flash of a half-remembered Captain

Beefheart song went through his head: 'Nowadays a woman's gotta hit a man just to let him know she's there.' And before he knew it he was sliding his hand over her hand on the table and leaning forward to kiss her hoping like hell she was going to respond.

And when she did, when clear and sober on a Sunday lunchtime, she opened her mouth to his, let her tongue flick against his teeth, Pete felt a lightness in himself that he didn't recognise.

13

Two weeks later Bobby was looking out the window, trying not to think about what was going on in the bedroom next door. This was one part of the new arrangement she hadn't really planned on. How close she was going to be to Maria when she was working, specially in these new flats where they made the walls out of papier mâché. You could hear everything if you wanted to. Or if you didn't want to.

Wasn't like she was squeamish about it. There'd been plenty of times she'd had to sort out problems with punters on the street. Some punter with his dick hanging out having a go at Maria round the back of Aspro's. Been plenty of times when Maria had had punters round her own flat, till Bobby put her foot down. But this was different. Every bloody time. You couldn't help thinking about it, what your girlfriend was doing in there. She could have put a Walkman on, of course, but then the whole point was that she could hear what was going on in case a punter turned nasty. So there she was, sitting at the table, trying to distract herself with last week's *Post* magazine, when something caught her eye. Just idly flicking through the pages, his face leapt out at her. Leslie St Clair. Just as vivid on the page of a magazine as the first time she'd seen him.

That was in Barrells seventy eight, seventy nine; she would have been sixteen or so trying hard to look older. Anyway, there she was dancing away in this little dyke club on the edge of town and the handsomest man in the world walks in. That was the first thing she registered, how good-looking he was. Maybe she was wrong but there weren't so many handsome people around back then. Men in particular used to look terrible. Bobby thought of the Seventies – the Sixties and the Seventies, all the time she was growing up – and she thought ugly ugly ugly ugly. And seeing this guy who looked like he'd come straight off the TV walking into your club, well it was a shock.

And of course he really had walked in off the TV, more or less, cause when she'd stopped gawping at how pretty he was – yeah, yeah, just cause you're a dyke doesn't mean you can't have opinions – she recognised him. Leslie St Clair. It was one of the sad things about living somewhere like Cardiff; anybody from the city ever did anything, the whole place knew about it. Back then it was Shirley Bassey, John Toshack, Andy Fairweather Lowe, Dave Edmunds and Leslie St Clair. Didn't have anything to do with liking their music or whatever. Leslie St Clair's music was horrible, real lounge-bar-smoothie shit like the 'Music to Watch Girls By' thing they have on the advert now, but he was on TV a lot, the sort of feller would show up doing the song on *Morecambe and Wise*. Regular housewives' favourite, really, light brown skin; you could take him for whatever you wanted. Though everyone in Cardiff knew he was a docks boy. Him and Shirley – the ones that made good.

Anyway, there he'd been, Leslie St Clair, large as life, walking through Barrells like it was the most natural thing in the world that this TV celebrity should be in a dyke bar, and he goes over to the DJ booth where Big Norma is playing the records and he nods his head and Norma gets someone else to take over playing the records and leads the way into the office and Bobby leans over to Roz who she's dancing with and says, 'Did you see that?' and Roz is like Leslie St Clair, oh yeah big deal, he's in here all the time. Then Roz paused and put her mouth closer to Bobby's ear and whispered, 'Talent spotting,' then burst out laughing.

At the time Bobby just laughed without knowing what Roz

was talking about. It wasn't long, though, before she got to know very well what kind of talent spotting Leslie St Clair was engaged in. Took a whole lot longer to forget it, though, all the things she'd seen and done with Leslie St Clair. But she'd managed in the end, hadn't thought about him in years. Even when she'd hear his name on the news, the way you did from time to time, she'd let it brush past her, no more than an echo of an echo.

She leafed back to the start of the article, started reading the story of this poor kid from the docks who'd worked his way up from boxing to showbiz to business and as she read and noted all the gaps, all the things not said, all the things swept under the carpet, she laughed, laughed the laugh that says don't go pulling the wool over my eyes, the laugh that says don't try telling me this whole world isn't full of shit cause I know better.

It was only when she put the magazine down and started to light up a fag that she saw her hands were shaking, realised that under the cynical 'well what d'you expect him to tell the papers, what do you expect the papers to print?' response, she was raging. Something about seeing him there, smug and rich and hardly looking a day older than twenty years ago, and talking about something called community capitalism, that made her want to rip that smile from his face, tell the world what Leslie St Clair was really about.

She put the paper down and went over to the computer. Working on her website had become a way of banishing all troublesome thoughts.

Today, though, she couldn't settle to it. Copy of *Web Design for Dummies* in her hand, she was trying to figure out how to connect up video files to the site, but then Maria's four o'clock turned up, classic married bloke on a business trip, and Bobby found her mind couldn't keep track of the complexities; thoughts of St Clair first kept returning. What was she going to do – tell her story twenty years too late to that newspaper guy Kim was seeing? Couldn't really see how that was going to do her any good. But maybe it would, maybe it would make the memories go away. Christ, the memories.

In another effort to distract herself, she logged on to the Internet and started aimlessly surfing around. She checked out Friends Reunited, laughed at the pictures of Donna and Jane trying to look slim, then started to wonder if the Net might help her find her dad.

Now here was something strong enough to drive St Clair out of her head. Busy rooting around for something, anything, that might help her find her dad, she barely registered the door slamming as Maria's punter left. Maria walked round behind Bobby, started massaging her shoulders and looking at the screen.

'What you doing, Bob?'

'Nothing,' said Bobby. Maria didn't say anything, but Bobby knew she knew what was going on. Knew all about Bobby's dad. How she'd never known him. How her mum had hardly known him either. How he'd fucked off well before Bobby was born. How her mum had waited till about three weeks afterwards before getting shot of Bobby herself.

Bobby knew where her mum was, though; they told her that when she came out of the home. Pam Ranger, now living in Essex. Bobby spoke to her once in a while, generally after a couple of Diamond Whites. Always asked what her dad's name was, but her mum wouldn't give it up, pretended like she couldn't remember. Bobby knew Maria was kind of hoping she'd just let it lie. After all, she kept saying to Bobby, she didn't know when she was lucky, not having her dad around. Maria's dad had been around all right.

But sod that, it had to be better to know than not know, and if she could just get a name out of her so-called natural mother then she was sure with the Internet she'd have a chance of running the bastard down.

'Not now, Ri,' she said, loosing herself from Maria's grip. 'I've got to make a phone call.'

'C'mon, Bob. Let's get moving. I want to go out.'

Finally. Bobby sighed with relief. She'd been on edge ever since she'd spoken to her mum, waiting to get back on the Internet, see what she could find out. The night had just crawled by, but now at last Maria was finished. What time was it? Quarter past midnight. The other girls were still off doing hotel visits. Bobby'd got a mate to slip a few business cards in the toilets in the Hilton, paid off nicely. Maria'd been looking after the punters wanted to come out. Last one was some Jap business feller staying at the St David's where they were really fucking hot on keeping the girls out. Now that was the kind of punter you wanted – loaded, no trouble – not like the kind of lowlife you got out on the streets.

And now he was out the door and Maria wanted to go out, which was fair enough, Friday night and all that. But all Bobby wanted was for Maria to go out, leave her in peace, check out this name her mother had finally given up.

'Give us half an hour, love, and I'll be ready.'

'Fuck that, Bob. I'm the one been fucking working all night. Six fucking punters, five hundred quid, and now I wants to go out.'

'Fine,' said Bobby, 'you go out. I'll see you down there.'

'Jesus, Bob, it's past bloody midnight already.'

Bobby hesitated for a moment. She knew she was being selfish, but right now she just felt like getting on with her search.

'I said half an hour, didn't I? You wants to go out, fine. Like I says, I'll see you down there.'

'Christ, you're getting to be a boring cunt these days, Bob.' Maria grabbed her bag and her coat and moved towards the door.

'Aren't you going to call a cab?' Bobby asked as she turned on her computer.

'Fuck do you care, Bob, I get raped walking into town? You just carry on playing with your bastard computer.'

Bobby turned round, angry now. 'Look, I said you wait a half hour I'll fucking drive us into town, all right? Just box up a fucking draw and watch the TV and I'll be done in a minute.'

Maria shook her head. 'I'm going out, Bobby. Going down the Hippo, see my mates, have a bit of a laugh. You do what the fuck you want.'

'The Hippo, you sure?' said Bobby, thinking maybe she'd feel like it in a bit. But the door had already slammed behind her. Bobby frowned for a moment, aware that she was in danger of cocking up the golden rule of pimping – you've got to have the carrot as well as the stick, a little dollop of sweet to set against the sour. But then who was she kidding? Her and Maria, it was long gone beyond pimp and hustler. They were like an old married couple these days, bickering all the bloody time. Christ, she was feeling her age; that was another part of it. Maria's idea of a big night out – couple of Es, few lines of coke, up till dawn at the Hippo or the Emporium or whatever they called the Top Rank these days – well, once in a while Bobby could handle it but mostly, to be honest, she'd rather stay in, takeaway and a couple of videos. Getting old, for sure. She was in the car these days, she found herself tuning into Radio 2 just cause there were some songs she remembered.

Bobby shook her head, banished these thoughts, then clicked on the Internet Explorer icon. Her mum had been drunk when she phoned her, as per usual for a Friday night, far as Bobby could tell, and she'd whined and cried but finally given up a name for her dad. Only trouble was it didn't sound like his real name. 'Troy Thursday,' she'd said he was called. Well, you had to laugh really, didn't you? What kind of stupid slapper would get herself up the duff with a bloke called Troy Thursday, think it was his real name? Her mum, that's what kind. But still it was something, Bobby supposed.

She typed in Troy Thursday, waited, and the screen came back with 126,000 answers. That couldn't be right. Bollocks, she'd forgotten to put it in inverted commas. She put the commas in, clicked on Go again and waited, suddenly aware she was holding her breath. Two seconds later the screen came up and fucking hell – eighty-five matches found.

Her excitement quickly faded when she realised that they all seemed to relate to some place called Troy somewhere in the States and things that happened there on a Thursday – you know, girls' softball team play next match in Troy, Thursday 10 April. But she kept on going and on page six of the results there it was. Some kind of Tom Jones fan page offering a list of all the gigs Big Tom had played. She clicked on the link and a huge list of venues and dates came up, starting in the year 1960. She scrolled down and almost immediately she saw it: 13 January 1961, Ocean Club, Caerphilly. Tom was fourth on the bill alongside Lorne Lesley, the Bombardiers and Troy Thursday.

Bobby felt her hair stand on end. Her dad. Shit.

14

Pete was starting to wonder if he was entirely in control of his life. He was sat in his latest weekend motor – this time a rather more subdued new Toyota – sharing a spliff with Kim – who he was starting to think of less as Kim and more as my girlfriend though he had to be careful about that, he could tell you didn't want to put too many fences round Kim – and Mikey – who seemed to have appointed himself as Pete's best mate.

They were parked on the edge of Mermaid Quay outside what had been the Tiger Bay Café, about the only locally owned and run place in the whole neighbourhood and would you believe it the first to close down. People didn't come down here after authenticity; far as Pete could see, what they wanted was chain bars and restaurants offering new concepts in Italian dining, the same ones being rolled out in waterfront developments and shopping malls from here to Bluewater. Anyway, they were sat in this car, the three of them, and it was coming up to midnight and they'd had a few drinks and Pete was now getting thoroughly stoned and they were trying to decide where to go next.

'We could go to the karaoke, over the Balti,' said Mikey.

Pete was about to say he'd rather listen to house music or nu-metal or absolutely bastard anything than go to a karaoke night, which was the kind of thing he just plain dreaded, but before he could get a word out Kim had chipped in with, 'Yeah, cool,' and dug Pete in the ribs and said, 'Be a laugh, eh?' and before he knew it Pete was trailing off after Kim and Mikey round the makeshift car park, across James Street, and a little way up Bute Street to the Baltimore Arms.

Once they were inside and upstairs Mikey peeled off to chat to the guy on the door and Pete headed to the bar with Kim.

'Now, let's get one thing straight,' he said. 'I am not singing. You can beg, you can plead, you can make me feel like a total wimp, I'm still not singing.'

Kim looked at him and shook her head in mock disapproval. 'You really are determined to be one boring bastard, aren't you?'

Pete shrugged, 'I told you.'

'Yeah,' said Kim, then, in an exaggerated Cardiff accent, she added, 'That's why I loves you, see,' and kissed him on the lips and Pete felt better and got the drinks in and was pleased he had made his stand, but then as the drinks got drunk and Kim went up and sang and Mikey went up and sang and Kim went up and sang again with a couple of other girls she seemed to know, and Pete sat there with his first pint still hardly touched and less and less to say, he couldn't help feeling like really he was a boring bastard and while he might be a bit of a novelty to a girl like Kim it wouldn't last, she'd have to find someone who was more of a laugh.

Watching her up on the little stage belting out 'Angels' with her mates, Pete couldn't help wondering what he was doing with a woman like this.

He'd slept with Kim three times now. First time had been the day they went out driving. They'd driven back to Kim's from the pub at warp speed. The excitement had carried Pete through the potentially awkward moments back at the flat, no shilly-shallying around making cups of coffee and stuff, but straight into the bedroom and unwrapping her clothes and his own clothes falling off and hands everywhere and just thrilled by the sight and the feel of an unfamiliar body after twenty years; a younger thicker body, not specially a better body than Viv's, it wasn't that, but a body that was responding with an eager lust not an easy familiarity.

It was only when things got down to the nitty-gritty that some weirdness crept in. The foreplay was fine; the foreplay was more than fine; it was – Pete couldn't help saying to himself – bloody great. It was what followed that was harder. When it came to the actual act Pete couldn't help but think of Viv, think of how Viv responded if he did *a*, wondered if Kim would like it if he did *b* because that's what Viv liked. Suddenly everything he wanted to do, every thrust or lick or bite, he realised he was doing because that's what he did with Viv, that's what Viv liked, and his head wasn't with Kim any more, it was thinking what would Viv think about this, and then wondering whether Viv had done this with someone else – a thought that hadn't crossed his mind before. He wasn't sure whether Kim had noticed or not – maybe she too was thinking of her ex – but suddenly, in the final stages, something was lost, some spark of intimacy and excitement was replaced by a sweaty ordinariness, and he was hit by a wave of utter misery.

It went after a while, of course, though if ever there had been a moment he wished he smoked that was it. And it wasn't long – in fact it was only a couple of hours – before they did it again. And it was good – less excited maybe but better controlled – and Christ knows it wasn't like there was any place in the world he'd have sooner been, but again there was that nagging sense of three of them in the bed and Pete knew that it would be a while before seventeen years of marriage worked their way out of his system.

Kim, to be fair, had been great about it. 'I bet you think of her, don't you?' she said after they'd done it that second time and Pete had squirmed and evaded and she'd laughed and said, 'Don't worry, I'm not asking you to do a comparison report, I was just thinking it must be weird for you, you know,' and Pete had managed a laugh too, and said yeah, weird was the word and that little moment had really helped to break down whatever barrier he'd been building up and suddenly he felt that much easier being around Kim, felt like she understood him.

Only trouble was, she might understand him but the way things were developing he was damned if he understood her.

Day after they'd been together he'd been thinking about her all the time. He'd phoned her up at work in the afternoon. God knows what the etiquette of these things was these days. Were you meant to wait weeks before you called someone just so they didn't think you were too keen, or was it only girls who were meant to do that? Anyway, he figured that he'd be pleased if she rang him so why shouldn't she be pleased if he rang her? So he did and it was a bit weird. It wasn't like she was unfriendly; she was perfectly friendly as ever. That was the thing. As ever. Friendly like she'd been the week before, not friendly like hey baby that was so gooood. But then maybe her boss was standing next to her when she took the call, maybe that was just her phone manner. Maybe, maybe, maybe.

He was plunged back into the thing he'd really hated about being single, never bloody knowing what was going on. Trying to figure out women like they were some alien species.

Shouldn't complain really, cause it made a change from trying to figure out Viv, as he had over the years, only to discover eventually that here was a woman who really was happy with her life – liked her job, liked her house, liked her kids, liked her washing machine, liked her husband, in about that order. Seventeen years figuring out someone who did exactly what it said on the packet. One thing about Kim, he was pretty sure there was more to her than met the eye.

Certainly, two weeks in, he wasn't getting much closer to figuring her out. Next time he'd seen her, the Thursday, she'd been fine; they'd gone out for a meal, Italian in town, gone back to hers again – and the sex had been good, definitely starting to get used to her, but then when he phoned her the next day to see what she was doing over the weekend she'd said she was busy the whole time which was a bit of a 'what the hell's that about', but had a kind of upside as it meant he did his duty and went to see Viv and the kids. They probably thought he was going completely mad cause he hardly said a word the whole time he was there, so weird had it all become now that he'd slept with Kim; it had somehow made the whole thing real, made him realise he really wasn't going back, this wasn't just a fantasy, this was his new life. And then he'd seen Kim again on the Monday and it had been fine, great even, and he could see that there was some kind of pattern emerging, some kind of dance, and one thing for sure, he wasn't the one leading it.

And now it was Friday night and Kim had come off the stage and people were buzzing around her and Mikey was sitting down at the table and introducing someone called Darren who was a moderately scary-looking white guy with prison tattoos on his forearm and a Cardiff accent so thick that even Pete who was born and bred had trouble with it, and then Kim was sat down too and had her arm around Pete and all the time the conversation seemed to be floating over or around him and then suddenly it was time to go and Pete was stood outside in the street and Kim's there saying that they could go back to her mate's place and Pete doesn't want to, all he wants to do is go back to Kim's place because when he's alone with her he feels fine and he can talk and be funny and alive but in a crowd like this he feels nothing but old and tired, so he says you mind if we go home, I'm really tired and Kim looks grumpy but says OK, but then when they get back to Kim's flat she turns to Pete and says, 'D'you mind not staying tonight? It's just I've got an early start in the morning' – first Pete had heard of this – 'and I've got my period and I just kind of need to be on my own. Is that OK?'

'Yeah,' said Pete, in that sense of 'yeah' that means 'not really but what can I do?'

'Oh God,' said Kim, 'you are sweet,' and leaned over and kissed him hard, let her tongue slide into his mouth, and then she pulled away and quickly got out of the car and waved goodbye, leaving Pete to drive off, the taste of her on his lips, completely unsure of where he stood.

15

Maria was late and Bobby was fed up. Maria hadn't come back from the Hippo till God knows what time the night before. Bobby hadn't minded too much about that cause she was still buzzing from finding her dad's name on the Net. Maria had blown out her two morning punters cause she was too hung over, and Bobby hadn't minded that either cause Tanya had filled in and Bobby spent the day making calls trying to trace her dad. But now it was well into the evening and Maria still hadn't shown up and Bobby was getting angrier by the minute. Tanya was off, Nikki was God knows where, there was a punter due any minute and Bobby's sweet high at finding a mention of Troy Thursday on the Internet had, with a complete lack of any further leads, steadily turned sour.

First she'd tried the Ocean Club where he'd played that gig long ago, but the Ocean Club wasn't there any more or at least it had changed its name half a dozen times and of course the manager now didn't have a clue what had happened in the Sixties. She kept on persevering, though, and eventually got hold of some old geezer who had been the manager sometime in the Sixties but he was worse than useless, he was one of those helpful bastards.

'You remember a singer called Troy Thursday, used to sing there back in the Sixties?' she'd asked.

'Yeah,' he'd said and her heart had leapt.

'Really?' she'd said.

'Yeah,' he'd said again.

'Well, d'you remember anything about him?'

'Yeah, he was a singer.'

'Well, what did he look like?' She could feel herself getting impatient now.

'Look like? I've no idea.'

'I thought you said you remembered him.'

'No, love, I said I remembered the name. Why, what d'you want to know?'

Bobby had felt like beating her brains out with the telephone; instead she pressed on, trying to get some sense out of him and getting precisely nowhere. He ended up giving her the names of a few other old-timers been on the club scene in the Sixties but they were useless and all. She was doing her best to face it. Her dad was a nobody who no one remembered. There you go. End of story.

The buzzer went. Bobby looked out the window. It was Nikki checking in for work, about eight bastard hours late. She sighed and got up from her computer, walked over to the intercom and buzzed her in. Time for a little chat.

Bobby waited till Nikki had plonked her bag down in the middle of the floor, sighing like she was exhausted from all the hard work of walking half a mile round to Bobby's place, then climbing a flight of stairs, even though she was still in her mid twenties and skinny as anything thanks to the fact that she lived on fags and tuna fish. She lit up a Marlboro Light the second she let go her bag, and Bobby walked over to the kitchen area, grabbed an ashtray and stuck it down in front of her.

'So,' she said once they were sat down nice and cosy across the coffee table, 'you like working inside then, Nikki?'

Nikki shrugged, flicked her ash just to one side of the ashtray. 'S'all right.'

'S'all right. That all you reckon it is? What d'you think walking up and down Penarth Road in the freezing fucking cold waiting for some punter to flag you down is then? That all right too?'

Nikki stared at Bobby. 'Same fucking thing, innit, Bob? Inside, outside. Still the same thing, innit?'

'No it fucking isn't. Out there, right; out there you're a slag. That's it. You're five minutes in the back of the car.'

'Two minutes.'

'Two minutes – that's your fucking attitude all over, right. Well, fine out there on the streets two minutes, yeah, fine. Get the money, get it done, get out of there. But this is different, right. In here, right, you're not a slag. You're like an escort, you're just a girl likes to show a bloke a good time.'

Nikki snorted with derision at this and Bobby barely resisted the temptation to grab her by the hair and smack her face.

'Come on,' she said instead, 'have a look at this.'

Bobby led the way over to the computer and opened up the Good Sex Guide website, clicked on Cardiff then showed Nikki the list of girls there.

'You see that? That's where all the blokes write down about all the different girls what they been with. Like reviews, right.'

Nikki wrinkled her face in a mixture of horror and disbelief. 'Reviews?'

'Yeah,' said Bobby. 'And this here, right, where it says Nikki, right, that's where this bloke writes about you. Now, let's see what he has to say, shall we?'

Course what the bloke says is none too complimentary. He doesn't say his name or anything but Bobby reckons she knows who it is. Feller looks like a teacher but drives a white van. Probably an electrician or something. Anyway, bloke's a semi-regular and he starts off saying he's been round to Bobby's place a few times and he's always had a good time; Tanya obviously got him off big-time and Lorraine was fine too. But Nikki – well, the feller was not impressed. Snotty, lifeless, looked at her watch after about ten seconds, wouldn't get on top, wouldn't let him touch her tits, would just lie there chewing gum and lit up a fag the second the bloke came. Ends up saying he was thoroughly disappointed, didn't know if he'd be going back there again.

Bobby waited till Nikki finished reading. 'Well?' she said.

'Well what? Who gives a fuck what some punter thinks? I'm not his fucking girlfriend, am I? I'm a fucking hustler. He wants a fuck, fair enough. But I'm not doing any of that other shit.'

Bobby looked at Nikki and her anger suddenly subsided. She could see the girl was actually upset at the thought of giving the punters any kind of intimacy. She sighed; she knew the story. Same old same old. Most of the girls she'd ever been with, the working girls, there was usually abuse one sort or another. Just because it was a cliché didn't mean it wasn't true. Lot of girls – not all the girls, definitely not – but a lot of the girls out there, they'd have some pretty fucking bad stuff to contend with. And Nikki was one of them, all right.

Bobby was on the point of saying something, probably something she would regret, like don't worry about it, girl, we'll keep on carrying you, when Nikki pulled herself together and spoke first.

'Anyway, Bob,' she said, 'I was talking to Maria last night . . .'

'Oh yeah?' said Bob, a note of menace in her voice, waiting to see if this was going where she suspected it was going.

'Yeah,' said Nikki, 'and she reckons you're not paying us enough.'

'She what?' Bobby stared at her. The deal Bobby gave her girls had to be the best in town. 'Fine,' she said. 'You don't like it, why don't you just fuck off out on the street, and the same goes for Maria and all. See how much fucking Scott or Chrissy Boy taxes you. Fact, fuck it, you just go and do that anyway. Had enough of you sitting round here looking like a miserable cow doesn't know a good thing when it's staring her in the face. Just fuck off.'

Nikki looked at Bobby in horror, her mouth dropping open, her eyes flicking from left to right as her brain struggled to find the words to make Bobby back down. Then the intercom went again. A regular punter. Bobby looked at Nikki. 'You're one lucky fucking cow, you knows that? Now, this feller comes round, you try and be nice, you got that?'

Nikki looked down, bit her lip and nodded.

Bobby shook her head. She'd believe it when she saw it. And as for Maria – she wasn't going to stand for that, no way. She was just about to put her headphones on, get back to her computer, blot out the sound of Nikki and the punter, when the phone rang. She picked up. It was the TV girl Kim, sounding all excited – her documentary was definitely happening. When could Bobby do an interview? Bobby thought about it. First reaction was it was asking for trouble publicising what she was doing. But maybe that was old-world thinking, Custom House thinking. Maybe now it would be cool to go on TV, tell the world you're a cyber pimp, free advertising basically. Plus right now she just felt like getting out of the flat and away from Nikki and Maria and the rest of them for a bit.

'Sure, darlin',' she said eventually. 'You just tells me the when and where, I'll be there.' And Kim says how about tonight and Bobby says OK and puts the phone down and then curses herself for not asking if there was any money in it.

It was late going on very late at night. The filming which had seemed to take for ever had finished hours ago and now Bobby was sat at a table in Floyd's bar right at the back by the window. She was right next to Kim who seemed to be somewhere on the cusp between drunk and very drunk or maybe she was putting it on a bit the way straight girls did when they put their hand on your leg.

It was surely up to Bobby now, how far she wanted to take it.

A week or two back, whenever it was she'd gone to meet her at the UCI, there wouldn't have been no question about it. She'd have had a bit of fun and forgotten her; she was a nice-enough-looking girl, no question, and you could just tell she'd be up for it in bed, wouldn't be one of those girls just lay there like they were doing you a favour just turning up. Now, though, Bobby didn't know. She wanted to take it light, but she had this scary feeling like maybe she couldn't do light any more, maybe light wasn't what she needed.

But then what she had with Maria was pretty heavy and that sure as hell didn't feel like what she needed either, so what the fuck. She leaned into Kim, found her mouth with her own, waited till Kim's tongue slid inside then bit down on it, not hard but firmly. She could feel Kim's whole body wriggle with anticipation. Oh well, maybe a bit of fun wouldn't be too terrible, thought Bobby.

And it wasn't either. They went back to Kim's place and it was like Bobby had expected, kind of grown-up student, loads of books and videos and CDs, stripped wooden floors. Bobby liked it too. In fact she almost felt like she was as horny for Kim's flat, Kim's nice safe life, as she was for Kim's nice round safe body. Whatever, it was a good time and Bobby slept better than she had for ages, which made it all the more surprising that when she woke up, Kim lying next to her snoring faintly, it was like someone had tipped a bucket of cold water over her, pure dread coming down.

It took her a moment to locate this dread. First thing she thought of was her father. Drawing a blank in her research for him. Nah, too old a wound. Maria? Not hardly; difficult to place too much value on sexual fidelity when your girlfriend's a hustler. So what was it? Getting older? Her uncertain future? Yeah, well all those things were worrying, all right, but none of them had the sharpness of this fear. Then she got it. Leslie St

Clair. Just saying his name to herself triggered deep and ancient pain. Leslie St Clair under her skin.

And lying there in the early-morning light, lying there in this nice safe flat with this nice safe girl, she realised she had no choice but to let herself remember. Remember it all.

End of the Seventies. Summer nights Bobby used to scrounge a bus fare off this social worker took a bit of a shine to her and head into town. She'd get off at the bus station and have a look in the Big Asteys café, see if anyone was about. Most times her friend Lee would be there, another half-caste kid – home used to be full of them back then, not like today when every other girl on the estate's got a little brown baby and nobody gives a toss.

If Lee was there, she'd go get a cup of tea and a Club biscuit, then sit at the corner table and take the piss out of all the old grannies down from the Valleys. That or talk about the football, who was coming up next, who was supposed to have a good firm. Living for Saturday afternoons the pair of them then.

It was obvious now, of course, became obvious pretty quickly even then, that they were both bent but neither of them was exactly broadcasting it. Lee specially. She supposed she'd known all the time what was driving him, what made him the vicious little fucker he was if it came to a fight. If you live in a home you hear all the stories, stuff Lee and a couple of other kids got up to, stuff they got up to with Mr Allen and all. But you ignored it, treated it like it was all a joke. And anyone called him a queer to his face – well, they didn't do it twice, not unless they wanted a taste of Lee's trusty Stanley knife.

Been a bit different for her, of course. For a start she never looked like the other girls, always looked like a boy, partly cause no one ever had a clue what to do with her hair and you never saw any girls in the magazines or anything weren't white, so she ended up having her hair short and she had this stocky kind of build and she liked sports – course that was the one thing they thought you might be good at – and she wasn't what you might call happy with her body shape, so she used to end up wearing tracksuits a lot, and so, basically, she looked like a boy and acted like a boy and in a funny sort of way it seemed only natural that she'd fancy girls like a boy – not just natural to her, seemed like everyone was expecting her to be a les. But all that said and done, it wasn't exactly an easy option – for one thing lesbians were like practically unknown back then. Least if you were a gay boy you could hang around the bus-station toilets and someone would soon show you what went where. Taken Bobby bloody ages to find out about Barrells.

That was where she'd go later on on Saturday night, nine, ten o'clock. But before that they'd just hang around, Lee and her. Asteys would turf them out after a bit. Sometimes they'd just stick around the bus station. Lee would stand around near the toilets, try and get money off of the old queers – give me a quid and I'll be in in a minute – now and again they'd fall for it if they were from out of town. Once or twice, and Bobby didn't feel good about it, they'd followed an old feller away from the station, waited till he crossed over the bridge then dragged him down on the towpath and robbed him. Never done any real harm, like, though the last time Bobby'd been a bit frightened by the expression she'd seen on Lee's face. So she hadn't wanted to do that again. And of course she'd found a new plan for them. Go round the Prince of Wales.

Tonight would be the fourth time they'd been there. First time had been funny. They'd hardly got in the door before the old bat in the ticket office was yelling at them to get the hell out of there, you dirty little bastards. Should have seen her face when Bobby said Mr St Clair asked her to come round. Woman kept shaking her head, looked like she was going to start crying or something. Anyway, in the end she showed them the way through the main doors into the foyer, pointed out the door that led upstairs, then left them to it. They'd made their way up this winding staircase till they came out on the top-floor landing, through another door and into a big room like a ballroom or something, all this old decoration on the walls and ceiling and that, and a bar at the back and a few tables spread around. St Clair was sat at the middle table, bottle of wine in front of him, people buzzing all around him, most of them not much older than Bobby or Lee. Made Bobby think of Fagin in *Oliver* – not that the kids were like pickpockets or anything. Well, some of them probably were but that wasn't the point – just that feeling of dodginess.

So, yeah, since then she'd been there twice and it was cool. Nothing much happened; St Clair was dead friendly, gave them Cokes and that, and it was just nice to be somewhere you didn't get any hassle. And of course Bobby knew there was going to be something St Clair wanted from her – or more likely Lee, she figured – she wasn't born yesterday.

Anyway, the fourth time they just gave the old bag a nod and headed straight up to the top floor. Moment they entered the big room Bobby could see something was going on. The tables had all been moved to one side and there was a guy Bobby hadn't seen before fixing up a couple of big lights.

St Clair spotted them immediately, came over and led them to the bar.

'Well,' he says, opening a Coke for Bobby and a barley wine for Lee, 'fancy you two dropping in. You like films?' He was looking at Lee not Bobby.

'Yeah,' says Lee and Bobby's just waiting for him to carry on with something really dumb like I thought *Earthquake* was really good, but then she sees Lee's eyes looking round the room and he just shrugs and glances at Bobby and they both raise their eyebrows a little bit like oh right, so this is what we've got ourselves into.

'That's good then,' said St Clair. 'Well, tell you what, why don't you two just sit down over here,' he waved at a little table set at the back of the room, behind the cameras, 'and watch what we're up to. Get a feel for how we do things round here, y'know.'

'Uh huh,' said Bobby and led the way over. Her and Lee just sat there for what seemed like hours while nothing much happened, both of them too edgy to say anything. Then St Clair walked over to the door and locked it. The lights were turned on and showtime began.

Bobby wasn't naïve. She figured she knew what to expect. After all, the Prince of Wales wasn't the Odeon, it was a porn pit. Not real porn, obviously, just innocuous crap about randy nurses. She knew; she'd sneaked in once or twice with the other kids, found out very quickly none of it spoke to her lust. She was pretty sure, though, that this would be different.

And it was. First off a couple of the lads she'd seen hanging around came on to the little set dressed in school uniform, despite being a good five years too old for it, both of them obviously trying not to laugh. She waited for the girls to come out, but they didn't; instead an older bloke dressed up as some kind of old-time teacher with a stupid fake beard on comes out and Bobby realises it's not going to be a boy-girl kind of a film. Which actually was a relief; she didn't know how she'd feel about watching that. Blokes with blokes, though, she could handle. In fact once they got going, the teacher guy starting to give his pupils the kind of lesson could get you on the front page of the *News of the World*, anyone caught you at it, she was disconcerted to find herself getting a bit turned on by it. As for Lee, his tongue was practically hanging out of his mouth. Bobby was sure St Clair wouldn't have much of a problem persuading him, he wanted to give old Lee his start in show business.

Whatever, the initial buzz wore off soon enough and the

proceedings became first comical – as the guy in the fake beard couldn't get it up – then boring – as the cameraman kept asking them to stop and do stuff again. Bobby had finished her drink so she got up, walked over to the bar and was just wondering if it would be OK to help herself to another Coke when St Clair materialised at her side.

'Not your scene, sweetheart?'

Bobby shrugged. 'Just thirsty.'

St Clair reached behind the bar and popped the lid off another bottle of Coke.

'How old are you, love,' he said, 'you don't mind me asking?'

'Sixteen,' said Bobby.

'Uh huh,' said St Clair, a flicker across his face, like he didn't believe her and was trying to figure out how old she really was. 'So where d'you live?'

'Rumney,' she said.

'Mum and dad?'

Bobby snorted with derision. 'Kids' home.'

'Oh yeah?' said St Clair and didn't say anything else about it, just left her till the filming finally finished and everyone was having a bit of a party and her and Lee were just going, and he slips up to her and asks, 'Don't suppose any of your girlfriends in the home be interested in being in one of our little films?'

And that's how it started. How she got from that – Bobby Ranger, screwed-up children's-home tomboy – to this – Bobby Ranger, top pimp, lying there in the early morning in a strange woman's sheets. And then she noticed that the strange woman was awake too and looking at her with concern and saying, 'Bobby, why are you crying?' and Bobby hadn't even noticed that she had been, and then before she knew it she was telling Kim, telling Kim all these secrets so long locked down, these secrets that had to come out before she choked on them.

16

Pete's phone rang for about the fiftieth time that afternoon. Cherri was lost somewhere near Ebbw Vale trying to find the Beaufort Theatre to interview Barbara Dickson, some idiot from the council's latest PR firm was hassling him to write something about some nautical festival they were having down the bay, the Subaru PR didn't know if she'd have a car for the weekend or not, could she let him know Friday morning, the ad manager had just rung with a couple of cancellations on page four so he'd have to dredge up some more news from somewhere and one way or another it was an afternoon of above-average hassle.

'Pete Duke,' he barked. But smiled when he recognised the voice on the other end of the line. Leslie St Clair. He'd rung up a couple of times since Pete's article had run, first to thank him for the piece, which was nice, wasn't often celebs bothered to do that.

'So what can I do for you today, Mr St Clair?'

'Les, man, for Christ's sake. I was wondering if you might like to come along to a little press conference we're having tomorrow. The WDA are hosting it, last big push for the Castle Market deal. Buffet and as much champagne as you can get down your neck. One o'clock at the St David's. You fancy it?'

'Sure,' said Pete, whose time on the *Post* had taught him never to walk away from a free lunch, and he put the phone down, already in a better humour. He worked his way steadily through the rest of the day's business, getting it all done by six, which was unusual. Now he felt like seeing someone, felt like seeing Kim, get things back on track. He dialled her number. She picked up quickly and sounded happy enough to hear from him, but she was all breathless and hyped up and busy filming something for her documentary, so she said she'd see him tomorrow which was good but didn't solve the problem of what to do now.

Pete thought about it for a moment, decided to head out into town, meet up with Randall. A quick trawl of the usual haunts failed to yield a sighting of Randall, however, which was a bit odd, so without really thinking what he was doing Pete found himself getting in the car and driving out to Whitchurch to see Viv and the kids.

Turning off Manor Way and heading up towards the close, he started to wonder if this was such a good idea after all. Viv was bound to be pissed off but he felt a real yearning to see them. Even if all they did was ignore him, they made him feel like he had some existence in the world, some solidity.

Sure enough, Viv opened the door and her face immediately turned to thunder. He could see her about to launch into a 'what the hell d'you think you're doing turning up here' rant but before she could say a word he'd slipped past her and into the kitchen where he sat down at the breakfast bar and waited for Viv to follow him in.

'Got anything to drink?'

'You what?' she said, staring at him and shaking her head. 'You can't bloody do this, you know.'

'I only asked for a drink,' he said, sounding like – who was he sounding like? – Randall he supposed, all fake innocence.

Viv shook her head again in disbelief but went to the fridge anyway, got out a big bottle of Coke, poured him a glass. Wasn't the kind of drink Pete had meant but he was getting soberer by the second and there was something achingly familiar about the glass of Coke.

'Kids in?' he said after taking a swig.

'Yeah,' said Viv. 'You mind telling me what the hell this is about?'

'Nothing much,' said Pete. 'Just thought it would be nice to see you.'

'Oh yeah, you just thought it would be nice to see us? Well, great. And how are we supposed to feel? Honoured? Look, kids, Dad's come back to see us. Well, you bastard.' She broke off, just stared at him. 'You got any idea what you've done to us, walking out like that?'

Pete looked around him, wondered if there was any evidence of what he'd done. Everything was just the way it used to be. The fridge had the same stuff inside it, the same fridge magnets on its door; the wipe-clean noticeboard had the same notices on it. A three-quarterful bottle of wine identical to the one that had been there the day he left was stood on the spotless work surface next to the cooking oil. Nothing had changed. If he let his eyes fasten on any more details he was sure he'd go mad. As far as he could see, it all just proved his point. There'd been no need for him there, the place had run perfectly well without him. Or had it? Up till now he'd repressed the idea that his leaving might have been devastating – he'd never thought himself capable of devastation. But what if the sameness of everything was not a sign of continuity but of trauma; what if that wasn't a similar bottle of quarter-drunk wine but the same bottle? What if he'd paralysed these lives that had been dearer to him than his own? What words to say then?

'You all right, love?' he said at last. Well, it was a start.

She looked at him like he was mad. 'What d'you bloody think, Pete? Your bloody husband walks out on you after seventeen bloody years, out of the blue, and you ask if I'm all right. Course I'm bloody not. And right when Becca's got her GCSEs coming up and all . . .'

Pete tuned out a bit at this point. He just had to believe that the kids were OK. They seemed OK whenever he'd visited them since. They said their schoolwork was going fine. He had to hang on to that. And he knew Viv, knew she'd try and work on his guilt. What she didn't seem to get was that it was his guilt over leaving her that was her better avenue of attack, but then maybe she was just like him, didn't think she mattered for herself.

'. . . and you leave me here stuck out in the middle of bloody nowhere . . .' exactly where you always insisted on living, thought Pete '. . . and you're off in bloody town and no doubt you got yourself a bloody girlfriend already . . .' She always said that but this time she must have noticed some reaction in Pete's face cause she stopped all of a sudden. 'Oh Christ,' she said, 'you have, haven't you? You've got a bloody girlfriend,' and then she burst into tears and Pete awkwardly tried to put his arm round her but she batted him away, just let herself sob and sob then turned to him and said through her tear-stained face, her face made ugly by crying, 'Who is it?'

'No one you know,' he said, stalling for time. He hadn't planned on telling Viv about Kim, not till he was a lot surer about it all himself. Best thing maybe would be to deny the whole thing except, bollocks, 'no one you know' kind of gave the game away.

'Yeah, well,' says Viv, half laughing, half hysterical, 'didn't think you'd be going off with Julie next door. C'mon, tell me who the bitch is.'

'Her name's Kim,' said Pete. 'She works for the BBC.'

'Well la-di-da. How old is she?'

'I dunno,' said Pete, wondering if she'd ever told him.

'Younger than me, I'll bloody bet. Have to be young to be taken in by a wanker like you.'

'She's about thirty,' said Pete, adding a couple of years on to what he guessed Kim's actual age to be. He should ask her, should find out her bloody birthday. Christ, how little he knew about her. How much he knew about the woman stood in front of him.

'Well, you want me to tell the girls, tell them about Dad's new girlfriend? Bet they'd be interested.' Viv's voice was getting louder.

'No, for Christ's sake. I wasn't even planning on telling you yet. It might be all over next week. You know what it's like . . .' Oh, why did he have to say that?

'No, I don't know what it's like; I'm stuck here with two kids. How'm I expected to know what it's like? Or d'you think I'll be hopping over the garden fence having it away with old Duncan?' She turned round, grabbed the bottle of wine, took out the stopper and poured herself a big glass. Pete watched her face carefully. If the wine had really been there for two months, no way she'd be able to swallow it. He felt a moment of idiotic relief when it seemed to go down smoothly. Life had been going on as normal. It hadn't all been paralysed by his absence.

'Look,' he said, 'I'd better go.'

'Yeah,' said Viv, 'you better had,' and then, as Pete was walking out the door, her door, their door, she shouted after him, 'And give my love to your girlfriend, tell her I'll tear her throat out I ever sees her.'

Christ, a bit of Cardiff creeping into Viv's hard-won accent. Pete drove off pondering her threat. Did it mean she still loved him? Did he want her to still love him?

17

Bobby and Jamal were in the health centre. Jamal had a bit of an earache, and Maria had a regular booked in at four, so Bobby'd taken him down after school. Jamal was sat there with a packet of crisps and Bobby was wrapped up in her thoughts, wondering what the hell had been going on in her head, blurting out all that stuff to Kim.

Anyway, she's sitting there minding her own business when this old feller comes in and sits down next to her, starts rabbiting on about the development and that, and Bobby's not paying a lot of attention cause it's not like she hasn't heard it all before about a million times, but then the feller – Noah his name was, she thought; old West Indian feller anyway – starts talking about the Big Windsor and what the hell are they doing just leaving it to rot? Heard tell they were going to turn it into a lap-dancing club – he laughs and stares at Bobby but nothing happens – and I remember when that place was jumping, all the entertainers used to come down there – and Bobby's ears prick up at this and she asks the question one more time.

'You ever hear of a singer called Troy Thursday?'

The old feller thinks about it. Bobby can see he's dying to say yes, but eventually he shakes his head and says, 'No, darlin', 'fraid not.'

Bobby just smiles and says, 'No worries.'

The old feller won't leave it alone, though. 'When was he around then? Fifties? Sixties?'

'Early Sixties,' says Bobby, her eye on the doctor's surgery door which is just opening, should be Jamal's turn next.

She can see the old feller ransacking the memory banks one more time but before he can speak the nurse calls out, 'Jamal Hughes,' and she stands up then taps Jam on the shoulder so he gets up too and they're heading for the doctor's door when the old feller finally pipes up and says, 'I know, darlin', I know who you should ask. Feller called Bernie Walters. That feller knows everyone in the entertainment business.'

'Yeah, thanks,' says Bobby, her first thought being what would I want to talk to that old cunt for, but then she thinks again and she has to face it. It's a good idea. If anyone could tell her who Troy Thursday was, it was probably Bernie Walters. Been booking acts in Cardiff since Moses showed up with the tablets. Funny she hadn't thought of him before, really — it was just that he was hooked up with Kenny Ibadulla and bloody Ken always treated Bob like she was something you'd stepped in. So, yeah, sure, Bernie Walters, but how was she going to get to him without going through Kenny?

It was a question she asked Maria later on, the three of them having their tea back at the home flat. And Maria surprised her by saying well why don't you just go round Bernie's office? It's only down on St Mary Street.

Just a little remark but it was one of those moments for Bobby, like someone just turned the lights on. Of course — that was all you had to do, look in the phone book to get his address and go round his office. What could be more obvious? It struck Bobby forcibly just how small-scale her existence was, how limited she'd let herself become by the hustling life. The world outside Butetown had become unreal to her. An outsider like Bernie Walters only really came into focus through his connection with Kenny Ibadulla.

But this one little unthinking remark of Maria's, it was like she'd been let out of prison. You just take it for granted that Kenny is the man, cause within Butetown, of course it's true, Kenny's the man. But let your horizons widen and what's Kenny? Another petty gangster whose territory amounts to a single crumbling housing estate. And if Bobby wanted to move up in the world, who was Kenny, who was anyone, to stop her?

'Ri,' she said then, 'what d'you think about moving?'

'Moving?' said Maria.

'I don't want to move,' said Jamal, suddenly tuning into the conversation, 'I'm watching *Simpsons*.'

'Not now, love,' said Bobby, ruffling his hair and waiting till his attention was focused back on Springfield's first family before turning to Maria. 'I was thinking maybe we could rent one of the other flats over the wharf, to live in, like. Be easier for work and stuff.'

Maria's eyes immediately flickered to Jamal. Bobby knew what she was thinking. Boy was nearly six now; one of these days he's going to be wondering where it is Mummy goes to work.

'Doesn't have to be the same block or anything. I was just thinking it'd be good to get away from here –' she waved her hand, not sure herself if she was referring to the flat or the street or the whole of bloody Butetown '– and they're nice, the flats, aren't they?' Christ, she sounded like she was an estate agent, trying to sell Maria the place – what was going on in her head?

'I dunno,' said Maria eventually. 'What's the point?'

And Bobby just shrugged, wondered if these changes she was going through, maybe they were going to take her away from everything. 'Fine,' she said, 'whatever. I'm going over the wharf for a bit.'

'Playing with your bloody computer again.'

'Yeah,' said Bobby, feeling once more like there was a chasm opening up between her and Maria, 'that's right.' She kissed Jamal and headed out into the evening.

On the street she turned on her mobile, listened to her messages. A couple of hang–ups, probably punters. One from the feller Pete asking for an interview. Christ, she'd have to think about that bit first. And one from Kim – you fancy coming round? Bobby grinned suddenly; she could think of something better to do than play with her computer.

She called Kim. Kim only had an hour before she had to go out but if Bobby wanted to come over like right now . . .

Bobby fancied it, all right. Fancied it like she hadn't in a long time. Fancied Kim like she fancied leaving her life behind. Hardly a word spoken between them the whole time, just hot and heavy from the moment she walked in the door. Came like a fucking train. Afterwards she did go over the wharf, played with the computer a bit, more than anything just to take the flush from her face before she had to see Maria again.

Next morning Bobby was up bright and early, made Jamal a cooked breakfast, took him to school chatting all the way there – how did he like his teacher? what did he think of the lunches? all this stuff – till the kid was looking at her like what are you on? And then she called up directory enquiries and got Bernie Walters's number, phoned it up and got an address in St Mary Street off the secretary.

She hung up and stood there for a moment, just knowing that Bernie would be the key.

Half of her wanted to stop now, go back to the flat, have a cup of tea, sort of savour the anticipation. Other half wanted to get it over and done with, plus to be honest she was nervous and she knew the longer she left it the worse she would get and before she'd realised she'd made a decision her feet were carrying her towards town.

On the way she wondered what excuse she could use to get to talk to Bernie. She'd met him once or twice over the years. Sixtyish feller but looked good on it; thick grey hair and a permanent tan, word was he owned a share of Kenny's club, Black Caesar's. She knew who he was, all right, but she doubted it was mutual. So what was she going to say? Maybe ask him about the lap-dancing, see if he was interested in her introducing some girls to him. Get a commission or whatever. Nah, she thought, as she reached the Monument and the beginning of St Mary Street, might as well go straight for it.

The secretary put on a bit of a show when Bobby walked in – like 'You want to see him today? Oh no, I don't think so' – but then she buzzed through and had a quick word, told him there was a young lady wanted to ask about an entertainer he might have represented back in the Sixties and obviously Bernie said send her right in, cause, after a little bit more fiddling about and making Bobby take a seat next to the framed photo of Dave Edmunds, the door opened and there was Bernie.

He walked over to shake her hand, clocking her as she stood up, stuck his hand out and said, 'I know you, don't I? But you're going to have to excuse me. I never forget a face, love, but I'm hopeless with names.'

'Bobby,' she said, 'Bobby Ranger.'

'Course,' said Bernie, 'Bobby Ranger . . . well, come on in.'

She followed him into the office, framed photos all over the place, everyone from Stan Stennett to Cerys Matthews. Her eyes passed over them quickly, hungrily, like she was expecting one of them to say Troy Thursday in big letters. Didn't, of course.

Bernie sat down on his desk, great big fuck-off computer on a table next to it, obviously brand new, the box was stood there in the corner. Bernie clicked on the screen and she saw a game of cards disappear.

'Nice computer,' she said.

Bernie shook his head. 'Probably. That's what my bloody nephew sold me the thing tells me. "Bernie," he says, "you got to get into the computer age, get your business on-line, get a website." So like an idiot I say yes and he sells me this stuff, five grands-worth of it, and be honest with you that was six months ago and I just about know how to turn it on, love . . . Makes me feel like I'm from out the ark. You understand this stuff?'

Bobby shrugged. 'I knows a bit.'

'Really?' says Bernie, brightening up. 'Cause I've been asking our old mate Kenny if he knows anyone could help me out and he's just been um-ing and er-ing . . .'

Our old mate Kenny. Bobby wondered who the hell Bernie thought she was. Still, now wasn't the time to set him right. 'Yeah, well,' she said, 'I'm not an expert exactly, but I might be able to help you out a bit, if you want to build a website or something. I've built my own . . .' she added, thinking why am I telling him this?

'Really?' said Bernie. 'That'd be great. If you could find some time in the next week or so. Wouldn't be able to pay you much, but . . .'

'Sure,' said Bobby, thinking Christ, looks like I'm the one getting the job. 'Sure.'

'Great. Now what was it you wanted to see me about?'

'Well,' began Bobby, 'I'm trying to trace this singer from the Sixties.'

'Oh yes?' said Bernie. 'What's the name?'

'Troy Thursday,' said Bobby, the name sounding ridiculous as ever, like she was trying to track down Scooby Doo.

'Troy Thursday,' said Bernie, frowning. 'And might I ask why?'

'Well,' said Bobby, launching into what was becoming a familiar spiel, 'I was adopted –' that was the first lie; what she really meant was I was left abandoned, unwanted '– and I'm looking to trace my natural parents and I found my mum, right, and she says my dad was a singer called Troy Thursday.'

'Hmm,' said Bernie, who'd suddenly gone all inscrutable.

'Well,' said Bobby, who frankly couldn't bear the suspense, 'you remember him or what?'

'Oh yes,' said Bernie, 'I remember the name, all right. Only trouble is there wasn't just one Troy Thursday; it's a name a few people used.' He looked up at the ceiling, frowned. 'Well, it was a name I invented, to be honest, and any time someone dropped out from a bill we'd stick Troy Thursday on instead. This was late Fifties, early Sixties, see, things were less sophisticated then: you could tell folks that Troy Thursday was a big name in London and they'd believe you. But really it'd be whoever was hanging around the office at the time – they would be Troy Thursday for the night up in Aberdare or Ponty or wherever.'

Bobby thought about this: typical of her bloody mother to get off with a guy who wasn't even real. 'You remember who any of them were?' she asked hopefully.

Bernie shrugged. 'Long time ago, you know, but I tell you what. You come back next week and have a look over the computer situation, I'll see if I can't get a little list together – how's that sound?'

'Fine,' said Bobby. 'How about if I ask my mum where the gig was she met him – would that help? You got any records or anything?'

Bernie laughed. 'Nothing that thorough, I'm afraid, but yes, if your mother can remember where it was, that might help jog the old memory bank. Amazing what sticks in there, you know. Well, to be honest, you get to my age it's easier to remember stuff happened in 1961 than stuff happened last week. So if you make an appointment with Marguerite on your way out I'll look forward to seeing you next week.'

Bobby shook Bernie's hand awkwardly and was just about to leave when something obvious struck her. 'All the Troy Thursdays, they were all black then?'

She could have sworn she saw a flicker of panic on Bernie's

face but if there was one he banished it quickly and all he said was, 'Look, love, like I say, it was a good old while ago, but yeah, quite a few of the Troys would have been black, always had a lot of docks boys on the books. And like I say, I'll get a little list together for you.'

'OK,' said Bobby, because what else could she do – beat the name out of him?, but as she walked down the stairs she reckoned Bernie Walters had a pretty good idea who her dad was.

18

Pete had slept really badly. Viv kept appearing in his dreams. Guilt coming down hard. Pete wasn't good with guilt. He couldn't bear to feel he had hurt someone else. Part of him, a big part of him, just wanted to go back home to her, put the shutters up and carry on with their nice quiet life. Kind of like those old guys who can't hack it outside prison; first thing they do when they get released is commit another crime, so they can go back to their nice comfy cell and a life without decisions.

He got out of bed before these thoughts suffocated him. He knew he was doing the right thing. Was sure that in the long run Viv would see he was doing it for both of them – saving them from a living death. Wouldn't she?

He was in work early and spent most of the day being, he suspected, a bit of a bastard. Right on everyone's case. Worked straight through lunch drawing up a three-month plan for the features pages and was just calling an arse-kicking meeting of his key writers when the phone went. Kim. And for the first time that day he felt happy. She said she wanted to meet him somewhere quiet, she had a story she wanted to tell him about, so he suggested the Conway and she said fine and just this brief exchange seemed to relax him, helped him get through the second half of the day a little more calmly than the first.

In the Conway Pete was almost at the bottom of his first pint by the time Kim showed up. As she walked towards him he wondered what Viv would make of her. She was younger than Viv – seven, eight years younger. Of course Viv kept herself in pretty good shape, a bit obsessive about it, if you asked Pete, while Kim didn't seem to care that she was carrying a few extra pounds. That was a lot of it for Pete, really; Kim just didn't seem to see life as such a bloody training course as Viv did. You could see it on her face that Kim was a girl liked to have a good time. But what would Viv think? God knows. Probably that she was a bit of a slapper. Well, thought Pete, maybe he was a bit of a slapper at heart too. He wondered what Kim saw when she looked at him. A bloke learning to relax a bit, he hoped. He'd gone back to the flat after work, changed out of his suit into jeans and a plain blue shirt from Gap. Nothing fancy but he wasn't trying to be fancy; all he wanted to be was a steady good bloke who knew how to have a bit of a laugh as well. And as Kim walked towards him and kissed him on the lips he felt sure this was a woman he could have a laugh with.

'So,' she said once they'd got a fresh round of drinks, 'you want to hear about my story?'

Sure said Pete so Kim launched into this long-winded account of how she'd done this, like, in-depth interview with this Bobby, you know the pimp, yeah, and that was all really good, yeah, really good material for Kim's documentary, but then she came out with this incredible stuff about Leslie St Clair.

'Oh yeah?' said Pete, his ears pricking up a bit.

'Yeah,' said Kim and told Pete all about the Prince of Wales and the porn movies.

'Christ,' said Pete when she finished. 'I'd heard a few rumours before. But never from anyone was actually in-volved. Shame she didn't come forward before I wrote my piece about him.'

'Well she couldn't have really,' said Kim, ''cause it was only reading your piece made her remember it all.'

'Wouldn't have thought you'd forget something like that,' said Pete. 'You sure she's not just making it up?'

'No,' said Kim, 'no way. She obviously just, like, repressed the memory or whatever.'

'Yeah,' said Pete, 'I guess. So what are you going to do about it? How's it going to fit with your documentary?'

Kim looked at him, shook her head. 'It's not for me, stupid. It's for you so you can do a follow-up story, expose the real Leslie St Clair.'

Pete thought about it. It was . . . well, potentially it was a great story. If it checked out, which was a big if. Controversial as hell, mind. Wales wasn't a place which liked to see its heroes taken down. So taking down Leslie St Clair wouldn't be something to do lightly. Most definitely controversial. And Graham wouldn't be keen on that. What Graham liked was good news, civic-booster stuff – under-35s vote Cardiff Britain's best city for getting completely arseholed in. 'I dunno,' he said eventually. 'Might be tricky to get it past the editor.'

Kim looked at him aghast. 'For fuck's sake, Pete, don't be such a gutless bloody wimp. Your editor doesn't want to know, take it to bloody London. Tabloids'll pay you a fortune.'

Pete thought about it some more. Yes. Well. Maybe anyway. But he wasn't at all sure that Graham would be happy to let Pete moonlight. So where would that leave him? Did he want to quit his nice comfy job and dive into the world of freelance muck-raking? Did he hell. On the other hand, he didn't want Kim thinking he was a total wimp. And anyway it was most likely just a load of ancient gossip would never add up to anything, so for the moment he figured he'd try and stick to his usual life strategy, trying to please everybody.

'Uh, yeah, of course,' he said, 'I'll check it out. You tell Bobby to get in touch with me she wants to take things further.'

'Great,' said Kim, 'great,' and Pete smiled at her and was just standing up to get another round of drinks in when there was a clap on his shoulder and he looked up and saw Randall standing there.

'Randall,' said Pete, 'what are you doing here?' which was a stupid question – like asking a dartboard what it's doing in a pub. So Randall just shrugged and Pete remembered his manners and said, 'Oh, this is Kim.'

'Robert Randall,' said Randall, sticking out his hand.

'Oh,' said Kim, 'from the paper? My nan loves your column.'

'Hmm,' said Randall, 'thanks,' not looking altogether thrilled by this information. Pete could see he still fancied himself as a bit of a ladies' man. But he recovered himself quickly and in no time was getting the drinks in. And then they were sat round the table together and it occurred to Pete that if anyone would know about St Clair and dodgy movies in the Prince of Wales, Randall would be the man.

'Oh yes,' said Randall. 'You know he used to own the Prince of Wales?'

'The old porn cinema,' said Pete. 'Yeah, I heard that.'

'Well,' said Randall, lowering his voice to conspiratorial level, 'I seem to remember there was a rumour at the time he wasn't just showing porn movies there, he was making them too, and none of your soft-core business either.'

'Yeah? So when would that have been?'

'Late Seventies,' said Randall. 'Lot of that stuff going on then. Porn stuff. There was a feller in Bridge Street used to have a trapdoor in his shop floor, let his special customers down to where he kept the hard stuff. It was all new then.'

Bridge Street, thought Pete. Heart of the old seedy Cardiff centre long since airbrushed out of existence. The new Bridge Street had a selection of multi-storey car parks and a bike shop in it; the old Bridge Street was a hundred-yard stretch of dodgy second-hand 'bookshops', smoky cafés, scrumpy pubs and 'medical supply' shops that lost half their trade when they legalised abortion. Pete used to haunt the street when he was a kid looking for *Marvel* comics, knowing he was trespassing into the forbidden world of adults. The Seventies: sin and perversion behind those doorways filled with blue and yellow streamers.

And then the conversation moved on to Kim's documentary; *The Secret World of the Lesbian Pimps* she told Randall it was called.

'Hmm,' said Randall. 'Always were a few of them around. Used to be an amazing woman in the House of Blazes, six foot tall if she was an inch. Sailors used to come in and . . .'

And Randall was off into tales of the old Tiger Bay. Kim sat there lapping them up, all this good stuff that never made it into *Randall's Rambles* – the hookers and pimps and Benzedrine addicts and blue movies made in the Prince of Wales.

Pete was happier, happier than he'd been for a while. Watching Kim and listening to Randall, he realised that a lot of the strain he found in being with Kim was they were always around her mates, who invariably made him feel straight and boring and old. Randall, on the other hand, made Pete feel like he was someone, someone dry and witty and experienced. Someone who could have a few drinks, tell a few stories.

They ended up staying in the pub till closing time. Afterwards, Pete announced he was starving, partly to try and head off a visit to the Cambrian, which was bound to be full of Kim's mates and could too easily break the evening's spell, and partly because it was the simple truth. He figured he'd walk back with Kim and pick something up from the takeaway, but instead Randall chipped in with, 'How about you two lovebirds come back to the flat for some bread and cheese and a drop of whisky?'

Pete looked at Kim and she nodded and smiled and then cooed with delight when she saw Randall's flat and turned to Pete and said why the hell haven't you brought me here before, this place is fabulous, and Pete for once didn't try to explain, just shrugged and smiled and soon they were sat in the kitchen eating bread and Brie and drinking tumblers full of single malt that tasted of peat and fog and chocolate and had one of those nights when everyone's laughing like hell and in between unburdening their deepest thoughts and no one can remember a thing about it in the morning, which is partly just as well and partly because it feels like the top of your head is going to come off.

At least that's how Pete's head felt at six the following morning. But feeling the warmth of Kim next to him helped and so did the Alka-Seltzers he fetched for them both and so did the sweaty, still half-drunk, sex that followed, allowing them both another hour's sleep, and after they'd breakfasted on strong coffee and kissed in the street before parting Pete felt great as he walked down past the stadium to work. Felt terrible but great too.

19

Bobby and Maria dropped Jamal off at school then walked over to Atlantic Wharf. Malcolm Hopkin was meeting them there at half nine to show them a potential new flat before they started work. Bobby was buzzing with ideas. She'd been on the computer half the night. First she'd finally sorted out how to upload her site on to the Net, and found a server who wasn't too fussy what kind of sites they hosted, which wasn't hard. It was starting to become obvious to everyone that there was only one sure-fire money-maker on the Net and that was sex. Funny, really, what happened to all those smart young entrepreneurial types. Six months ago they'd all been chopsing on in the papers about how their new site selling designer perfume or handbags or offering a unique service to the Jewish, lesbian, whatever community was going to take the world by storm, and now they were all busy getting their hands dirty, trying to actually generate some revenue. Well, good luck to them, but Bobby couldn't help but see the irony. She'd spent years on end being the object of general disgust – the evil pimp – and now the world was awash with cyber-pimps in Armani-framed glasses. Now she was looking forward to getting back over there, tweaking the site some more.

'Bob! Earth to fucking Bob? I'm here, you know.'

Bobby came to, looked at Maria, smiled vacantly.

'Sorry, doll, miles away.'

'You're always fucking miles away. You're living on another planet, Bob. It's doing my head in.'

'What?' said Bobby. 'You happier working out on the street? You don't think it's a better set-up we've got now?'

'No, Bob, course it's better. All that side of it, course it is. But you, Bob, it's like I don't know who you are any more. You never bloody speak to me. You're always on the bloody Internet. Jamal's complaining how you're never there at bedtime like you used to be. And I'm sick of telling him don't worry, love, Auntie Bob's building a nice website so your mum can screw more punters.'

'Christ, Ri, I'm only doing it for you. Make life easier.'

'Yeah, right, like you don't take half the money. Anyway, that's not the point; I don't want to talk about that. All it is, Bob, is I don't want a fucking website, I wants you to talk to me, I wants to have a laugh like we used to.'

Bobby didn't say anything, just hunched her shoulders up in her jacket and walked on ahead.

Maria laughed, ran after her, put her arms around Bobby. 'Christ, Bob,' she said, 'you look just like a little boy sometimes.'

Bobby rolled her eyes. She gave Maria her wintriest, oldest smile, a smile devoid of joy. 'Yeah, girl,' she said, 'never heard that before.'

'Oh, fuck off, Bob. That's exactly what I mean. You're so serious all the time. Lighten up, why don't you?'

Bobby kept her mouth shut, strode on towards the Atlantic Wharf flats. Didn't say another word till she saw Malcolm Hopkin waiting outside.

'All right, Mal,' she said and he raised his arm in greeting.

'All right, Bob,' he said.

'Yeah, not bad.' Bobby turned and saw Maria walking away, over towards the work flat.

'Something the matter, Bob?'

'Fuck knows. Time of the month? Who knows? Women, Mal. You know what I mean?'

Bobby had a good look around the new flat with Malcolm Hopkin. There wasn't anything special about it — it was pretty much identical to the one she was already renting, but Hopkin liked to haggle over money. You could see he got off on the game of it and, to be honest, Bobby found she liked being around Hopkin, liked the way he seemed to know everyone, know how to get things done, and yet he stayed in the background. She was sure she could learn a lot from a feller like that. How to survive, even. It was bothering her a lot these days. She'd wake up in the night worrying about shit she'd never even thought of before. What would she be doing in ten years' time? What would she be doing when she was old? How would she live? Suppose when you're young, you don't care about that stuff. That's why you get fucked up. But here she was pushing forty and the amazing thing really, when she thought about it, was how un-fucked-up she was. No drink or drug problems and she was fit as she'd ever been; didn't go to the gym or nothing but she walked a lot, she supposed. So she might as well face it; all the signs were she was going to be around for a bit.

'You got a pension, Mal?' she said as they left the flat, the rent agreed at a quarter of the figure she was paying for the other place ('One word you're doing any business in there, Bob, though, and you're out, right').

Hopkin laughed. 'Course I have, love.' He pointed to his head. 'It's right in here. Certain people don't look after me, I'll be writing my memoirs; well, dictating them anyway, you know what I mean?'

Bobby laughed briefly. 'Seriously, though.'

Hopkin raised his eyebrow. 'I am being serious, love. But if you're serious, I'll give you the number of a financial adviser won't rip you off too bad.' He looked at her quizzically. 'You feeling all right, Bob?'

'I dunno, you just gets tired sometimes.' Then she mustered up a smile and said, 'Yeah, well, back to work.'

Hopkin headed off to meet someone in the Wharf. Bobby headed for the work flat.

When she got there, there was no sign of Maria, just Nikki and Tanya sat in front of the telly watching MTV Base.

'Seen my girl?' said Bobby.

Nikki and Tanya looked at each other.

'She went out,' said Tanya eventually.

'Oh yeah?'

Tanya didn't say anything, apparently under the impression that 'out' was a good enough answer. Bobby let Tanya's eyes drift back to the TV, Destiny's Child high-kicking their way through 'Survivor', then bent down and yelled in her ear, 'Where the fuck did she go?'

'Christ, Bob,' said Tanya, sitting up. 'I don't know, do I? Phone rang and then she said she was going out.'

'Christ sake,' said Bobby, shaking her head. Then Nikki spoke up.

'Town, I think, Bob. She said to whoever it was she was going to meet them in town. Somewhere called Space, she said. You know where that is?'

'Space?' Bob thought about it, knew she'd heard the name, couldn't think where it was. 'All right,' she said, 'thanks, Nikki. Now, who wants to do the silly cow's one o'clock?'

'Can't, Bob,' said Tanya. 'Got an outcall over in Cyncoed.'

'I'll do it, Bob,' said Nikki. Amazing how she'd got it together since being given that talking to.

'All right, girl, nice one. It's a regular. Mr Jones, middle-aged feller, no problem. I got to go out for a minute but don't worry if I'm not back; he's all right.'

Bobby headed back outside. She wanted to be by herself for a moment to think. Where the fuck had Maria gone and who with? She called Maria's mobile number; it rang a couple of times then went on the voicemail. Bitch must have clocked Bobby's number. She called Maria's flat – nothing. Who the hell had she gone to see? She decided to go check out the flat anyway. Five minutes and she was round there. Let herself in with her key. Nobody home. Started to look through Maria's stuff for some clue as to where she'd gone, then stopped herself. What on earth was she doing? Maria would turn up later on; she was just acting like the unreliable bitch she always had been. Question was, why was Bobby taking it so serious?

Lot on her mind, that's what the trouble was. Nothing to do about it but calm down and get on with the job. She took a few deep breaths, let herself out of Maria's flat and drove back round the wharf, parked outside the pub. As she got out of the car she saw Malcolm Hopkin come out of the pub, meeting over presumably. 'All right, Mal.' She nodded her head at him.

'All right, Bob.' Malcolm waved her over and as he did so another fixture came through the doors: Malcolm's meeting. 'Bob, you ever met my friend Leslie St Clair?'

Somehow Bob got through it. Handshake, mumble. Long time, mumble. See you. She turned away and walked towards the flat. Felt like she was underwater. But her calm was well and truly shattered now. She couldn't go in, couldn't face Tanya and Nikki for a bit. Instead she waited till Hopkin and St Clair were gone then walked back past the pub to the canal.

Bobby sat by the wharf, aware that time was passing, aware that she should go back inside, take charge, make sure Tanya and Nikki were doing what they were supposed to, make sure the punters were behaving. After all, that was her job, wasn't it? Pimping. Taking control of the lives of dumb lazy girls would sooner lie on their backs than do a proper day's work. Course it was. It always had been, ever since . . . Bobby couldn't stop them coming now, couldn't stop the memories, couldn't move from her post, sitting above the dirty water, her legs dangling, a fag between her lips, her mind stuck twenty-odd years back in the past.

Late Seventies again. Coming out of the Prince of Wales that day, Bobby and Lee were in hysterics, couldn't stop laughing. You see that guy with the false beard? Laugh. Couldn't get it up, could he? Laugh and laugh. Desire kept at bay. But not for long. Ten minutes later walking up Caroline Street, sharing a bag of chips, looking at the stuff in the window of the army-surplus shop, Lee says, 'You reckon they get paid?'

'Course,' says Bobby. 'Course they get paid.'

Lee had another couple of chips. 'How much, d'you reckon?'

'Fuck should I know,' says Bobby, leaves it a beat then adds, 'Why? You thinking about having a go?'

'Fuck off,' says Lee. 'I'm not a fucking queer.'

'Course not,' says Bobby, little bit sarky, risking a punch off Lee, and when he doesn't react she knows for sure he's thinking about it. 'Anyway,' she says then, 'maybe they're not always queer films.'

'What d'you mean?'

'What d'you think I mean? Maybe they do films with girls and all.'

'What, lezzos?'

'No, are you fucking thick or what? Ordinary fucking sex.'

'Oh right, yeah,' says Lee. 'You reckon?'

'Yeah, maybe,' says Bobby, but she doesn't tell Lee what St Clair said to her about seeing if any girls at the home would be interested. She wanted to think on that a bit first.

And she did think about it and a couple of nights later when this girl called Debbie, barely sixteen, comes back to the home looking a right state and she's boasting about how she's just had sex with five boys in a tent over Butetown one after the other and

Bobby's listening to this thinking that's disgusting and then the old lightbulb goes off and she figures the girl's doing that kind of shit for free, might as well make a few quid out of it. So next day she goes up to Debbie and has a little word and next time her and Lee are up town they go round the Prince of Wales as per usual and Bobby can see Lee's a bit disappointed that things are back to normal but St Clair's there and when Lee's off playing pinball with a couple of other boys Bobby leans over and says how she has a friend might be interested in doing a film and St Clair says wonderful, wonderful, bring her along, and it works out we'll see you get a little finder's fee, yeah, and Bobby says that'd be good – oh and there's just one thing: it's got to be black boys; Debbie – I mean my mate – she doesn't go with white boys. Oh, says St Clair, black girl is she, looking a bit disappointed, and Bobby says oh no blonde as anything and St Clair says oh really and he's almost licking his lips and Bobby's sitting there feeling a bit sick to be honest but still thinking a finder's fee sounds good.

And it was too. Twenty quid St Clair slipped her after Debbie had done her thing under the lights, whole bunch of hard black boys St Clair had rustled up from somewhere, couple of faces Bobby knew from the football in amongst them. Twenty quid: best part of a week's wages back then. And it wasn't like Debbie minded; she was all over Bobby afterwards thanking her. Debbie got fifty quid, see, for doing what came naturally, couldn't thank Bobby enough, insisted on giving her a tenner out of the money. Bobby didn't feel the need to mention she'd got paid already. Second she pocketed that tenner, saw how keen Debbie was to pay her, that's when Bobby realised she had a job for life.

A job for life. Back in present time, 2001, Bobby thought about it. Her job for life. Twenty-odd years taking money off girls too dumb or lazy or screwed-up to make it any other way. And all of them grateful. Yeah, grateful. Sure, they'd all have their moments of chopsing on about how Bobby was ripping them off, how they were doing all the work, and all that. But even if they broke off with her like one or two did – only one or two, mind – they'd soon enough be hooked up with some real shark and be forking over even more than they were with Bobby. Cause they needed to. They had to give the money up; they had to be doing it for love. Otherwise they couldn't handle it. Stupid bloody slags.

Bobby hated them. Loved them, hated them. All those girls, girls like Maria. Didn't know what they wanted, ended up casually chucking their lives away. How different would it be she was living with a nice girl like Kim, didn't need to go out on the streets and give blokes blow-jobs to earn a few quid. Instead of Maria, who was doing Bobby's head in, pissing her around like this.

Or was she? Was it really Maria was the problem here or was it Bobby herself? Didn't she know deep down the way things were going? Maria would mess about one time too often and Bobby would cut her loose, like she'd cut all the others loose. When it got deep down Bobby was sure she had ice in her heart.

Bobby pulled herself together. What alternative was there? Wasn't like any civilian was going to get involved with the likes of Bobby, was it? OK, now and again a girl like that Kim might like a little walk on the wild side, but that was as far as it went.

Bobby dialled Maria's mobile again. Left a message – short and none too sweet. Phoned the flat – nothing. She had another thought, called Maria's sister Mandy, she'd know all right. Wouldn't necessarily tell Bobby what was going on, but she'd know. Bobby dialled the number. It rang and rang and eventually Mandy picked up, great wall of noise in the background. She was a DJ, Mandy, well into all this two-step stuff.

'Who's that?' she yelled into the phone.

'Bobby,' said Bobby.

'Oh yeah, hang on.' A pause while Mandy walked away from

the phone, turned the music down and came back. 'You looking for Ri?'

'Yeah,' said Bobby.

'Well, I don't know where she is,' said Mandy, a bit too pat for Bobby's liking but they were sisters, what could you do, 'but she asked if I could pick up Jamal for her.'

'Oh yeah,' said Bobby, 'and when's she planning to collect him from yours?'

A pause at the other end of the line, Mandy obviously thinking about it. She sighed. 'Well,' she said eventually, 'she said could I have him for the night, like. Thought she was going out with you, like, Bob.' The lie quickly tacked on at the end.

'Thanks, Mand,' said Bob and hung up quickly before her throat caught. The bitch was leaving her. It really sounded like the bitch was leaving her. Maybe the script had changed.

She stood up, chucked her fag into the murky water and started walking randomly, trying not to think about what it meant if Maria could leave her, just like that, trying to be strong Bobby, Bobby the leaver, Bobby the pimp, one of the boys, not giving in to Bobby the lost, Bobby the left behind, Bobby the motherless, fatherless child. Now more than ever she needed something, someone to hang on to.

20

Pete made it to the St David's Hotel for half twelve, determined to put Leslie St Clair on the spot over these porn-film allegations. Inside, the press conference was every bit as lavish as St Clair had promised. The champagne and canapés kept on coming and, nervous at the unfamiliar prospect of asking hard questions, Pete kept on going back for more.

By the time they were all herded into the conference room, Pete was feeling the worse for wear. He collapsed into a chair at the back and struggled to focus on the speeches. First some bloke from the WDA stood up and blahed on about what an exciting bid this was, how happy he was to support one of Wales's leading entrepreneurs, and there's a big round of clapping and up gets St Clair and goes into this long spiel about his community capitalism idea and how it was crucial to the rebirth of Cardiff and how proud he was to be in the forefront of it all, and there was more clapping and Pete forced himself to take some notes and that helped him sober up a bit and then they all trooped back outside – back to more champagne, more canapés.

Pete was hoping to get straight over to St Clair – couple of questions and out of there – but he could see that there was little chance of that. St Clair was surrounded by a group of cronies – the Welsh Development Authority feller; a man Pete recognised as Malcolm Hopkin, political fixer, had been around since the ark or at least the Sunny Jim days; the head of the council planning committee, pompous jerkoff in a bow-tie; and a big black guy with a crop, didn't look like a politician at all.

He hung around for another ten minutes or so, stoking up on the canapés and sticking to orange juice, doing his best to make small talk with a couple of girls from Red Dragon Radio. But there was no sign of St Clair's little group breaking up and Pete certainly didn't want to just barge in and start throwing embarrassing questions around. He decided to knock it on the head for the moment, just say a quick hello, try and fix up some other occasion to meet. First, though, time for a piss and he was just in there admiring the designer urinals when he found himself standing next to St Clair himself.

'Mr Duke,' said St Clair. 'How the hell's it going, man?'

'Good,' said Pete, 'good,' thinking this is hardly the place to start asking questions.

'Great,' said St Clair, then as they were walking out together, 'C'mon, let me get you a drink, from the private stock, like, and you can meet the boys.'

And so, within seconds, Pete was stood holding a glass of Cristal that he knew he shouldn't be drinking, being introduced to St Clair's mates. First the Welsh Development Authority feller, Dai Thompson, an instantly forgettable suit; then Malcolm Hopkin who gave Pete the professional great to see you again, butt, treatment. Next up was the council leader who Pete'd had the limited pleasure of rubbing shoulders with dozens of times over the years and who could hardly be bothered to hide his uninterest at this latest meeting.

Finally St Clair turned to the last member of the group. 'Well,' he says to Pete, 'seems like I'm introducing you to all your best mates already, but maybe you don't know Kenny Ibadulla of Ibadulla Holdings. Kenny, this is Pete Duke, finest journalist in Wales.'

'How you doing, mate?' says this Kenny Ibadulla, and sticks out a hand the size of a dinner plate, friendly enough but eyes like slate.

'All right,' says Pete and shakes Ibadulla's hand trying to figure out why he knows the name.

Pete's arrival seems to provide the catalyst for the group to break up. Immediately the council leader and the WDA bloke say their goodbyes to St Clair and head off towards the chauffeured cars waiting outside.

St Clair waits till the council leader's out the door then smiles and says why don't we all step outside on the terrace where a man can smoke a cigar in peace and next thing they're all out there looking over the bay with a bucket full of Cristal on the table and Hopkin and St Clair lighting up the Monte Cristos and St Clair is waving his arms about and saying, 'I still can't quite believe how all this has changed.'

'Tell you what, Les,' says Hopkin, 'thing I can't believe is how much it's all cost and how little we've got for it. You look around here, what have we got really? A shopping mall with no shops in it hardly, a half-dozen or so restaurants and a nice hotel. Don't seem like much of a return on a billion pounds, eh? Looks nice enough in the summer – OK, they raised the water level so you could sail your yacht over to the hotel, fair enough – but I liked it fine when the water went up and down, one day water one day mud, and I still don't see too many yachts, you know what I mean, Kenny?'

Kenny Ibadulla gives a not-entirely-hostile grunt which Pete supposes passes for approval.

'That's right, Ken,' Hopkin carries on. 'Some of us don't mind a bit of mud now and again, long as it doesn't stick, eh, Les?'

Les's turn to laugh. Pete watched his face. Didn't give away a thing. Yep, if there was one feller knew all about mud not sticking it was Leslie St Clair all right. Pete looked at his empty glass. He knew he should be getting out of there while he can still drive. Asking St Clair questions could wait.

'Listen,' he says, 'I should get going. Work to do.'

'Nonsense,' says St Clair, 'you just call your editor, pass the phone on to me, I'll sort him out for you.'

And, blame it on the Cristal, that's what Pete does. Calls Graham's number, speaks to Mags, then passes the phone on to St Clair who mouths what's his name and Pete says Graham, then St Clair's talking. 'Hi, is that Graham? Ah, right, Leslie St Clair here . . . we met at the Celtic Manor . . . Yes, yes, that's right, wonderful course, for sure . . . Now listen, Graham, I'm afraid I've kidnapped one of your staff, the irreplaceable Pete Duke . . . No, no, only joking, but we're having a bit of an extended interview here . . . yeah, yeah, that's what I thought . . . OK, I'll put him on, all the best.' St Clair winks and hands the phone on to Pete who takes it and moves over to the edge of the terrace away from the others.

'Graham?'

'Pete, looks like you're moving in rather exalted circles all of a sudden.'

'Um, yeah, listen is that all right, I'm not back for a couple of hours?'

'No, don't worry, you just get the story. You've done the page layouts already, so there's nothing the subs can't take care of.'

'Spose not,' said Pete and wound up the conversation, put the phone back in his pocket and rejoined St Clair and his mates, suddenly confronted with the dizzying prospect of being a free agent on a weekday afternoon.

More champagne was the first step, St Clair continually refilling everyone's glasses. Then any remaining illusions Pete had about the probity of public life and those in the spotlight were further dismantled when St Clair suggested they head up to the suite for a little straightener.

Again it wasn't that Pete was entirely naïve; when Kenny Ibadulla tipped the pile of white powder on to the table, Pete knew it was cocaine all right. He watched TV, he'd seen *Scarface*. It was just that somehow he thought this stuff happened elsewhere, not in Cardiff.

Kenny cut the powder into lines, took the first one himself and nodded happily like a satisfied goods taster then gestured at St Clair who, in turn, looked round at Pete and said go on my son and there he was right on the spot unable to think of any excuse that wouldn't sound unforgivably wussy in such company and next thing he knew he was accepting the rolled-up twenty from Kenny and trying hard to look like he'd done it many times before.

Pete gave way then to Malcolm Hopkin and retired to a chair in a corner of the room waiting for the heart attack that he felt sure would inevitably follow such lunatic behaviour.

But it didn't come. In fact nothing much seemed to be happening; there was a bit of a funny taste in the back of his mouth but otherwise Pete couldn't see that very much had changed at all. God knows why people paid fifty quid a gramme or whatever for this stuff. On the other hand he did feel like another drink and these were an interesting bunch of fellers so he was happy enough to stay here and chat to them.

It was only after an hour or so of chatting with rather more animation than he normally displayed, finding himself telling indiscreet stories about assorted colleagues and laughing hard at St Clair's jokes, and then seeing Kenny preparing the next round of lines and feeling considerable enthusiasm for another go of this stuff, that Pete figured maybe it was doing just a little bit more than he had realised.

After another straightener, a half hour or so later, the mood turned restive. The Cristal had run out and St Clair was clearly itching to get back out into the world, a feller who loved an audience.

'How about the Hilton? You fancy the Hilton, Kenny?'

Kenny shrugged. Even after the coke Kenny seemed to be a man of remarkably few words.

'How about you, Mal? The Hilton all right?'

'Food,' said Malcolm. 'Food would be good, Les, I reckon, first.'

St Clair nodded. 'All right then, food. What d'you fancy? Le Monde? Fish? That suit you, Pete? Fish?'

'Yeah, sure, I dunno,' said Pete, thinking that this really would be a good time to leave, but somehow unable to face the prospect of being on his own.

'Nah, bollocks to that,' said Kenny suddenly. 'We should get some serious food.'

Men of few words, when they say something people tend to listen – well, they do if they are big menacing men of few words like Kenny; men of few words like Pete just seem to fade into the wallpaper, but there you go – so half an hour later the cab dropped the four of them off outside Kenny's choice of restaurant, a nondescript-looking French place on the edge of Pont-canna.

Inside the restaurant Kenny took charge, had a word with the waiter who greeted him with effusive respect, ordered steaks all round and a couple of bottles of what looked like serious Bordeaux. No pissing about with starters, salads or mineral water; this was big-boys' food. Pete could see a few of the other punters, mostly couples looked like they were on their wedding anniversary, giving this bunch of loud blokes a quick shufti, but none of them were in a hurry to catch Kenny's eye and anyway before long St Clair was out of his seat and working the room.

Then the food came, and you couldn't fault it. You wanted steak, steak you most definitely got, and they all tucked in with relish. Pete couldn't help feeling like suddenly he was on the big-boys' team.

Steak finished, two more bottles of wine ordered, Hopkin turned the conversation to football.

'Still thinking of buying the City then?' he asked St Clair with what looked to Pete like a wink.

'Course I am,' said St Clair. 'You read the papers don't you, Mal?' He winked at Pete this time.

'Bit of a long shot, innit?' chipped in Kenny. 'Seems like the Ayatollah's doing a fair old job there.'

St Clair put his hands up. 'Yeah, fair enough, Ken, he is that.' A little pause. 'Doesn't hurt the old profile to register an interest, though, you know what I mean?'

Pete sat back in his chair, getting it and feeling pleased with himself. The Cardiff City thing was just St Clair blowing smoke, a way of upping his profile while he got on with his real business, this new development or whatever. Nice. He was enjoying seeing how the world worked.

Next step in his education came a half hour or so later. The meal done and dusted, conversation turned to where to go next. St Clair fancied a champagne bar on Mill Lane, but Hopkin was emphatic that somewhere called Cupid's Lounge was the place to go. Then Kenny said yeah the manager was a mate of his, like, and so that was agreed.

In the taxi, sandwiched between Kenny and Malcolm, Pete remembered what Cupid's Lounge was – a lap-dancing joint round the corner from the New Theatre.

Soon as they get to the club the manager greets Kenny, has a quick word and then they're ushered into a private sanctum and this time Pete's in there like Flynn just as soon as Kenny's chopped out the lines and then it's downstairs into the club proper and soon they're sat in a booth in the VIP section and there's the inevitable bottle of champagne in the ice bucket and a good view of the dance floor where, Christ, a naked girl is writhing around a pole as the DJ plays Seventies disco records and all around the room there's other women in various states of undress gyrating in front of parties of blokes, mostly twentysomething suits. And the state Pete's in, instead of looking at his shoes as he'd ordinarily be doing in such a situation, he's checking the girls out.

'She'll do, all right,' says Malcolm Hopkin, pointing over his shoulder at one of the older performers, a thirtysomething blonde who seemed to be making up for in enthusiasm anything she conceded to her colleagues in age as she shimmied around in front of a couple of junior execs who looked like rabbits in the headlights in the face of this full-on sexual display.

Soon as she finished with the execs, Malcolm was waving a twenty-pound note and the blonde who said her name was Liza gave him and Pete her full attention. All Pete's sober instincts told him not to stare at the increasingly naked woman in front of him. On the other hand, surely it would be ruder to look away; after all Liza was putting everything into it so the least a gent could do was show some appreciation. And well, blame it on the coke, blame it on the champagne, when it came down to it he really didn't want to look away. He was one of the big boys now; he could look where he liked.

One thing about big boys' games, though, is that they're played by big boys' rules. After watching a couple more dancers, Kimberley and Danielle, Pete was in the midst of an animated conversation with Malcolm Hopkin who was telling him about the old days when strippers were strippers and not entertainment consultants, when, his tongue well loosened, he saw an opportunity to ask the question he'd been working up to all day. 'Oh yeah,' he said, 'talking of strippers, wasn't St Clair involved in something like that?'

'How d'you mean?' said Hopkin. 'Don't think old Les ever used to take his kit off.'

'No,' said Pete. 'Years ago, in the Seventies, didn't he make films or something? In the old Prince of Wales?'

Hopkin paused, then looked at Pete carefully. 'Don't know who you've been talking to, son, but I'd recommend you don't believe everything you hear.'

'Oh yeah, well,' said Pete, dimly aware that probably he shouldn't be blundering on with this conversation, 'it's just someone's come forward, said Les was involved in some pretty nasty shit back then.'

Hopkin lowered his voice, focused in on Pete. 'A word to the wise, Mr Duke. You be careful when you're nosing around because you never know where your nose might take you. After all, there's some people might say the stuff you've been up to today was some pretty nasty shit.' He laughed humourlessly. 'Some people, believe it or not, don't appreciate that girls like our Liza over there are really highly skilled entertainment consultants, you know what I'm saying?'

Pete nodded slowly. A sinking in his stomach said he understood all too well. He'd just had the bill for the day's entertainment.

21

Amazing how fast five years can unravel. All weekend Bobby had been brooding on it. Two days ago, the only way she could see her and Maria splitting up was if she, Bobby, decided it was time. Bobby had been utterly sure of her control of the situation. Sure, she'd been having her little thing with Kim and, to be honest, wondering if it mightn't turn into a big thing. Yeah, Bobby had been going through some changes all right. But Maria was just the same girl she'd always been, wasn't she? Sweet if you caught her right, but vain and lazy and under Bobby's thumb like all the rest. She'd have put cash money on it.

Well, how dumb did she feel now? Hadn't she noticed the way Maria was always going out clubbing? How she never came back till the early hours? Hadn't she thought the other morning that she smelt someone on Maria and hadn't she just decided the dirty slag was losing it, not washing properly after work? Hadn't she been thinking she was so cool, nipping out for a quick one with Kim without Maria noticing? Well, guess who'd been the blind one.

Maria had told her it straight. She'd had enough of Bobby, her moods and obsessions; she'd met someone else. A bloke. At least it was a bloke. Maria'd found another woman, Bobby would have fucking killed them both. A bloke, though, you could see that was different. Didn't have to like it to see it was different.

Course the bloke in question sounded like a right peach. Macca, one of the DJs down the Hippo; Bobby knew the name, could just about put a face to it. His little brother played for the

City. Second team, no one you'd heard of. Macca'd been inside a couple of times; one of the guys, you know. Bobby didn't have to know him; she knew the type all right.

'How many kids he got then?'

Maria shrugged. They were sitting in the new flat on their own, Tanya out on call, Nikki not due in till after lunch. Bobby had been there all morning fiddling with the website, trying to think of nothing, when Maria had shown up around eleven, her mouth set hard.

'Probably doesn't know himself. How many other women he got?'

'Leave it, Bob, you don't know him. He's not like that.'

'Course not. They never are, are they? Not till you ask them for some child support anyway.'

'Fuck off, Bob – just cause you can't have kids.'

Bobby froze; the words hung there between them for a brief eternity. Then Bobby flipped, dived straight at Maria, grabbed her by the throat, started banging her head against the floor, screaming at her, not even screaming words, just the guttural gut-wrenched sounds that lie behind every bitch or cunt or fuck you ever yelled, and then Maria kicked her hard in the kneecap and Bobby relaxed her grip and Maria took her chance and ran white-faced and tear-stained out the door, Bobby lying on the ground panting hard, the sound of Maria's feet on the stairs carrying through the open doorway.

Later, maybe a half hour later, when Bobby had got her breathing back to normal and washed her face in the basin, letting the cold water pour down till her skin was numb with the cold of it, and she was sat at the table clutching a cup of tea and ignoring the ringing phone, she almost felt grateful to Maria. Cause that was it. The line was crossed, there was no going back, no making up. Over, over, over.

Over and no regrets. Over just in time before it got really

ugly. And wasn't that deep down what she wanted, to be free? Yeah, yeah, probably, but who was she kidding? She was hurting now, all right; no one wants to be the one that gets dumped, the unknowing fool whose lover has betrayed them. And suddenly she was thinking about Jamal and tears were rolling down her face. If the vindictive little bitch stopped her seeing Jamal she'd kill her. She stood up possessed by rage, then stared around blindly as if trying to sense her adversary's presence in the room, then sat down again, tried to calm herself. Of course she'd see Jamal, she'd pick him up from school, she'd buy him clothes, she'd . . .

Suddenly she knew what she had to do next. She had to go and see Bernie Walters and this time she wasn't leaving till he told her who her dad was.

Bobby was sat in Bernie Walters's office, a whole mass of computer equipment laid out on the desk in front of her, drinking a glass of wine and listening to Bernie talk about the Sixties.

She'd felt a hell of a lot calmer the moment she stepped into Bernie's office. Walking over there, she'd been well out of it. She'd called Maria's mobile three more times: cow wasn't answering. Walking past the building site where the Custom House used to be brought her to tears. Crying over some evil bloody dump full of alkies and hookers; what was the matter with her?

So, yeah, she had been in a bit of a state when she showed up at Bernie's door. Only just about held it together when she was talking to the secretary who gave her the same old bollocks about Bernie being a very busy man, but a bit more half-hearted this time, and sure enough Bernie was obviously absolutely delighted to have someone come round, stop him from playing Minesweeper on the computer. And so Bernie ushers her into the office, beaming away, and asks if she'd like a drink and Bobby says yeah – cause she wasn't that much of a drinker by and large but right then she needed one – and he opens up a little fridge, gets out a bottle of white wine and fusses around finding a couple of glasses and he's nattering away, all this stuff about how Dame Shirley used to come here all the time when she was a slip of a girl and Bernie's wife used to take her out shopping for clothes and then he starts rummaging around finding all these boxes with scanners and printers and software in them and treating her like she's a bit of an expert on this stuff and Bobby just feels liked and useful and the weight of the day starts to drop off her.

So much so that she'd been there a couple of hours, had pretty much connected up Bernie's system and installed all the software, had the scanner and printer up and running, was just trying to explain how to operate it all to Bernie, who was more interested in telling her a long involved story about Matt Monro and a hotel chambermaid while opening another bottle of wine, before she remembered what she was doing here in the first place.

So when Bernie stopped talking for a second to concentrate on pouring out more wine, she said, 'You have a think about Troy Thursday then, Bernie?'

That shut him up. He put the bottle down carefully, looked at the floor, looked at the pictures on the wall, looked at the ceiling, then finally looked at Bobby.

'Are you sure this is your father, the man who your mother calls Troy Thursday?'

'Sure as I can be,' said Bobby, hoping to hell it was true and not some stupid lie her so-called mother had made up to keep her off her back.

'And you're sure you want to know who he is? You realise you could be in for a lot of heartache if he doesn't want to know?

He might not be very happy to find you coming out of the woodwork.'

Bobby looked at Bernie, oddly touched. How often had anyone taken her feelings into account? 'Yeah,' she said, 'I want to know. Whoever it is can't be worse than all this not knowing.' That much she was sure was true; she felt like it was one of the things holding her back in life, all this not knowing who she was except for Bobby Ranger – top pimp.

'Well,' said Bernie, taking a big swig of wine and looking terribly serious all of a sudden, 'I must say I had a feeling I knew who your Troy Thursday was, as soon as you mentioned it was a black feller. But I thought I'd better check. And as far as I can see, there were only two black guys ever did a Troy Thursday gig for me. Now one of them, Lance, God rest his soul, wasn't ever likely to be getting no girls pregnant, if you know what I mean. But the other one – look, you're really sure you want to know this, cause this is a hell of a name I've got for you here?'

Bobby nodded, her throat too tight to contemplate speaking.

'OK then,' said Bernie. 'Well, the other one just used the name once or twice when he was trying out a new act and anyway, well he's a feller, whose name you'll know already. Leslie St Clair.'

Bernie paused to let this revelation sink in.

'Oh Christ,' he said as he watched Bobby faint clean away in front of him.

22

The last couple of days Pete'd felt unsettled, remembering what had happened the Friday before. It all felt unreal. It wasn't what he, Pete Duke, did – champagne, cocaine, lap-dancers. But it had felt good. And perhaps he could be a player too, he saw that now; all he had to do was learn how to look the other way from time to time. And how hard was that?

He called Kim, back at work after a weekend in London. She picked up straight away, sounded pleased to hear from him. Apparently she'd just shown her boss a rough assemblage of her lesbian-pimp documentary and it had gone down a treat.

'Great,' said Pete and told her about his day out with the big boys.

He was planning to stop short of the lap-dancing club but somehow he couldn't round off the story without it and as it happened it turned out to be Kim's favourite part.

'Well, Pete,' she said at the end of it, 'you naughty boy.' Then she lowered her voice, went all husky on him. 'They turn you on then, those lap-dancing girls?'

Pete said nothing, just turned red, glad he was on the phone. She carried on. 'I'll bet they did. I was going to give it a try one time, you know. You think I'd be good? You fancy a little private dance later on?'

'Mmm,' he said uncertainly.

'Mmm,' said Kim. 'I'll give you mmm. Don't know why I waste my charms on you. Anyway, did you get anything direct out of this St Clair guy or was it all just good background stuff?'

'Well,' said Pete, grateful to be getting on to his reason for phoning, 'I certainly didn't get anything direct. Couldn't really just blurt it out in the middle of dinner. "Oh by the way, Mr St Clair, did you use to make porn films?" '

'Don't see why not,' said Kim. 'I would've.'

'Yeah, well,' said Pete, 'maybe you would, but I did ask one of his mates about it – said I'd heard these rumours and the guy basically threatened me.'

'Threatened you?'

'Well, kind of implied that if I tried to investigate this stuff they'd say I'd been taking drugs and all that.'

'Bollocks,' said Kim. 'You just say you were working under-cover, only pretended to take the drugs, got the story at great personal risk, you'll be a bloody hero.'

Pete thought about it. Probably she had a point. Probably if he had the guts that's what he would do – tough the whole thing out, get the story and take the consequences. Trouble was, first off, he didn't think he had those kind of guts and second he wasn't sure he wanted to do the story anyway. Some stupid idea that if he'd taken St Clair's hospitality he shouldn't shaft the guy afterwards, whatever he'd done.

'Look, Pete,' said Kim in mind-reading mode, 'you got to remember that this St Clair isn't Father Christmas, he's a seedy degenerate fraud. Those kids made those movies they were only sixteen, seventeen some of them. One or two of them might even have been under age from what Bobby says, runaways from the kids' home and that, and the whole experience traumatised a lot of their lives and he just exploited them.'

'Yeah,' said Pete, 'but . . .'

'But bastard nothing,' said Kim. 'You and me, Pete, we're going to work this story. It could be huge, you know, get both of us out of this town for ever. It's a London story, Pete, this one, a big London story.'

Pete hesitated. He could see she was right. Big London story – get out of this town for good. That what he wanted? He wasn't sure. But Kim was what he wanted, he knew that all right.

'OK,' he said at last, 'you're on.'

He put the phone down and checked his watch. Lunchtime. OK, he decided to kick off his investigation right away, before he lost his nerve. First step – find Randall. He caught up with him by the lift and said, 'You know that stuff you were telling me about Leslie St Clair? D'you know anyone might know about any of it like first hand?'

Randall frowned like he was deciding whether to let Pete in on the secret or not, then shrugged and said, 'Well, why don't we go and have a bit of a look-see?'

Randall led them off at a cracking pace across town, through the Royal Arcade, down what remained of Bridge Street, over Churchill Way and right into Guildford Crescent, past the Thai House and the Ibis Hotel they'd built where the swimming baths used to be, then down the alleyway alongside the prison wall and, for a moment, Pete thought they were going to see someone inside but instead Randall headed over the main road towards the Vulcan, a pub that Pete could have sworn had closed down years ago.

In fact it hardly looked open from the outside but Randall pulled on the door and led the way into the snug and suddenly Pete was transported back twenty years into the pubs of his youth.

The room was tiny, just three or four tables and a bar, and the minimum amount of space needed to house a dartboard. The bar itself offered the classic trinity of Brains Light, Brains Dark and Brains SA. Randall ordered himself a pint of Skull Attack; Pete took a pint of light and surveyed the clientele. Nobody under sixty. Couple of Arab-looking fellers in the corner, old-time sailors Pete reckoned; old couple by the dartboard doing the

Mirror crossword. Fat bald bloke with a big moustache, looked like an old-time wrestler, sat by himself at the table next to the door watching Pete and Randall with interest.

Randall waited for Pete to remember his role and pay for the drinks, turned round and waved to the fat bloke. 'George,' he said. 'Good Lord, man, you're looking big as a house. Fancy a drink? Young Pete here's getting them in.'

George raised his half-full pint of dark towards Pete who sighed and turned back towards the barman. 'Get him a large whisky while you're at it,' said Randall and Pete did as he was told.

They sat down next to the enormous George and Pete left it to Randall to kick things off, so the next ten minutes or so were spent discussing third parties that Pete had never heard of with unlikely old-school sobriquets like the Nailer and Jack the Hat. Then, just as Pete's attention was drifting off, wondering what on earth Randall was expecting to learn from this surprisingly camp old slugger, Randall suddenly said, 'The Brolly Man, he used to work for St Clair and all, didn't he?'

'Yeah,' said George. 'Well, now and again, like.'

'Pete here met old Les the other day, you know.'

'Oh yeah?' said George. 'Hope you checked your wallet after, son.'

Randall chuckled. 'Pete works on the paper with me. Doing a bit of an in-depth story on old Les, in fact. And he was asking me about the films Les used to make.'

'Oh yeah?' said George, still smiling but his eyes turned watchful. 'Long time ago, that was.'

Pete jumped in. 'You know about them, though?'

'Oh aye, used to work security for Mr St Clair at the time. I'd be there now and again, make sure there wasn't any trouble on set.'

'Got a bit more involved than that, George, from what I remember you telling me,' chipped in Randall.

George looked round at Pete then back at Randall. 'Well . . . it was all a bit of fun, really. Boys will be boys, you know what I mean.'

'Well, I can imagine,' said Randall, 'though I rather think I'd prefer not to. You don't know if any of these films are still in circulation, do you?'

George shrugged, 'Long time ago, like I said, butt, and it was all on, what d'you call it, Super 8? And I can't say I saw any of them myself even at the time. Old Terry used to flog them over in Bridge Street and I heard some got sent up to London, but like I said I never saw them myself, more of a doer than a watcher me, least back then I was.' George picked up his pint and took a reflective sip from it.

Pete looked at him, wondering what memories were flicking through his mind.

'You don't have any idea who might have copies, do you?'

'What, apart from old Les?' George thought about it, knocked back the whisky, looked pointedly at the empty glass. Pete took the hint, got another large one and came back to the table.

'Good man,' said George. 'Well, I suppose old Jock might still have some. He was the cameraman, like.'

'You know where we could find him?' asked Pete.

George looked at Pete, then over at Randall. 'Well, I might have an idea, but it strikes me it's worth more than a couple of whiskies to tell you fellers.'

Randall raised his eyebrows at Pete. Pete frowned. He'd made a point throughout his career of not paying people for information. True, it was less an integrity matter than a budget one, but still Pete felt it was a sound principle. On the other hand, he really did want to be calling Kim up, minute he got back to the office, telling her what a great lead he'd got.

Anyway, while he was hesitating, Randall weighed in. 'Well, George, it's hardly hot news, is it? Everyone's heard the rumours.

All this is just a bit of dotting the i's and crossing the t's, if you know what I mean. But still I'm sure Pete here would see you right for a drink, wouldn't you, Pete? Sure you've got twenty for old George.'

'Twenty?' said George in a grumbling growl, but, when Pete dug the note out of his pocket, he accepted it with the air of a man for whom twenty quid was still an amount to be respected.

'Right then,' he said. 'You want Jock, you try the Fisherman's Rest.'

'Out by the lighthouse?' said Randall.

'Out by the lighthouse is right,' said George, 'and tell you what, you get to see him, don't tell him I sent you.'

23

Bobby was still feeling shaky and spacy as she walked back to the flat. She couldn't believe she'd fainted. Never fainted before in her life but, Christ, what a shock. She hadn't really been able to say anything to Bernie; he was just looking at her all worried and his secretary, Marguerite, had been dabbing water on her face and she'd just said, 'You sure?' and he'd said, 'Yeah, that's why I checked, didn't want to lead you up the garden path on that one,' and she'd said thanks and sorry but she had to go home and she'd be in again tomorrow, sorry about leaving the computer in such a mess, and Bernie had said forget about it and she'd laughed cause she knew that wasn't what he meant but the one thing she couldn't do was forget about it. Though part of her wished she could, wished she'd never heard him say that name. All this time she'd wanted so much to know who her dad was and now she knew and shit she'd never thought she'd have wished she didn't know.

Leslie St Clair. At first, walking back, the name just kept buzzing through her mind like a tape loop she couldn't make sense of it; it was just here frying her brain. Gradually, though, she started to break down the enormity of it. Was it right? Was her mum lying? She didn't think so. It was too weird to be a lie. Did her mum know who he really was, this Troy Thursday? A harder question. One for later.

So was he her dad? Did she look like him? She thought about it. He was a fine-looking man, she was a pretty odd-looking woman, but . . . but she could see it. Her mouth, her eyes. Christ.

OK, maybe she looked a little like him – the strange-girl version. But was she *like* him? Well, there was a question she didn't want to answer.

This was really too much. She needed to talk to someone. Maria. She walked up the stairs and into the flat. Maybe Maria would be there, back waiting for her. Ha, ha. There was just Nikki sitting in front of the TV and she could hear Tanya in the master bedroom giving it some welly with a punter. Christ. She nodded to Nikki then put her headphones on and logged on to the computer, looking for distraction.

She soon found it in the shape of her email inbox which had received an avalanche of mail. Hundreds of new messages were waiting for her – 249 in all. The last few days the website had really started to take off. She'd got it linked up to the Good Sex Guide website, placed a few little mentions on the newsgroups, nothing that looked like spam, and you could see there was demand out there from the response. But 249 emails! This carried on, she'd be full time in front of the screen answering them. Just at the moment, though, she didn't mind at all.

Most of them were crap, of course. About half were one sort of spam or another; if it wasn't people trying to sell her scanners for only $29.99, it was other sex sites imploring her to watch their secret dorm-room cams. Yeah, right. Or offering free membership to increasingly implausibly named sites – finding an original name was clearly a bit of a nightmare which was why Bobby was pleased to have solved the problem with cardiffescorts.com, a site that did exactly what it said on the can. Anyway, she deleted all the spam, then started going through the messages from actual punters. Most of these were crap too, either abusive or pornographic and probably written by some fourteen-year-old in Australia. An inability to let go of the CAPS key was generally a bit of a giveaway. A few of them were genuinely pretty shocking, even to Bobby; the Net's anonymity surely did bring out the freaks. Anyway, weed out the kids and the nutters and what Bobby was left with was about twenty more or less bona fide enquiries. Which was fine. Say two of them turned into genuine punters: well, two new punters a day you were laughing. Kept on for long she'd be renting the whole bloody block. And now she felt tired of all these sad little missives from sad little lives. Had she ever felt so miserable? Where was Maria when she needed her?

She took the headphones off, turned round to talk to Nikki.

'All right, girl, how's it going?'

'All right, Bob,' said Nikki, looking alarmed, like Bobby was about to launch into her again. 'I've been trying harder, Bob. Have you noticed?'

'Yeah, Nikki, you've been doing great,' said Bobby and suddenly she felt faint again, sitting there talking to this poor dumb, frightened girl, doing her best to act like she was happy screwing whoever came through the door with fifty quid in their pocket. Jesus. Right now Bobby felt like she literally couldn't live with herself. This was unbearable. She forced herself to stand up, went into the bathroom. She looked in the bathroom cabinet: nothing there that would be any good to her. She thought quickly, made up her mind.

She came out of the bathroom and told Nikki she had to go. Her and Tanya could lock up after Tanya's punter left. Bobby left the flat, walked over to Butetown in a daze, completely oblivious to traffic or passers-by. She let herself into the old flat, Maria's flat, called out once, forlornly, 'Ri,' got no answer, went into the bathroom, found Maria's Temazepam, necked half a dozen of them and laid herself down on Maria's bed, waiting for unconsciousness to come, not caring if she ever woke again.

24

Pete and Kim were driving east out of Cardiff down Newport Road where the old Cardiff suddenly gives way to the brand-new strip-mall Cardiff, the procession of Allied Carpets and Burger King, TGI Fridays's and PC World, electrical stores and bowling alleys.

A right at the end of the strip, and Pete steered down through Rumney, nosing his way to the coast road. Never a big deal, the coastal road that threaded through the marshlands between Cardiff and Newport was now almost entirely hidden amongst the mushrooming industrial estates, so it took a couple of wrong turns before Pete found himself heading out past the car breakers and in sight of the sea wall.

The countryside. Well, of sorts. After a mile or so of ugly scrub, Kim looked out of the window and said, 'Bloody hell, Pete, where do you call this?'

Pete shrugged. 'Marshfield, I think.'

'Sounds about right,' said Kim, laughing.

They sped through a couple of villages that were doing their best to spruce themselves up, pretend they were in the Vale, but not really pulling it off, no matter how many riding stables they had. They couldn't get away from the fact that they were sited on a strip of no man's land bounded by the giant sink estates of St Mellons to the north and a horribly unappealing seafront of mud and industrial waste to the south. There was a hotel and a golf course, new since Pete had last been down there, and a thoroughly tiched-up pub-restaurant welcomed them into St

Brides, the last village on the road before it hit the Usk estuary and turned north into Newport.

Pete was looking out carefully for the turning now, trying to remember the directions he'd been given. Finally, just as the road was curving north and Pete was preparing to retrace his route, he saw a sign saying the Fisherman's Friend, breathed a sigh of relief and turned right. The road brought them out by the sea wall, and there it was, a big shabby pub, its car park home to a handful of beat-up white-trash motors. Beyond the pub the road dead-ended in a caravan site.

'Jesus Christ,' said Kim. 'People come here for holidays?'

'Funny old world,' said Pete. 'Funny old world!'

'OK then,' said Kim, as they walked round to the front of the pub. 'So we're looking for a man named Jock?'

'That's right,' said Pete.

'Any idea what he looks like?'

'Not really,' said Pete. 'I was kind of hoping he'd be an elderly and obvious degenerate wearing a kilt.'

Kim smiled up at him. 'You know what, Pete, you really are starting to lighten up.' And with that she kissed him and Pete kissed her back.

Inside it was every bit as rough and ready as the outside. There was a stage area festooned with the remnants of party decorations and a band entirely composed of short bald bearded blokes in their forties were just setting up their equipment. There were a handful of punters scattered around the place, a couple of traveller types were sat by the door, their kids running in and out, and a bunch of older blokes stood round the bar.

Pete took a deep breath, went up and ordered a pint of bitter for himself and a gin and tonic for Kim. As the barman gave him his change, he decided it was now or never and, casual as you like, said, 'I'm looking for Jock.' And just as casual the bloke said, 'Well, you've found him, haven't you,' and yelled out, 'Jock, over here'. And with that one of the fellers along the bar turned to look at Pete. Easy, he thought.

Then he got a good look at the man called Jock's teeth, all three of them. If the state of a man's mouth was any pointer to the state of his soul, then this Jock was one serious reprobate.

Teeth aside, Jock was sixtyish, six foot-plus, dishevelled, scrubby beard and a bush of hair with old-fashioned tortoise-shell-framed glasses. He gave the vague impression of a dissolute schoolteacher. He wasn't Scottish. The first words out of his mouth – 'Who are you then?' – placed him as a hundred per cent South Walian.

'You're not Scottish,' said Kim, like this might be news to him.

'No,' he said. 'Worked up there years ago. Now, you know my name but I don't know yours.'

'Kim,' said Kim.

'Pete,' said Pete, and then, 'We're journalists. We were hoping to talk to you about Leslie St Clair.'

Right then the band chose to kick off their soundcheck with a drum roll and the opening chords to 'Sweet Home Alabama.'

'Who?' said Jock.

'Leslie St Clair,' shouted Pete just as the band came to an abrupt stop.

'Easy, butt,' said Jock, 'no need to tell the whole world. Now, how about you buy me a drink and I'll sit down over there with the young lady.'

Pete nodded, ordered up a pint of Guinness for Jock and then remembered Randall's tip and added a large whisky to the round.

It didn't make much difference. Jock started out garrulous enough. Turned out he'd worked for St Clair on and off for years. He was happy to tell tales of how St Clair had set him up with work for porn mags, specialising in fake readers' wives: 'Just used a crap camera and made sure you could see the pattern on the carpet and the spots on the girl's bum.' But then, when Pete said it was the Prince of Wales days he was interested in, old Jock shut up like a clam.

'You were the cameraman on his films then?' Pete pressed.

'What films, son?' said Jock. 'Don't remember no films.'

'That's not what I've heard,' said Pete.

Jock laughed humourlessly. 'One thing I'd have thought you'd learned by now, son, in your line of work and all – people don't half talk a lot of shit.'

Kim had a go then, changed the subject subtly but effectively. 'You think I'd make a good model, Jock?'

'You, darlin'?' said Jock, giving her a good old-fashioned leer. 'You bet.'

Kim smiled like this was her lucky day. 'Really, cause it's always been like a little bit of a fantasy of mine . . .'

Both Jock and Pete were staring at her now, Jock obviously wondering if this was a put-on, but still unable to stop his mouth opening, his tongue starting to poke out.

'Yeah, you know, if it was shot by a real professional and all, something to remember when I'm old and saggy. You know what I mean?'

Jock smiled like he knew just what Kim meant.

'You're not still in the business, are you, Jock? Don't have a studio or anything?'

Jock swallowed hard. He obviously suspected he was being stitched up, but on the other hand it didn't look like he had too much else going on.

'Well,' he said at last. 'I have got a little bit of a studio set-up, as it happens.'

'Oh yeah?' said Kim. 'Is it far? Could I have a look?'

Jock frowned again, then made up his mind, knocked back

the rest of his pint and with a curt, 'C'mon then,' led the way out
of the pub.

'You want a lift?' said Pete, heading over towards the car, but
Jock grunted a no and inclined his head towards the caravan
park. Kim walked alongside Jock, keeping up a stream of chatter
while Pete followed a few paces behind, marvelling at her ability
to improvise and wondering how far she was planning to take
things. He wouldn't put it past her to suddenly whip her clothes
off; the thought immediately made him feel just a little bit
possessive and a little bit absurd too.

Jock's place was a full-scale trailer home parked right at the far
end of the park backed up against a large hedge. Jock opened the
door and the three of them entered what turned out to be a
surprisingly spotless environment dominated by a large black
leather sofa at the far end and an enormous TV in the corner.
Jock indicated that they should sit on the sofa then went round
the room pulling down blackout blinds over the windows and
door. He fiddled with some switches and the room was bathed in
bright white light.

'Ta da,' said Jock. 'Instant studio.'

'Very nice,' said Kim. 'So is there any of your work I could
have a look at?'

Jock frowned at this, then walked over to a filing cabinet by
the far wall. He unlocked it, pulled out a drawer and started
rummaging around. As he did so Kim moved up behind him
looking over his shoulder. Jock immediately withdrew a couple
of magazines and slammed the drawer shut.

'There you go, love,' he said, handing Kim what looked like a
bog-standard top-shelf title. 'You look at the centrefold girl in
that one, blonde piece, don't know what they called her in the
mag, Michelle's her real name. Anyway, I took them.'

Kim flipped the magazine open, looked at the photos of the
bottle-blonde with her ankles round her neck, squinted at them

hard as if imagining herself in the same high heels and garter-belt get-up, then handed it back. 'Very nice.'

'Yeah,' said Jock, 'very nice indeed. Used the old Nikkormat for that one, came out a treat, didn't they? So you ready to go, love?'

'Oh God, not now,' giggled Kim, 'but I'm definitely interested. You think it would be all right if I came over on my own sometime?'

Jock's face made it clear it would be more than all right. In no time he was scribbling a mobile number on a piece of paper and then they made their excuses and Pete stood up and led the way out.

Once they were in the car Kim could scarcely contain herself.

'He's got them, Pete. In the filing cabinet. Loads of little film boxes; you know, the old-fashioned sort, like for home movies. They were there, Pete.'

Pete leaned over and kissed her. 'Bloody hell, girl,' he said. 'You were brilliant.'

'Yes indeed,' said Kim. 'Good little team, aren't we, Pete?'

'Yeah,' said Pete, thinking I hope so, I really do hope so.

As they drove, Kim spun ever wilder plans to steal the film reels while Pete tried to raise reasonable objections.

'Anyway,' said Kim as they swung left out of the Boulevard de Nantes, heading past the castle walls, 'how about if I go round there, say I want to do the photo shoot and then get him off into the bedroom or somewhere?'

'Christ's sake, Kim, be serious.'

'I am serious,' said Kim. 'You think I can't handle an old lech like him? All I have to do is keep him out of the way for a minute or two and you nip in and get the films, then I go, "Oh sorry, changed my mind."'

Pete shook his head. 'Way too dangerous. Much simpler and safer if you just meet him in the pub, keep him in there, and I, uh, I break into the trailer and get the films.'

Kim pouted comically. 'Oh and I don't get to have the nice pictures taken.'

Pete laughed, hoping she was joking. 'You want any nude photos taken, I'll take them for you,' he said and he angled the car into the car park round the back of Randall's mansion block.

Kim laughed. Pete was just about to park when he saw another car a few spaces along still with its lights on, a big black Saab. He glanced casually across to see which of the neighbours it was and instead found himself staring straight into the face of Kenny Ibadulla.

Kenny opened his window. Behind him Pete could see three more guys. Pete opened his own window and tried a smile, got nothing back.

'You two-faced cunt,' said Kenny. 'You drink with a man one day, go sneaking about digging up ancient history the next. You think that's all right?'

'You what?' said Pete.

'You fucking heard. Now, you stop digging and we'll forget all about it. That's what Les said to tell you. I told him I should break your fucking arm, make sure you got the message, but Les said no. Next time, though . . . Well, you better make fucking sure there ain't no next time. You got that?'

Pete nodded, the power of speech temporarily lost to him, and with that Kenny closed his window and backed the Saab out of the car park before accelerating off into the night.

'Christ,' said Kim. 'Who was that?'

'A man called Kenny Ibadulla.'

'*The* Kenny Ibadulla?'

'I suppose.'

'Wow, Pete, looks like we're really stirring some shit up here.'

'Wow?' said Pete, getting out of the car, his legs trembling underneath him. 'You think this is exciting? It's not, it's stupid and it's dangerous.'

Kim got out of her side of the car, came round and put her arm in his. 'Course it's dangerous, darling. It's a big story, didn't we know that already? A big story, a big get-out-of-Cardiff story.' And Pete felt her tongue snake its way into his ear and he shuddered at his own helplessness.

25

Bobby Ranger was dreaming. She was dreaming about flowers. Lots of old flowers, a whole carpet of flowers, a whole wall of flowers, a whole world of flowers – roses, tulips, orchids, daffodils, carnations, chrysanthemums, daisies, sunflowers, poppies, violets, lilies, anemones, pinks, poppies again, flowers she didn't know the names of, flowers bright, bright colours, red, yellow, purple, flaming scarlet, yellow, blue and white, white, white, flowers everywhere, flowers left and right and up and down, flowers in her eyes, flowers in her mouth, flowers.

26

Pete couldn't sleep. It was three in the morning and Kim had left an hour or so before, left after they'd had the most intense, the most abandoned, dangerous sex of his life. From the second Kenny Ibadulla had threatened them she'd been all over him; they'd gone straight to the bedroom, her desire pervasive, sucking the air out of the room. For a moment he'd felt nauseous, afraid, sure he wouldn't, couldn't respond, but even as he was thinking that he realised he was responding, that the same cocktail of danger and transgression had its effect on him too, and then he was locked together with her, inside her, outside her, all over her, her biting scratching screaming and him feeling no pain, into her like drowning, and barely stopping at all between the first time and the second time.

And then she was gone and now it was three a.m. and Pete got out of bed and went down to the kitchen and once again thought it must be nice to smoke a cigarette at a time like this. Instead he made a cup of Nescafé and was overcome by a backwash of disgust at what he'd just done, the sex suddenly seeming not mystical and revolutionary but like too much chocolate: sickly and decadent. And as for his 'mission', it seemed sordid, pointless, grubby muck-raking, the reverse of what journalism had come to mean to him, which was order and structure and . . . and a quiet life, he supposed. Looking at his coffee in the cold of three a.m. he wondered if he wouldn't do best to run and hide, run back to Viv and the kids and beg their forgiveness.

Pete heard the front door to the flat open and then a burst of cheery whistling. Randall was home; the Cambrian must have finally tipped him out.

Seconds later Randall was in the kitchen.

'Peter, good Lord. What keeps you awake at this ungodly hour? Not woman trouble, I hope?'

'No,' said Pete, 'not that.'

'Good, good. She's a gem that one. Trouble, all right, you can see that, but worth it, I'll bet. So if it's not that, then what? Ah, you've been out adventuring, have you? On the trail of the lonesome Jock, perhaps? Did you find him?'

'Yes,' said Pete, and filled Randall in on the evening's events.

'Hmm,' said Randall when Pete had finished. 'Well, for God's sake don't rob the place yourself.'

'Who else is going to do it? Can't exactly send one of the reporters out, can I?'

'No,' said Randall, 'but you can do what people normally do when they've got a particular problem: call in the professionals. The toilet breaks, you call in a plumber; you need a burglary doing, you call in a burglar.'

'Yeah, yeah, sure,' said Pete, 'but I don't know any burglars. Don't exactly advertise in the *Thomson Local*, do they?'

'No,' said Randall, 'you just have to move in the right circles.' He checked his watch. 'C'mon, get yourself dressed. We'll go have a bit of a shufti, see who's out and about.'

Ten minutes later Pete and Randall were out on the street, skirting the Millennium Stadium and heading for the Tudor Road bridge over the Taff, Pete shivering from the cold, Randall seemingly oblivious to it. Must be all the alcohol in his system, thought Pete. The amazing thing with Randall was the way he never seemed to get any drunker. Not after the first few lunchtime pints. He seemed to have some way of gauging the optimum level of mild drunkenness and maintaining it indefinitely. A skill the youth of today could profitably learn, Pete thought, as he stepped over a pool of vomit.

Over the Tudor Road bridge they carried on into Tudor Road itself. The first couple of blocks were Cardiff's Chinatown, the next couple were a free-for-all for recent immigrants into the city: Somalis, Bengalis et al. On the south side of the street was a sari shop and a tattoo parlour and then a sign saying Tudor Pool Hall. Randall went up to the door, which looked to have been recently kicked in, and pressed the intercom. A voice said, 'Who is it?' Randall replied and the door buzzed open. 'After you,' said Randall and Pete led the way up a flight of stairs into the pool hall.

There were ten or so pool tables: half a dozen pub-sized and three or four big blue American ones. Only one of them was in use, a couple of Somali boys just setting the balls up. There was a bar over to the right with a couple of tables in front of it. Half a dozen guys, most of them Chinese-looking, were sat round one of the tables playing cards. A genial-looking bloke with un-mistakably Cardiffian mixed-race features turned to look at the newcomers.

'Randall,' he said. 'How're you doing, man?'

'Good, good,' said Randall. 'This is my friend Pete, works on the newspaper.'

'Hiya, Pete,' said the bloke, then looked at his watch. 'Bit late really, but seeing as it's you . . . what can I get you?'

'Large whisky, Naz, please and . . .'

'Bottle of Beck's,' said Pete.

Naz walked over behind the bar and got the drinks together. Randall and Pete followed him.

'So what brings you gents out this time of night?'

'Well,' said Randall, 'as it happens, my friend Pete here has need of a couple of young lads to do a little job.'

'Uh huh,' said Naz. 'Well, no disrespect to your friend, right, but why don't you and me have a little chat in private?'

'Fine,' said Randall and headed back behind the bar and into the office.

Pete stood sipping his Beck's, trying not to catch anybody's eye, saw a discarded copy of the *Mirror* on a banquette and picked it up, idly flicking through to see if there were any stories he should have picked up on. Pete in general was dead against the way that happenings in *Big Brother* or *Popstars* were counted as news even in the broadsheets, but he knew and Graham knew that you couldn't move too far away from the spirit of the times. OK, the *Post* was meant to be a bit of a fuddy-duddy paper, safe for farmers from Carmarthen to read without having apoplexy, but still. Even farmers from Carmarthen watch the soaps.

Pete suddenly looked up to see Randall and Naz emerging from the back office.

'Thank you, sir,' said Randall to Naz and then ushered Pete over to a neutral table where he passed across a scrap of paper with a mobile number and a name: Daniel.

'Not to be melodramatic or anything,' said Randall, 'but it's probably best if you just memorise it.'

Pete nodded, feeling oddly detached as he gently crashed through another ethical and legal barrier. Suborning a felony? Why the hell not?

27

Bobby woke up screaming then gagging, her fingers in her mouth trying to empty it of nothing.

'Stop it, for Christ's sake.'

Bobby looked round, her head spinning, trying to take in what was happening. She wasn't dead, she was alive, and Maria was standing over her looking furious. What time was it? Christ, what had she done? What kind of a bloody idiot had she made of herself? She started to sit up, but she still felt terribly tired and her head was aching like she'd drunk a bottle of vodka.

'Lie down, you stupid cow,' said Maria, no trace of sympathy on her face. Well, Bobby could understand that. 'How many have you taken?'

'How many what?' said Bobby, then, feebly, 'I haven't taken anything.'

'Course you haven't.' Maria waved the empty bottle of Temazepam under her nose. 'C'mon, how many?'

'I dunno,' said Bobby, feeling utterly miserable, defeated, unable to bear the switch-around of roles that was going on. 'Six or seven. Is that dangerous?'

'Well, you're not dead, are you?' Maria paced over to the window then walked back. 'You better go down the hospital anyway, get them to check you out. But I'm not bloody taking you, you already screwed my night up. I brings Macca back and he sees you snoring on my bloody bed and he pisses off just like that.'

'Sorry, Ri, I'll tell him for you.'

'Oh shut it, Bob, I'll sort it out. Anyway, why don't you give her a call, get her to take you?'

'Who d'you mean?'

'Who d'you think I mean? That BBC bitch you been screwing the last month or whatever it is. Or d'you think I didn't know?' Maria looked at Bobby closely. 'How stupid have you been taking me for all this time?'

Bobby closed her eyes, wished Maria would go away. But she was right: she'd better go down the hospital.

She told Maria the number.

'Fine,' said Maria, picking up the phone. 'What's the bitch's name?'

'Kim,' said Bobby and repeated the number as Maria dialled, thinking, Kim, just you be there, girl. I'm needing an angel right now.

Bobby was on one of those trolley beds in a cubicle somewhere in the A & E ward in Llandough Hospital, the old-fashioned one on the hill, looking back down over the bay. She was feeling really, really stupid. She was going to have to tell Kim what it was all about; she couldn't see any choice unless she wanted the girl to think she was a total bloody loser.

Be fair to Kim, she'd been magic so far. After Maria had called her, she'd come round straight away, even though it was six a.m. Hadn't freaked when Maria had given her the iceberg treatment; instead she'd sent Maria packing, got on the phone and had an ambulance round. Then she'd talked to all the doctors and that while Bobby lay there still a bit woozy, to be honest, and quite glad she was in the hospital cause it was a pretty scary idea, really, that you might just shut your eyes and never wake up again, though that didn't seem likely. Didn't seem like the doctors were too bothered at all, sounded like Temazepam wasn't really the way to go, you wanted to top yourself. Paracetamol'd be a whole lot more effective. The nurse had given her the full horror-story thing with Paracetamol you took a load of them; they might get you into the hospital and that and you'd be all right and just thinking what the hell was all that about and I must get my life back together and then day or two later your liver packs in and that's the end of you.

Bobby didn't want this to be the end of her. She just felt ashamed of herself and soon as Kim came back from making some calls or whatever, she'd tell her what it was all about and maybe Kim would have some idea what she should do. It was so nice for once to be around someone else who was, like, capable, could sort stuff out. All her life it seemed like Bobby had been the one sorting everything out, always been, like, the man, and right now she was feeling a bit sick of being the man. She was, don't laugh, feeling like a little girl. Needed a bit of looking after.

Ah, thank Christ, there was Kim now, talking to the nurse, smiling. She came up and squeezed Bobby's hand.

'Nurse here says you'll be fine, Bob.'

Bobby smiled, dragged herself up into a sitting position. 'Yeah. Does that mean I can go now?'

'Just wait till the doctor comes round,' said the nurse. 'Then he'll check you over and sign you out, I expect.'

'How long will that be?' asked Bobby, hating her voice as it came out like a whiny kid's.

'Not long,' said the nurse and moved off to the next bed, leaving Bobby alone with Kim.

'I've never done this before, you know,' said Bobby.

Kim put her hand on Bobby's. 'Don't worry about it.'

'No,' said Bobby, 'I do worry. I just want you to know: this isn't me. I'm not one of those girls always pretending like she's going to kill herself any time she don't like her haircut, it's just . . .'

'Yeah?' Kim looked at her. 'Just what?'

'Just . . . I've had a bit of a shock.'

Then Bobby told her, told her who her dad was, and Kim said fucking hell in a tone of reverence and Bobby said fucking hell is about right and they both just sat there quietly for a bit and finally Kim said, 'Well, what are you going to do?'

'I dunno,' said Bobby, telling the simple truth.

'Well,' said Kim, 'you still want to go after him over the Prince of Wales stuff? Oh God, don't answer that now.' She shook her head. 'Talk about a mind-fuck, that was your dad.'

'Yeah,' said Bobby. And then the doctor showed up and gave Bobby a bit of a lecture while Bobby bowed her head, then he said she could go home and she walked out to the car and Kim said, 'D'you want to come to mine?' and Bobby had never felt so grateful for anything in her life. 'Yes please,' she said.

28

It was lunchtime before Pete called Kim. Been a godawful morning. Cherri was off sick again, and Graham had decided to weigh in with some ideas. Graham's ideas were always things he'd picked up at some dinner party the night before and Pete would send someone off to write them up and then, likely as not, a few days later Graham would spike them all, having completely forgotten he'd commissioned them in the first place. And today Pete was really not in the mood for it. He needed his sleep, that's what Viv always said, and as with so many things she was right. That was what he missed at the moment, being with someone who knew him that well, who knew he needed his sleep – oh God, he was thinking about his mother not a lover. Maybe that was the problem? Maybe he'd treated Viv like she was his mother and now aged forty he was leaving home. God, that was a scary thought: age nought to twenty living with his actual mum, then twenty to forty, more or less, with Viv. Now was he doomed to do the whole thing all over again? Christ, he hoped not. Maybe, just maybe, he was finally a grown-up. He thought about Kim then: was she a mother figure? Not hardly.

He dispensed jobs right, left and centre, then sat back at his desk and phoned her, sure she'd be excited to hear about his adventures in burglar recruitment.

He rang her work number first, got her chirpy voicemail, then tried her mobile. She picked up on the third ring, sounding distracted.

'Yeah?'

'Kim, it's me, Pete.'

'Oh, hi Pete . . .' Then Pete could hear someone saying something to Kim and her sounding irritated replying, 'OK, OK,' then, 'Hang on, Pete, I've just got to go outside.' Sound of her footsteps then, 'Hi Pete, sorry about that. Bloody hospital won't let you use the mobile.'

'Hospital?'

'Yeah, long story, Pete. Bobby's here, you know the pimp, yeah?'

'Yes.'

'Well, basically she took an overdose – don't worry, she's all right. But, uh, basically she called me to give her a hand and I feel a bit responsible, like what with the docco and everything, like maybe I put her under a lot of pressure with the St Clair stuff and all.'

'Yeah,' said Pete, not really taking in what Kim was telling him. 'Yeah, about the St Clair stuff. Randall knows someone reckons he can get the stuff, you know, that we were talking about last night.'

'What?' said Kim. 'What are you talking about?'

'Oh, forget it,' said Pete, realising that this really wasn't the sort of thing he wanted to be blurting out on the phone while sitting in the middle of a newspaper office. 'Listen,' he said, 'how about we meet up after work and I'll tell you about it?'

'Um, yeah,' said Kim, sounding like she wasn't sure, 'except it depends a bit what's happening here with Bobby and that. I'll bell you later, right.'

'Right,' said Pete, but already he was talking into dead air. Probably got cut off. He frowned. Why was Kim helping this Bobby out at the hospital?

Her mobile seemed to be switched off all afternoon so, after work, Pete decided he'd walk round to her place, see if she was in and, if not, leave her a note.

Took him fifteen minutes to get there. He rang the bell, waited for a bit, nothing seemed to be happening. He was just starting to write a note when the door opened and there was Kim standing in her dressing gown, just like the first time he'd called round there except that was on a Sunday morning and this was a Tuesday evening.

'Hi Kim, you all right?'

'Yeah,' said Kim, looking flustered. 'I was just having a bath. What d'you want?'

'Got some news for you, you know about the films.' He inclined his head towards the stairs behind her. 'Let's go in, I'll tell you about it.'

'Uh, yeah, OK,' said Kim, 'but be quiet, yeah, cause I've got Bobby staying here.'

'Oh,' said Pete, 'right. Is she OK?'

'Yeah, she's fine, I think, just a bit shaken; you know, bit disorientated or whatever.'

Pete followed Kim up the stairs thinking she was certainly carrying through with the Florence Nightingale bit, taking Bobby home with her. It was just then that he flashed on a drunken memory of Kim snogging Bobby on the last night of the Custom House. He shrugged it aside; everyone had been well out of it. It came right back into focus, though, the minute they got inside Kim's flat and Bobby, wearing one of Kim's old T-shirts, stuck her head out of the bedroom and said, 'You coming back to bed, darlin'?' Then she saw Pete and just closed her eyes like a kid, thinking if they can't see you, you can't see them, and shut the door again quickly and quietly.

Pete just stood there staring at the closed door, then he turned to look at Kim, wondering if there was some way he could be jumping to conclusions here. Couldn't think of one. He started to speak. Kim cut him off.

'Don't start, Pete. You're not my fucking mother, you know what I mean? We have a good time together, right? So don't say a word, yeah, don't screw it up. I don't ask you what you get up to when I'm not around, you don't hassle me.'

Pete just stood there, mouth opening and closing like a goldfish. Words running through his head but none of them right. Finally he just shook his head, turned and walked back down the stairs.

Back outside, the evening now seeming not brisk but bloody freezing, he pulled up his collar against the wind and headed back towards town. As he walked he had a Wham record maddeningly stuck in his head, 'I don't want your freedom, I don't want nobody else' – maybe that wasn't right but that was what was going through his head. Thing was, he did want his freedom but he felt like he wanted Kim as well, and not on a timeshare basis either, so maybe he didn't want his freedom after all. Maybe the only kind of relationship he could consider was just a straight–ahead monogamy deal.

Shit, shit, shit, he thought. He really wished what had just happened hadn't. Cause on the one level he could handle the idea that Kim had a life outside of him; even that she might have other affairs. It was just coming smack up against the reality of it so suddenly that he was finding hard to handle. But then, as he walked, he started to feel less angry and hurt and more philosophical. Because deep down he was pretty sure he had more sticking power than most people. If he really wanted Kim he would fight and fight for her and he'd wear down the competition, he was sure of that. You wanted dogged, you came to Pete Duke. He set his face against the wind, mustered a bit of a smile. He knew what he was going to do: he was going to press on with the investigation, get on with it by himself and present it to Kim, show her what he was made of.

He got out his mobile, dialled the number Randall had procured for him.

'That Daniel? . . . Good. Yeah, I got your number from Naz, said you might be able to help me out with a little job.'

29

Bobby woke up feeling better than she had in months. Stronger, clearer. Kim wasn't in the bed. Bobby called out: no reply. She looked at the clock: quarter to ten. Kim must have gone to work. She padded into the kitchen. There was a note from Kim on the table. Make herself at home. The level of trust implied by this made Bobby feel like crying. She had a bath, a piece of toast, took her time, savoured being in the flat, let herself think once more what it would be like to have this different life.

Then reality started to crowd in. First off, she had a business to run. She hadn't been there for two days and she'd been in a right old state before that. God knows what would be going on over the wharf. Was Maria planning on keeping on working? How about Nikki and Tanya? She had to get over there, sort it out one way or the other.

She called a cab. Came five minutes later. Time was, when the old Cabbies Club was still going, she knew all the drivers, more or less . . . Now, though, she got some Sikh feller she'd never seen before, didn't say a word.

Went to her own flat first, had a shower, put some fresh clothes on, then opened the work flat up. She couldn't settle. Made a cup of tea, didn't drink it, got her website up on-screen, couldn't face working on it. Too much shit in her head. What was going on with Maria? What was she going to do about St Clair? Questions circling round and round, driving her mad.

She willed herself to act. Got out her mobile and called Maria first. Switched off. Shit. Tried Tanya next. Alleluia, she picked up.

'Tan?'

'Bob, that you? Where are you?'

'At the wharf.'

'You feeling better, Bob?'

'Yeah, yeah. You coming in this morning?'

'Just doing a bit of shopping, Bob. I'll be over soon. What time's first one?'

Bobby checked her appointment book. 'Twelve,' she said, 'but I may have to go out before that. You handle it?'

'Course, Bob. Been handling it all right the last two days.'

Bobby laughed. 'Yeah, I know, and thanks a lot, girl.' She paused, thought about something then carried on. 'Tell you what, Tan, sometime soon we should talk about you becoming a partner, like.'

'Yeah?' said Tanya. 'You serious?'

'Sure,' said Bobby, 'later, yeah,' and clicked her phone off, feeling like she was making a start. Letting go of a bit of control; it felt good. Now for the next stage, the big one.

Bobby took a deep breath, picked up her phone again and dialled Bernie's number. Thankfully he wasn't in yet. Bobby persuaded Marguerite to dig in her Rolodex and find a number for Leslie St Clair. There were half a dozen of them including a mobile number she said was written in red, which Bobby figured would be the one to go for.

Without giving herself time to think twice, she dialled the number. Two rings and there he was on the other end of the line. Leslie St Clair, corrupter of her youth and most likely her dad.

'Hi,' she said. 'This is Bobby Ranger, don't know if you remember me.'

A laugh at the end of the phone. 'Bobby Ranger! I remember you, all right. What can I do for you, Bobby?'

'I was wondering if I could come and see you about something.'

'Mm hmm. What sort of something might we be talking about?'

'I'd rather not say on the phone.'

St Clair's voice hardened. 'I hope that isn't some kind of threat.'

'No,' said Bobby, 'nothing like that. It's just something, I don't know, personal.'

'How mysterious. Well, I dare say I can fit you in. You still down the docks?'

'Yeah,' said Bobby.

'Excellent,' said St Clair. 'Well, let me think, where to meet?' He laughed again. 'Tell you what. For old times' sake, how about we meet in the Prince of Wales? Twelve thirty all right with you?'

'Yeah,' said Bobby, her mouth suddenly so dry she could barely speak. 'See you there.'

She got there early. Stood on the other side of the road, outside the Cardiff Jeans Co., looking at it. The Prince of Wales. Now it looked so innocuous, all sandblasted stone on the outside, plate-glass doors and loads of signs advertising deals on drinks and food. Lot of the girls liked to go in there, she knew that. Herself, though, she'd always begged off. Too many memories she didn't want to face up to. Well, now she was going to be facing them. Big time. Bobby checked her watch: still ten minutes early but what the hell, she could have a little look around the place, prepare herself. She squared her shoulders and crossed the road then walked into what used to be the foyer. Suddenly she could smell the ammonia in the cleaning fluid they used to use, could feel the dread and excitement of twenty years before.

As before, there was a choice; head straight into the downstairs or take the stairs up. Bobby decided to start at the bottom. She headed on through the foyer into the body of the building, where the stalls used to be. The space disconcerted her at first. Where there used to be a Stygian darkness lit only by the flickering of *Swedish Dentists on the Job*, now there was a big light open space, dotted with tables and chairs, a long bar approximately where the screen used to be. She turned and looked up. Weird, they'd kept the circle more or less intact, even the upper circle, which, Christ, seemed to still have cinema seats on it.

She felt dizzy suddenly, unable to separate past from present. What was strange was the powerful nostalgia she felt for the old building, the old days. You looked round it now and it was nice enough, a big city-centre pub just starting to fill up with office boys and girls after a cheap lunch and a couple of drinks to take the edge off the afternoon in surroundings which if you didn't know looked like some lovely old theatre: the old Prince of Wales, in fact, the legitimate theatre it had been before Bobby was born, where Ronald Reagan once trod the boards. Was nostalgia completely indiscriminate? If she went back to the home they'd stuck her in, would she feel the same? She shook her head. No way. But this place, this place she felt something for. Maybe it was because this is where it had started: her life, the life. Bobby Ranger, top pimp. Gold teeth to prove it.

She had to see more, go upstairs. There was a big new staircase taking you up from the stalls, but she ignored that and made her way back to the front door. Took the old staircase up, and then headed into the circle. More seats, another bar. She looked up at the upper circle, realised it was closed off, just decorative with its rows of original seating, hopefully now thoroughly disinfected. She stood there for a moment wondering what to do next, was just going over the new walkway towards the bar when she noticed they had kept two of the boxes, one on either side. The one to her right held a couple in office junior get-up, her hands all over him, him looking bored. The box on the left had one occupant sitting there, watching her. Leslie St Clair.

He raised his glass to her, motioned for her to join him. She looked around, spotted the passageway that led to the box and followed it, her heartbeat accelerating.

St Clair stood up to greet her, kissed her on the cheek. 'Bobby Ranger. Well, well, well. You want a drink?'

Bobby shook her head, not trusting herself to speak just yet; instead she sat down at the little table they'd squeezed into the box and St Clair followed suit. She scanned his face. He was still a handsome man, all right, even at sixty-odd. Light brown skin, not much darker than Bobby's, really. Sharp regular features, a bit like Johnny Mathis or someone; his nose was a bit more Afro than hers but the eyes, his piercing green eyes − they were her own eyes looking back at her. She wondered if he had ever noticed, ever thought.

St Clair smiled at her. 'So what can I do for you after all this time?'

Bobby dived in, involuntarily closing her eyes as she spoke. 'Were you ever known as Troy Thursday?'

'Troy Thursday?' St Clair looked at her in amazement. 'It's a long time since I heard that name.'

'Thirty-eight years,' said Bobby.

St Clair sat back in his chair and stared at her. 'Thirty-eight years. That'd be your age, perhaps. Are you trying to tell me something, girl?'

'Yeah,' she said, her voice coming out as little more than a whisper. 'My mum, she said . . .'

But before she could finish St Clair was out of his seat and pulling Bobby out of hers, opening his arms to her. 'She said I'm your dad, didn't she?'

Bobby shrank back instinctively from St Clair's approach −

nothing in her memory banks welcomed such an approach from any man – but then something deeper kicked in – some primal need – and suddenly she just gave it up, all the years, all the lifetime of holding back from the embraces that were never offered, and with an audible groan she let herself go, like a vertigo sufferer giving in to the joy of falling, and collapsed into the waiting arms of Leslie St Clair.

Bobby was doing her best to keep her sense of perspective, but she could tell that she had a big stupid grin on her face and her eyes were shining as she listened to him talk. Her dad.

He'd been great so far; she could hardly believe it. No denials, no doubt; he had just opened his arms to her, pulled her in and held her.

Eventually they broke apart and St Clair ordered a bottle of champagne and they sat there in the box looking out over the ground floor of the pub and St Clair entertained her, told her showbiz stories, business stories, told her about his big plans for Cardiff, this thing called the Castle Market that was going to make him a fortune, went on about what an exciting time it was to be back in the city. More stories, stories about his childhood, the old Tiger Bay, and Bobby just sat there looking at him, looking at his skin, his hair, his eyes, thinking: my skin, my hair, my eyes.

Only little disappointment was he didn't seem to remember a thing about Bobby's mum. Oh, he talked like he did, but you could just see he was blagging it. 'Lovely girl, used to come to all the gigs . . .' he started, but then visibly ran out of steam. Well, it was no more than Bobby expected, but still it would be nice to think your conception was more than just ten minutes out the back of the Embassy Ballroom, Pontypridd. And yet that was the amazing thing: one stupid meaningless little fuck between some stupid young girl and some horny chancer and you end up with a human being. St Clair had a fit of coughing, then went off to the toilet and Bobby looked around the pub feeling a bit drunk now from the lunchtime champagne.

It was no wonder she'd never wanted kids herself, she thought. It wasn't just she was a lesbian, lot of lesbians got kids, not the point at all and she liked kids, loved Jamal, but she'd never wanted one growing inside her. Never wanted that responsibility. Weird thing was, though, when she had the hysterectomy, couple of years back, she'd cried for a week. Who'd be a woman, eh?

St Clair, Les, her dad, came back from the toilets, sat back down and lit up another fag. 'So you know old Bernie, then?'

'Yeah,' said Bobby. 'How d'you know that?'

'Oh,' said St. Clair, 'Bernie gave me a call, warned me that there might be a surprise in store, didn't want me having a heart attack on the spot.'

'Oh,' said Bobby, feeling a little cheated by this news, wondering why he'd gone through that little charade of pretending not to know, a familiar little flicker of suspicion in her mind. She looked at her watch and saw it was closing in on four. 'Time I was getting back to work,' she said.

'Work?' said St Clair, raising an eyebrow. 'What line of work are you in, then?'

'Well,' said Bobby, pausing, caught between the desire to chuck the realities of her life in the face of this never-was father and the desire to impress him, make him proud of his never-was little girl.

'Computers,' she said finally. 'Helping people set up their systems, web design, stuff like that, got my own business doing it. Doing a little job for Bernie Walters at the moment, as it goes.'

St Clair nodded, gave her a proud-father smile. 'Good line of work to be in. Lot of my business is on the Net these days. Don't suppose you'd like a job working for your old man, would you?'

Bobby looked at him, trying to keep her face neutral. 'Really?'

'Sure,' said St Clair. 'Good web designers, always a demand for them.'

'Yeah, course,' said Bobby, wondering why this all seemed a little too good to be true.

30

Pete woke up with an overwhelming sense of guilt, that awful sense that you've done something terrible the night before but you can't quite remember what.

Then he remembered. He'd phoned up Daniel. He'd met Daniel in an estate pub in Llanrumney, kind of place you really didn't want to catch anyone's eye. He'd told Daniel what he wanted and Daniel had said yeah, Naz had told him more or less. Some fucking nonce needed turning over. No problem, mate. And Pete had said yeah, but no violence, just a burglary, just these films the guy had. That'd be enough to turn him over to the law, and this Daniel had nodded and said no problem, boss, and had taken fifty quid from Pete with the promise of another fifty when the job was done and Pete had explained which trailer it was and which pub the cameraman drank in and had gone back to the flat to wait and Randall had suggested popping out for a quickie and even though Pete knew full well what a quickie was he'd said yes and gone and got completely hammered and he'd told Randall all about finding Kim with Bobby and Randall had just looked a bit embarrassed and said well that Kim she's certainly not a girl for the fainthearted and that was about the last bit of conversation Pete could remember. Till about half two walking back from the Cambrian, completely out of it, his mobile had rung and eventually Pete had managed to find it and answer it and the kid Daniel had said he'd got the stuff, when did Pete want to pick it up, and Pete had said how about lunchtime, one o'clock in the car park of the pub they'd met before, and Daniel had said fine.

And so, feeling like his life was spiralling out of control, Pete dragged himself out of bed and into work. Then he dragged himself through the morning, behaving like the original sore-headed bear, well aware that he was drawing on years of accumulated goodwill.

One o'clock Pete was in the car park. Ten minutes later Daniel turned up and jumped over the wall from the estate, a carrier bag in his hand. Pete had a quick look, saw a bunch of little white boxes with film reels inside, handed over the next fifty quid to Daniel who said thanks boss, then laughed and said served the old pervert right and all and Pete said yeah sure and drove back into town feeling like the feller from *Taxi Driver*, cleaning up the streets at whatever lunatic cost. Except Pete lacked the comfort of madness, so basically just felt out of his depth. He shook his head; what was the matter with him? He'd got the films, had an out-and-out scoop for the first time in his journalistic career. Big story, as Kim would say. Big London, get-out-of-Cardiff story.

As he pulled into the office car park, it struck him that it might be an idea to check what was on the films first, before he went in to see Graham, told him he'd got the scoop of the decade, then realised all he had was a bunch of home movies: Jock on the beach at Porthcawl.

Who would have a film projector? His dad used to have one but they'd chucked everything out when they moved. He was pretty certain Randall didn't have one. Randall seemed to have gone through life acquiring a bare minimum of possessions, a couple of shelves of books and three sets of clothing. Maybe the ex-wives had all the stuff. The BBC? Surely the BBC would be able to lay their hands on one. He took a quick deep breath and dialled Kim's number.

'Kim?'

'Yeah. Pete, that you? Look . . .' Her voice was immediately awkward.

'Yeah, it's me, and it's OK, I'm not calling about last night, leave that for the minute. Listen, I've got the films.'

'The films? Christ, Pete, how d'you do that?' Kim sounded excited.

Pete smiled. 'Don't ask,' he said – well, wasn't he the cool one? – then followed up, 'listen, have you got a film projector there, something we can watch them on?'

A pause. 'Yeah, I'm sure I can find something, but let's not watch them here. Why don't you come over to mine about four?'

'Make it five,' said Pete and rang off, feeling like he was getting back in the saddle here.

Back in the office Pete was just settling in again when Terry on the police desk passed him a little story, asked if he was interested. A caravan had been burnt out in the trailer park at St Brides, the words Fuck Off Nonce found painted on what remained of one of the walls. Nobody hurt, but a fair bit of property damage. What did Pete think? Single para, or go a bit bigger, maybe link it to all that paedophile vigilante stuff from last year?

Pete found himself staring at the story, the two paras of notes, unable to speak. This was his doing.

'Well, boss?' said Terry, impatient.

Finally Pete found his voice. 'Single para will be fine, don't want to reopen all that can of worms.' Terry said OK and walked off, giving him a little bit of a look but nothing special, and Pete sat back and wondered at himself.

His phone rang then. Pete picked up. Malcolm Hopkin. Pete was immediately on the alert and Hopkin didn't beat about the bush.

'Pete, boy, what the hell has got into you?'

Pete said nothing.

'You're running around town like Clark Kent all of a sudden. Your boss Graham there assures me you're Mr Sensible, Mr Quiet Life, and now you're trampling all over the prize rose bushes.' He paused. 'Or should I say prize caravan parks?'

Pete shuddered but managed to stay silent.

Hopkin sighed.

'OK, lad, well you obviously reckon you're on to a bit of a story here, and I suppose you're right, but what I'm asking is whether you might be able to listen to the other side. You prepared to do that, son? Listen?'

'I guess,' said Pete, guardedly.

'Good man,' said Hopkin. 'How about six o'clock at my office?'

'OK,' said Pete. 'Where's that?'

Hopkin laughed. 'The Wharf, son, pub by the dock. Six o'clock, yeah?'

'Yeah, OK,' said Pete, frowning.

31

Bobby was sitting in Bernie Walters's office, a glass of wine in her hand, her head spinning. Les – her dad – had had to shoot off on some urgent business and she'd just sat there by herself for a bit in the Prince of Wales wondering just how different her life might have been if her mum had told her, if her mum had known, if her mum hadn't given her up the second she saw what colour she was, if her mum and dad had wanted each other, had wanted her. Bollocks, this was the kind of self-pity she'd long since learnt you couldn't afford; known since she was six years old there was no one in this world you could rely on but yourself and she'd made peace with that but now this feeling that she'd had a dad all this time, a dad who did want her, who was pleased to see her, who didn't reject her, well it hurt, left her feeling scalded and raw to the world.

And that was without even thinking about the other stuff – who he was – the things that had happened all those years ago, happened right in that pub. She'd had to get out of there, stood up, realised she was well on the way to being drunk. Out in the fresh air she'd considered going home, but her head was buzzing too much and she felt like another drink, needed a bit more of a blanket between her and the world. Then she'd looked across the road, seen the light in Bernie's office and thought Bernie'll have a drink, Bernie knows my dad, and in she'd gone and it was like he'd been waiting for her. She walked in and she was just going to say hello to Marguerite when Bernie's door opened and he just gave her this big hug and led her into his office and there was a bottle open and an empty glass waiting and Bernie was smiling at her and she felt . . . cared for.

'When did you realise, Bern?' she asked him.

Bernie looked at her. 'The moment you asked if this Troy Thursday was black. Course, my apologies, I should have thought of that at once, but I'm not as swift as I once was. Anyway, moment you asked that I thought of Les and then I looked at your face and thought well, the truth's staring right back at me. But of course I had to check it out a little bit, see how the land lay, if you know what I mean.'

'You told him, didn't you?'

Bernie squirmed in his seat a little. 'Well, yes, I felt it was best, really. Didn't want you getting hurt, and I didn't want Les getting too much of a shock either, not in his state.'

'What d'you mean, not in his state?'

Bernie shook his head quickly. 'Oh nothing, he's just had a few health problems lately.'

'He didn't say anything about that.'

'No, well, probably not the main thing on his mind, not when he was seeing you. And it went all right, did it?'

'Yeah,' said Bobby, 'great, I think, but odd, you know?'

Bernie nodded. 'I can imagine. You going to see him again?'

'Yeah, tomorrow. Wants me to meet him at the Castle, show me his plans.'

'Great,' said Bernie again, beaming effusively and refilling her glass. 'Going to hear on Friday, isn't he, whether he gets it or not.' A frown quickly passed over Bernie's face but was summarily dismissed. 'Anyway, forget business, this is wonderful.'

'Yeah,' said Bobby, coasting on the alcohol high, well aware that she might be in for an almighty comedown, but just for now letting herself enjoy it.

32

Pete was round at Kim's flat. She was assembling the Super 8 projector and he was watching her. They were both being fastidiously polite to each other, skating round the huge crater that was the Bobby business.

Finally Kim had the first film threaded into the spools of the projector. Pete had closed the curtains and cleared the pictures off a white wall that would serve as the screen. Kim switched the projector to play and Pete turned the lights out.

The film started. It was colour but faded and badly lit. There was a big table and some sort of banquet in progress. There were all these older blokes sitting round the table with masks over their eyes and these younger blokes in shorts and T-shirts serving then. Very quickly and without any attempt at dramatic explanation the sex began. Pete and Kim looked at each other. Pete tried a grin like it's all right, this was all a long time ago and it's just a rather kitsch artefact now. Except it wasn't; there was still something shockingly illicit in what they were watching.

Pete tried to neutralise it by concentrating on whether any of the masked men could possibly be St Clair. He stared at the screen; the masks made it hard to be at all sure, but even so none of the older men seemed to have St Clair's colouring. He reeled back in shock then as the screen cut to a close-up of a penis entering a mouth.

'I dunno,' he said to Kim to cover his embarrassment. 'Can't see St Clair in there.'

'Must have stayed behind the camera,' said Kim, her attention not wavering from the screen, apparently unbothered by what she was watching.

'Yeah,' said Pete, 'suppose so,' hoping the film would run out soon.

'We can just keep looking through the others,' said Kim brightly. 'Maybe he appears himself in the straight ones. After all, it must be girls he's into if he's Bobby's . . .' Kim's voice tailed off.

Pete looked at her. Bobby's what? What was she talking about? Before he could ask, though, Kim let out a yell.

'Fucking hell!' She was pointing at the screen, as an acned blond youth was lying back letting a fat bloke in a mask go down on him. 'I know him.'

'Who is it?'

Kim waved his question away, eyes still fixed on the screen. She watched till the blond boy got off, then she walked up to the screen as the camera panned up to his face cracking into a big grin. Then the reel ended and the film started flapping about in the projector till Kim switched it off and turned to Pete.

'That's Lee Fontana.'

Pete looked at her blankly.

'You know. The chef. He's got his own show on HTV, has his own restaurant out in Radyr. I worked with him on *Good Morning Wales* a couple of years back.'

Pete nodded. The name rang the faintest of bells; probably the bloke had done the Dish of the Day feature in the Saturday magazine or something, wasn't like Wales was overburdened with celebrity chefs. Anyway, that was hardly the point. 'You sure?'

'Yeah,' said Kim. 'Well, ninety-nine per cent anyway.'

'Christ,' said Pete. 'Well, if he confirms St Clair was there, then . . .'

'Then we've got him, yeah.' Kim had a huge smile on her face. 'Jesus, Pete, this story just keeps on getting better and better. Lee Fontana, that is so brilliant. This could be a bloody *Panorama* special, this could. I will just be so out of here.'

Kim came over to Pete, put her arms round him from behind and whispered in his ear, 'That was one brilliant piece of work, Peter Duke. You fancy a little celebration?' She slipped her hand down his chest, found his nipple and squeezed it then turned him round to face her, kissed him hard.

Pete wanted to resist but failed completely and allowed himself to be dragged to the bedroom. Just then her mobile rang, making them both jump. She switched it off immediately but it gave Pete the opening he needed. 'Look, Kim, we've got to talk. What's going on with you and Bobby?'

She carried on unbuttoning her shirt, smiling. 'Nothing you have to worry about, Pete. She was just in a bit of a state and I brought her home and . . .' She laughed. 'You know what I'm like, Pete, terrible old tart, but it's nothing. Hardly like I'm going to go off with a lesbian pimp, am I? Be serious. But if it bothers you that much, I'll knock it on the head.'

She looked at him, all fake sincerity and sweetness, and she unhooked her bra, then gave him another smile and said, 'Or maybe you'd like to watch, that it? You one of those fellers desperate to see two girls getting it on?'

'Piss off,' said Pete, but even as he said it he was moving towards her, letting her undo his buttons, letting himself sink into it, feeling that if something was this much fun what did it matter if it was wrong, and thinking that sounded like the lyrics to a country song, maybe it was the lyrics to a country song and then he wasn't thinking about lyrics any more, wasn't thinking of anything more complex than touch and taste and sight till it was over and he was once more wishing he smoked. Then he turned to look at the clock by the bed and it was five to six and he remembered he was meant to be meeting Malcolm Hopkin in five minutes.

'Oh God,' he said. 'Sorry, look I've got to go.'

'Oh right,' said Kim, mock-outraged. 'Well, just leave the money on the mantelpiece, is it?'

'Sorry,' said Pete again. 'It's just I've got to meet Malcolm Hopkin — you know, St Clair's mate. Says he's got some information for us.'

'Like hell,' said Kim. 'He'll just be trying to buy you off.'

Pete shrugged. 'C'mon, got to get all sides of the story.'

'Yeah, well. Anyway, while you're doing that I'll try and set something up with old Lee Fontana. You want to come along?'

'Sure,' said Pete.

'Fine,' said Kim. 'Well, call me on the mobile later on . . . Oh, and you know when you meet Hopkin?'

'Yeah.'

'Well, there's any bribes going, you make sure you get one for me and all.'

Pete made it to the Wharf at half six, hair still wet from the shower. Malcolm Hopkin was sat at the bar with a copy of the *Echo* in his hand, a pint and chaser next to him.

Hopkin looked him up and down quizzically. 'You just fall in the canal, son?'

'No,' said Pete. 'Just had a shower.'

'Oh aye,' said Hopkin. 'Afternooner, was it? Married, is she?'

Pete spluttered haplessly. Hopkin clapped him on the back. 'Only joking, son. What are you drinking?'

'Pint of light,' said Pete and waited for Hopkin to get the drink and lead them over to a table in the raised area looking out over the water, near where a band was soundchecking – later on the Wharf would be packed. Any night there was a decent band on, the Wharf was full of men and women Pete's age, the kind of people who'd been squeezed out of the town pubs by the youth revolution.

The band were running through something mellow, sounded like a Bobby Blue Bland tune, and the lights from the Holiday Inn Express further up the wharf looked almost pretty.

'Did it ever strike you, son,' said Malcolm, lighting up a fag, 'that Cardiff's really like an American city?'

Pete took a pull on his pint, raised his eyebrows.

'You think about it. Listen to the music – American music, right. People been hearing that in Cardiff since for ever. Cause of all this.' Malcolm waved at the docks. 'Sailors brought the music in. And that's the other thing to remember; it's a new city, hardly more than a hundred years old.'

'Hundred and fifty,' said Pete.

'Hundred and fifty, whatever. Same age as Chicago. And an immigrant city too. People came from all over to work here. Africa, China, England. All over.'

'Uh huh,' said Pete, thinking about it. Well, the Chicago comparison was apt enough, at least when it came to the way local politics ran. Chicago – the natural home of the political fixer. 'Yeah,' he said, 'I'd have thought Chicago would be your kind of place.'

Hopkin laughed. 'I know what you're saying. But what I'm saying is this city is changing. You grew up here, didn't you, son?'

'Yeah,' said Pete. 'Well, Whitchurch way.'

'Exactly. So you know how the city was, you remember it before all this development, right? And you've seen it change, yeah?'

'Yeah,' said Pete, wondering what on earth this was all about.

'Yeah, of course you have, and let me ask you, you think it's changed for the better?'

Pete scratched his head – flashed on St Mary Street on a Saturday night, a neon strip of theme bars and blokes in

Aquascutum shirts throwing up. 'I guess,' he said. 'More jobs, more money, you know.'

'Sure,' said Hopkin. 'You're right there. No question. And I like to think I've played my part over the years helping bring the investment in. But that doesn't mean I have to like it all.'

'Yeah,' said Pete, 'I know what you mean, but I don't exactly get why you're telling me this, if you don't mind me saying.'

'Not at all, cause the reason you don't get it is cause I'm taking a bastard long time to get to the point, and that is that if you run the story that I suspect you've got about old Les and his dirty doings half a bloody lifetime ago, well, what'll happen — more than likely — is the bid will be screwed, Globalcast Holdings or whoever will nip in through the back door and you'll have another bloody drive-thru Burger King and an Allied Carpets and you'll have played your part in bringing that about.'

'Yeah,' said Pete, 'that's all well and good and, be honest, I don't disagree with a word you've said, but that still doesn't mean I can condone what St Clair did.'

'No,' said Hopkin, 'fair enough. If you've got evidence that Les did wrong — and I suspect you haven't really got much more than a load of tittle-tattle — well, fine, go ahead and print it, but let me just say that if you waited till next week, once the contract's been awarded, you'd be doing the city as a whole a big favour.'

Pete didn't say anything, just kept on looking out at the water, thinking that what Hopkin said was reasonable enough.

'Doing your bank balance a big favour and all, I wouldn't be surprised,' Pete said in the end, 'but, fair enough, the story's been waiting twenty-five years to come out, couple more days won't kill it.'

'Good man,' said Hopkin, all but sighing with relief before carrying on. 'And of course our friend Kenny will be relieved and all. Not a man you want to get on the wrong side of, is our friend Kenny.'

'No,' said Pete, kind of wishing Hopkin hadn't said that, had allowed Pete to feel like he was acting out of magnanimity and not out of fear.

33

Bobby tried Kim's mobile again around eight and finally got an answer. She seemed really pleased to hear from Bobby and sure she'd love to have a chat; why didn't Bobby meet her back at her flat in about half an hour?

On her way round Bobby found herself thinking about the Pete feller, wondering how serious it was between him and Kim. Stupid – what was she doing feeling jealous? Not like the thing with Kim could ever go anywhere, and anyway didn't she have enough on her mind already? But still she could tell she was going to have to talk to Kim about the Pete feller. In the past it didn't bother her too much a girl she was seeing was sleeping with some bloke; she always felt like the girl would see sense before long, see who gave her the best time. Yeah, well. That's how she'd always been; arrogant, y'know. Up till lately. Now all she was was vulnerable.

Then Kim opened the door and saw Bobby and gave her this big oh-dahling hug and kiss and led her into the front room and they sat on Kim's nice sofa and Bobby told her how it had gone with her dad, badly wanting, she realised, Kim's approval.

She didn't get it, though. Kim kept shaking her head and when she finished just looked at her and said, 'He's got a nerve, thinking he can just swan back into your life like that.'

'Yeah,' said Bobby, suddenly feeling apprehensive, 'maybe you're right. But I dunno, it's not like he abandoned me on purpose; he never knew I existed. And he's a nice guy really. I'd forgotten that; a real charmer, like. You don't know, you never met him, have you?'

'No,' said Kim, 'but I think you may be losing your sense of perspective a bit here, Bob. Remember how angry you were when you came to me first, told me about all the abuse you'd suffered?'

'Well,' said Bobby, 'it wasn't me who suffered it really.'

'Oh come on, he abused you all one way or another. Look, I've seen the films. Did I tell you that I've got the films?'

'No,' said Bobby, 'Jesus,' and then she realised that she'd been staring idly at a Super 8 projector, a film loaded up.

Kim followed her gaze. 'Yeah, that's one of them there. You want to have a look?'

Bobby didn't say anything. She wasn't sure if she did or she didn't. But Kim didn't wait for an answer, just turned the film on anyway.

Suddenly she was sixteen again. And she was caught exactly halfway between laughing and crying. Laughing cause it had all been a laugh back then, sixteen and without a prospect in the world, but still somehow invincible and at last amongst her people, Leslie St Clair's circus of outsiders. Crying because it was so long ago and where were they now, all those hard and pretty boys – Lee Fontana, Darren Jones, Perko and, Christ, wasn't that Rizla in the corner just sitting there watching, a stoned grin on his face? She walked up closer to the wall, trying to make out anyone else.

'Recognise anyone?' asked Kim.

'Yeah,' said Bobby. 'That's Jonesy, Darren Jones, giving the fat guy a blow-job, and that's Lee Fontana there just taking his shirt off.'

'Yeah,' said Kim, all pleased. 'I recognised him already.'

'You didn't? Lee!' Shit, she hadn't seen Lee in years, always feared the worst for him.

'Yeah, you know he's a chef now, has his own restaurant, does a lot of TV stuff.'

'You taking the piss?'

'No, it's true.'

'Well, fucking hell.' Bobby shook her head, feeling slightly happier. God, if Lee Fontana could make it . . .

'Anyone else?'

Bobby shrugged. 'Few people. You see that guy there with the little 'tache, that's Frog. I still sees him now and again.'

'Oh yeah, how's he doing these days?'

Bobby frowned. 'Smackhead. Used to be a rentboy years ago, but he got a bit past his sell by.'

'Oh yeah?' said Kim. 'That's awful. You wouldn't know how I could get hold of him, would you?'

'Dunno,' said Bobby. 'Lives up the Valleys somewhere, but he goes in the White Hart now and again. His Auntie Liz works there.'

'Thanks, great,' said Kim, 'and he goes by Frog, does he?'

Bobby laughed. 'No, not to his auntie. He's Paul, his name is Paul Richards. Why d'you want to know, anyway?'

'Oh,' said Kim, 'just been following up a bit on what you told me about St Clair – your dad, I mean.'

Bobby waved the correction away. 'Yeah, St Clair is fine, Les, whatever; not like he's been a dad to me, is it? So, what, you're making a documentary about him?'

'Oh yes, well, maybe, see how it pans out.'

Bobby stared at Kim for a moment, wondering how she felt about St Clair being exposed on the TV. Confused. That was how she felt. 'I tell you I'm going to see him tomorrow?'

'Yeah?' said Kim. 'Really? Oh, you don't think I could . . .'

She broke off but Bobby could guess what she wanted to ask, something like can I come along and film you with him, and she felt a heaviness inside her; maybe there was no straight world, maybe everyone was on their own hustle after all – TV, brothel-keeping, whatever – maybe it all came down to individuals trying to screw as much as they could get out of each other. There was a line she'd used often enough to her girls: least you know you're getting screwed with what you do, and you're getting paid for it. You try working in McDonald's, you're getting screwed there and all and you're getting four pound an hour for it. Said it once, she'd said it a hundred times, but now, looking into Kim's eyes seeing the calculations going on there, she felt its truth. She couldn't help it, her face crumbled and she was reaching out to Kim like a bloody baby.

'Don't push me,' she was saying and then Kim was putting her arms round her and saying, 'Hey, girl, I'm sorry. Always working, that's my trouble,' and Bobby didn't try to analyse that for sincerity, just took the comfort offered, and then she let Kim put her to bed, half expecting that, tired though she was, she wouldn't be able to sleep, and if she did there'd be nightmares all the way, but instead she was asleep the second her head hit the pillow and if she dreamed at all she didn't remember it when she woke up a full twelve hours later.

She woke up feeling like she was newborn, an extraordinary lightness upon her and her whereabouts utterly strange. Second by second, though, the world came back to her. First her surroundings came into focus; the clothes spilled on the chair, Kim twisting in her sleep next to her, then a rush of pleasure. She was meeting Les – her dad, Les, her dad, Les – at twelve, then a rush of fear, an old familiar lesson learned; don't get your hopes up, girl, cause that's how you get hurt.

And then it was nine am, time to go, and Kim said softly in her ear, 'Go on, Bob, you better go see your dad,' and Bobby clutched on to her hard then let go and headed out the door and down the stairs and off to meet her father.

34

Pete and Kim were driving out into the Vale, on their way to see Lee Fontana. Pete was driving his latest review car; he'd finally managed to wangle a Subaru Impreza and as they passed Culverhouse Cross heading up the Tumble Hill he put his foot down and fairly hurtled past the other motors. He looked over at Kim, saw her smile back at him but her mind was clearly elsewhere – on the story, no doubt, the big story – and he had a stabbing sense that no matter how fast a car he was driving he was never going to keep up with her.

Lee Fontana lived in a converted chapel in Llancarfan, one of the little villages off the A48. Kim had phoned him the night before to say that she was making a docco on Leslie St Clair and his name had come up and she told Pete that he'd said, 'Oh fucking hell, love, I was wondering when someone would finally dig that whole business up, why don't you come over for breakfast?'

So nine forty-five there they were, ringing on the doorbell of a very tastefully converted chapel. Seconds later the door was open and a big hospitable bloke, with a sharp suit straining a little over his ample stomach, was ushering them into the kind of place Pete had only ever seen in the Saturday magazine. All burnished hardwoods and brightly coloured Sixties-looking furniture.

'You must be Kim, then,' said the bloke, smiling, his accent dead Cardiff but camped up a bit. 'I'm Lee and you're the photographer, are you?' he asked, turning towards Pete.

'No,' said Kim. 'This is Pete, he's from the *Post*.'

'Oh right,' said Lee with a little sigh. 'Oh well, the more the merrier, I suppose. Come on in.'

They followed Lee across the open-plan interior through a living area which had Kim exclaiming, 'Wow, Lee, is that all Memphis?' and Lee saying, 'Yes, well a few bits and bobs,' but looking dead chuffed and then they were over in the eating and dining zone and there was a big plate of croissants in the middle of the table next to a pot of coffee and they each took a plate and a cup and Kim did a bit more ooh-what-a-gorgeous-place chitchat and then it was down to business.

'So,' said Pete, taking on the pro-journalist role, 'you're not denying your involvement with Leslie St Clair?'

'No,' said Lee. 'Why would I want to do that?' He frowned. 'I was wondering how you got to know about all that, though.'

'Uh . . .' said Pete, wondering how much to reveal.

'We saw one of the films,' chipped in Kim, clearly not bothered about showing their hand.

'Oh bloody hell,' said Lee, laughing out loud. 'Well, I suppose it's a compliment you recognised me. Bit skinnier back then, wasn't I?'

'A little bit, maybe,' smiled Kim. 'How old were you?'

'Oh, I dunno,' said Lee. 'Depends a bit which one you saw. Was it like a dinner party – God, it's all coming back to me now – with masks, was that the one?'

'Yeah, that's it.'

'Oh bloody hell, well do let me have a copy when you've finished with it. I've got to show it to Stefan; he'll never believe how fit I was back then. Oh God, how old was I? Sixteen definitely; you're not having me saying I was under-age.' He paused, looked from Kim to Pete and back again. 'Is that what this is about, you trying to say Les was using people were under-age?'

'Well,' said Kim, 'obviously if some of the performers were under-age . . .'

'No, no way,' said Lee. 'Absolutely no way is that what was going on there. That was the best bloody thing ever happened to me, meeting Les and his crowd. I was a right little hooligan back then, if you can believe it. Out of touch with my sexuality is what they'd say now. First person ever treated me decent was Les St Clair and once I saw what was going on I'd have bloody killed to get into those films. Well, you've seen them – did it look like anyone was forcing me to do it?'

'Well,' said Kim, laughing despite herself, 'not exactly but that doesn't mean it was appropriate.'

'Appropriate!' Lee burst out laughing now. 'C'mon, love, what the fuck has appropriate got to do with a good shag? No, you won't find me saying one word against Leslie St Clair – he put me in the films, he introduced me to people, he made all this,' Lee waved a hand at his elegant living space, 'made it all possible. Before I met Les my life was utter shit. Since then, well, it's not been all wine and roses, but there's been a hell of a lot more up than down. So if that's all you wanted to know, I've got work to do.'

And that was that, really. Kim tried to get in a couple more questions but you could see that the more Lee thought about what was going on the more pissed off he was getting and in no time they were out the door and Pete was driving them back to Cardiff.

'Well?' said Pete.

'Well what?' said Kim, sitting next to him frowning hard. 'Look, it doesn't matter if Lee bloody Fontana doesn't want to co-operate; he's admitted he was in the film, that's dynamite for starters. All we have to do now is find some of the other people who were in it and we're in business.'

'I dunno,' said Pete. 'It was a long time ago and, like Lee there

213

said, it doesn't seem like anyone was frightening the horses exactly.'

'Pete! It's a big bloody story, all right? Network are really excited about it. I spoke to someone in London about it last night; they're ready to run with it the minute I've got a couple of witness statements. Pete, you got to keep your head screwed on here. We're talking major fucking break. For both of us. You been on to the tabloids yet, have you, Pete? *News of the World*'ll love it.'

Pete didn't answer, just revved up the car as they pulled out of St Nicholas and a stretch of open road loomed, trying to become one with the motor, miles away from the muck-raking.

35

He was waiting for her in the Louis, an old-fashioned full-service café, looked like nothing from the outside but went back about a mile once you got inside. All daily-roast specials and puddings with custard and all the waitresses looked like your nan, place Bobby had completely forgotten existed, place you walked past thousands of times without even registering it any more, and there was St Clair sitting at a table near the front, chatting to the manager, finishing up a cup of coffee. And you could tell, she was sure you could tell, that he was pleased to see her and she was pleased to see him but scared too and wary and in a minute they were out on the street and he started talking to her, talking in a different voice from any she'd heard before, a quieter, more thoughtful voice. He asked her what she knew about the history of Cardiff and she said not much and he said, 'Well I've made quite a study of it. You know there was hardly anything here two hundred years ago?'

Bobby nodded; she wasn't stupid, she knew it was a Victorian city, an industrial city.

'Hardly anything at all here till one man came along. The second Marquess of Bute. His family already owned the castle, what there was of it then, just a falling-down keep and a half-built manor house really, plus all the land around it. Then they discovered coal up in the valleys and Bute had the vision to turn his land into the biggest port in the world.

'He had the vision, the second Marquess, but he died before it all really got going. Left a baby son – the richest baby in the world, they called him – John, the third Marquess. Imagine that – you're born fabulously rich and all the time you're growing up you're getting richer and richer. Coal and shipping is making you relatively speaking about the richest man there's ever been. Can you imagine that?'

'Hardly.'

'Me either, girl, me either. You and me, we come up the other way. And yeah, yeah, before you start I know I never helped you, but how could I when I never even knew you existed? But anyway, imagine you had all that money, what would you have done with it?'

Bobby shrugged.

'Well, this feller, he built himself castles. He built this one, for starters.'

By now they were at the foot of St Mary Street, looking across the road at Cardiff Castle. Bobby found herself blinking at it, thinking how strange it was that things that were frankly pretty extraordinary, like this great big castle stuck right in the middle of town, should become so familiar that you hardly even notice them. She had to think for a moment to remember if she'd ever actually been inside. All she could recall was a school trip to the Tattoo when she was a kid, a load of soldiers firing off cannons and stuff. She'd been scared but she hadn't shown it, wet the bed in the home that night. She couldn't remember anything much about the castle itself.

Well, now she was going to see it all again. St Clair walked over the drawbridge, had a quick word with the security guard and led her into the big open space in the middle.

The castle basically had these huge walls, made a square about a hundred yards across. In the middle was the one original part, a big Norman keep. The south wall where they came in had a tower in the middle with a military museum. The east and north walls had nothing much on them. It was the west wall that had all the main buildings, a whole hotchpotch of towers linked together by galleries.

St Clair gave her a whirlwind guided tour. He led her through these rococo rooms decorated in crazed Victorian gothic style like a fairytale castle come to life.

'You've got to remember the third Marquess was only eighteen when he started building all this stuff. He found this opium-fiend architect called Burges and they built this. You see that,' he pointed at a table in the middle of what was called the small dining room, 'you see that hole in the table? He had a bloody vine growing up from the floor below, came up through the table so they could pick grapes off it at the end of the meal.'

'Right,' grunted Bobby, kind of enjoying this new side of St Clair, the historian, but also wondering what the point of all this was. Leslie St Clair wasn't a feller did things without a point.

And sure enough, after they'd whisked through half a dozen more over-elaborate rooms, St Clair led the way back outside, into the central area.

'OK,' he said then, 'one last thing I want to show you.'

She followed him past the peacocks towards the castle keep. Over the inner moat then up a steep flight of stone stairs and they were inside. Up two flights of wooden stairs then into the tower. Up a winding staircase and then they came out at the top. The whole city of Cardiff spread out before them on a cold bright spring lunchtime.

'You see this?' St Clair flung his arms out wide. 'This is our city, girl, yours and mine.'

'Yeah,' said Bobby, like yes it's Cardiff, I know.

He turned to her. 'I'm not joking, girl. This is my city now; anywhere I go people know me, people respect me. Wasn't like that when I was coming up. Back then they wouldn't serve you in the pubs in town; you was supposed to stay back past the bridge, specially at night. Ever since the race riots all those years ago we had our place, which was a great bloody slum down there – ' he pointed towards the docks and the strip of housing that separated the town centre from the docks: Butetown '– and they had all the rest of it.'

Bobby nodded. She knew this.

'Course,' he said, 'you don't need me telling you all this; point is we've raised ourselves up, you know what I'm saying?'

Bobby nodded again, her mind suddenly occupied by an image of herself, raised up all right, standing on top of a pile of girls – Maria, Tanya, Nikki and all the ones who'd gone before – and St Clair next to her on a much bigger pile.

'Now then,' said St Clair, 'look over there.' He pointed beyond the banqueting hall and the castle wall and the river to the point where Llandaff Fields dead-ended in what used to be the Sophia Gardens exhibition centre and was now a makeshift car park. 'That's where it's going to be.'

'Your new shopping mall?'

'It's not a shopping mall, girl, it's a community development – the Castle Market, loads of incentives for local businesses to get involved.' He paused. 'Fucking hell, who do I think I'm talking to? Yeah, course it's a shopping mall. I know – just what the city needs, whatever. Point is, this deal comes off it's one big bloody payday.'

St Clair turned to look at Bobby. 'You think I'm rich, girl? Well, think again; I've got the biggest overdraft you ever heard of. All the magazines are going down the pan – the computer mags are losing me an arm and a leg. Everyone thinks they must still be coining it but there's so much competition these days, and the advertising market's gone to hell. Soon as a decent accountant gets anywhere near the books he'll close down the whole shooting gallery.

'But if this comes off,' he waved once more towards the

notional new development, 'well, I'm back in business. So I'm just holding my breath till Friday. We sign the deal, then I close the whole publishing thing down and I'm into the property business big-time.'

He put his hands on her shoulders then looked deep into her eyes. She looked back into his, could see nothing there, just a blackness. 'And not just for me — for you too.'

'Oh yeah?' said Bobby, mustering up a bit of front of her own. 'Written me into the will, have you?'

Then she turned her head away from St Clair's siren voice, looked back out over the Castle Field, sure she could see the two human pyres there, his victims and hers, and then she had an awful sense that she could see figures detaching themselves from the pyres walking towards her like zombies or the undead or something, all crying out: poor bloody Frog standing outside the Glendower trying to sell his shrunken junkie body; poor bloody thick bloody Debbie on the game from sixteen, carved up by some psychotic bloody punter when she was twenty-two; and all the rest of them, all walking towards her.

36

Pete was sitting at his desk fielding phone calls from Cherri, who was waiting for Bryn Terfel to show up, finishing the layout for tomorrow's arts page, and doing a bit of work on the St Clair story which was suddenly a hot priority.

He'd gone in to see Graham after the rocket Kim had put under him earlier on and just sort of mentioned that if Graham didn't want it, would it be OK if he freelanced it to one of the tabloids, the *News of the World*, maybe? Well, he'd never seen Graham so animated. No way was Pete taking the story anywhere. This was terrific principled journalism and that was what the *Welsh Post* stood for – subject to the lawyers approving it, of course.

'Of course,' Pete had said and he'd gone back to his desk feeling oddly depressed. He could see it was the right thing to do – what St Clair had done was morally repugnant, whether or not some of the participants had survived the experience apparently unscathed. But still, raking it all up now; well, he wasn't too sure who it was going to help exactly. But it would surely sell newspapers and that at the end of the day was his job so he was sitting there staring at a brand-new Word 97 document trying to assemble the facts of the story when the phone rang yet again.

'Pete.'

'Oh, he arrived yet, Cher?'

'Pete, it's not bloody Cher, it's Kim.' She sounded excited. 'I've found another witness, Pete, and this one's not going to be telling us how great it all was. Apparently he's a real fuck-up, lives near Blackwood. You up for it?'

Pete sighed; he supposed he had to be. 'Yeah,' he said. 'Where are you?'

'Beeb.'

'Right, I'll pick you up from there, front entrance in forty-five minutes. OK?'

Forty-five minutes later, right on the dot, Pete was there; another half hour and they were making their way up the valley north of Newport and they were either in Risca or Cross Keys – Pete could never figure out where one started and the other finished – and Kim was map-reading and telling Pete all this stuff she'd got from . . . Well, she didn't want to admit it but it was pretty obvious she must have got it from Bobby so Pete had called her on it and she said yeah, yeah, she had seen Bobby, but it was strictly business, Pete didn't have to worry, which of course meant he was worrying like mad cause he didn't know what it meant, didn't feel like he knew what anything meant just at the moment, and the rain was starting to come down and one slate-grey Valleys town looked the same as the next and boy could it get depressing up here, even now it was all greened over to the point you came from Mars or London or somewhere you would scarcely imagine there had ever been coal mines here, or slag heaps big enough to bury a school.

Finally they were in Blackwood, and a quick word with a passer-by who actually knew something about his town and they were knocking on this feller called Frog's door, an upstairs flat above a newsagent. A minute or so later they could hear someone coming down the stairs and then the door opened a crack. 'That you, Daz?'

'No,' said Kim.

The door opened and a desperately skinny, toothless apparition, red blotches all over his face, stood before them. 'Who are you then?'

'I'm Kim,' said Kim, 'and this is Pete. I'm from the TV.'

'Oh yeah?'

'Yeah, we're making a documentary about Leslie St Clair.'

'That bastard.'

'Yeah,' said Kim, a grin coming to her face, 'that's right, that bastard. Now is it OK if we come in?'

'Oh yeah. OK,' said the apparition, 'it's a bit of a tip, like.'

It was more than a bit of a tip; it was a sofa and a carpet and a huge pile of newspapers and all of it doubled as an ashtray and Pete was damn sure he wasn't going to sit down anywhere but just put his tape recorder on the table and stood staring out the window at the rainswept street outside wishing he was any place else. Kim, though, played the bloke like a trouper. She told him they'd seen the film and she couldn't believe such a respectable figure as Leslie St Clair, such a role model to kids, had been involved in such sordid goings-on and the bloke certainly caught on very quick and was soon agreeing that yeah, it had been terrible, traumatised his whole life, and Kim was lapping it up and Pete was thinking yeah, well the guy was certainly in a hell of a state. But then, when the guy suddenly had a lightbulb moment and asked Kim if she thought there might be any compensation available for a person who'd suffered like he had and Kim said she was sure there was and the bloke's ravaged face took on a certain serenity and the terrible details of addiction and self-destruction started to mount up, Pete started to feel sick cause God knows on one level the guy wasn't lying, he was fucked – you could see that from a mile off. But on another level you wondered whether it was all down to being in a porn film when he was a teenager and really, to be honest, in the end Pete felt like he'd rather not know about all this; it just made him feel sick and depressed and despairing of humanity and really nostalgic for his nice house and nice wife and nice kids and he couldn't stand it any more. He went outside to wait in the car and he sat for another half hour listening to Johnny Walker on Radio 2, Johnny Walker's voice reminding him of being thirteen again and listening to Mott the Hoople on Radio 1, and finally Kim came out holding Pete's tape recorder and all but hugging herself with delight. 'Bingo,' she said, 'absolute bloody bingo. We've got him on toast. I'll take a copy of the tape, play it to my boss and we'll be back up tomorrow with a film crew.' She leaned over and gave Pete a great wet kiss on the cheek, her hair smelling of fags, of junkie squalor.

'Let's go,' she said.

'Yeah,' said Pete, putting the car into gear, and was just about to add something about how glad he was to be getting out of there when he had to pull over slightly to get out of the way of a car coming fast in the opposite direction. And as he did so he saw it was a black Saab, but it was past him before he could see the driver.

He turned to Kim. 'You see that?'

'What?' said Kim, who was looking down at the tape recorder, rewinding it a little to make sure the sound quality was OK.

'Nothing,' said Pete. 'Just looked a bit like Kenny Ibadulla's car, the one passed us back there.'

'Really?' said Kim momentarily alarmed. Then she relaxed, patted the tape recorder. Well, he's too late, isn't he. We've done it, Pete. We've got him.'

'Yeah,' said Pete, 'I suppose we have,' but he didn't stop checking his rear-view mirror till they were back in Cardiff.

37

After her talk with her father Bobby had wanted to be by herself. She'd walked and walked and walked, found herself heading east, down Newport Road under the bridge where the old AA headquarters was morphing into a block of luxury flats, past the Jane Hodge Foundation and what was left of the old infirmary, past Clifton Street and Summers Funeral Home, past the Royal Oak, and a memory of Charlie Unger, the nearest she'd come till now to a father-figure, dead these past three years, past the commercial zone, past the car showrooms and over the round-about and up Rumney Hill, before she realised what she was doing: walking back to the home, retracing the footsteps that had first led her to Les St Clair those years ago, set her life on course.

She got as far as the corner, the street where the home was. Was it still there? Was it still a home? She hadn't a clue. There wasn't exactly a big old-girls' club, got together for reunions. That was it, though; she could go no further. She looked around her, saw a bench on the pavement outside a curry house, and fairly collapsed on to it, suddenly aware of how much her feet were hurting. She looked back down the hill; for the second time that day she could see the city spread out before her. But there was a difference: with Les she'd been in the centre looking out; now, on her own, she was on the outside looking in, and this was the view she trusted. After they'd come down from the tower Les had laid out his plans. He'd told her he was serious; if she wanted it, he would groom her as his heir. But then again if this big deal tomorrow didn't come off he was history.

And he was worried about the Prince of Wales stories getting around. Cat's out of the bag there, he told her. He didn't say it was her fault but she was sure he must have guessed, cause the next thing he said was obviously a message – we can keep it out the news a couple more days then it should be OK; after that they can say what they like cause I'll be back in business.

So that was what he wanted. It was almost a relief discovering that he wanted something. Only question was what she was going to do. Sat on top of Rumney Hill she pondered it. Did she owe more to Frog and poor dead Debbie and all the rest of them or to this new-found father? On the bus back into town she decided. She'd try and have it both ways. She'd put the brakes on Kim for a day or two, let Les's deal go through. After that Kim could drag the truth out into the open and che sera sera.

First thing she had to do was get hold of Kim. She called her at the flat. Got the machine. Called her mobile. Got the voicemail. Left messages on both. Then she got a call from Tanya: she was needed back at the flat.

She tried Kim's numbers every hour or so through the evening; still no reply. Finally she figured that nothing was going to happen till morning so, after she'd seen the back of Nikki's last punter for the day and replied to the last of her emails, she closed the work flat up and went upstairs to sleep.

Kim finally answered her phone at eight in the morning, sounded exhausted, said she'd been up all night working on the programme. Bobby asked if she could stop by and have a quick word about that. Kim sighed but said OK if she could get round fast.

Bobby was round there in fifteen. Kim was all power-suited up and doing her make-up and though it had been the last thing on her mind Bobby couldn't repress a thrill of desire at the sight of her, something really dead sexy about that whole Ally McBeal trip, especially coupled with Kim's curves.

She did her best to be a bit subtle, asking when the programme was coming out like she was just making conversation, but when Kim said she'd seen Frog the day before, got a dynamite interview with him and they were thinking of maybe using part of it on *Wales Today* tonight, she had to weigh in.

'Why don't you keep it back a few days till it's all finished?'

'Too much of a risk,' Kim said. 'HTV might get wind of it. Got to get something out tonight, put the marker down that it's my story.'

'How about tomorrow night?' said Bobby, thinking that the contract was being announced at lunchtime, so any time after that should be OK.

'Why?' said Kim. 'What's it matter to you?'

Bobby tried to think of a plausible lie, couldn't think of one and resorted to the truth, told her that after all this was her dad, and it was bad enough the story coming out without screwing him on his deal and all.

'Oh right,' said Kim.

'And,' said Bobby, feeling desperate now, 'you do it tomorrow I'll give you an interview and all.'

'Yeah?' said Kim. 'Really? That'd be excellent.' She paused, thought about it. 'Look, Bobby, I'll have a word with my producer, see what we can do, yeah? But, to be honest, your real worry isn't me, but Pete, you know. He saw Frog and all and we've got a bit of a deal going – I go tonight on the TV, he leads off tomorrow morning in the press. So you really want to put a lid on this till tomorrow night, you best speak to him.'

'Yeah?' said Bobby, thinking this was starting to feel like pushing water upstream. 'You think he'll listen?'

'Worth a try. He's a decent bloke. Honest, go.'

38

Pete was transcribing the tape of Frog's interview, still flip-flopping between pity and disbelief, when he got a call from reception. It was Albert, using the tone of voice he reserved for announcing obvious undesirables. 'There's someone down here,' he said, 'wants to speak to you.'

'Oh yes?' said Pete, seized with immediate dread, sure it was Kenny Ibadulla. He'd hardly slept all night, convinced Kenny would be banging his door down. He paused, waited till he felt as if he had his voice under control. 'Who is it?' Even as he spoke he was wondering what he was going to do next. Rely on old Albert to deal with Kenny? Hardly.

'Bobby Ranger, she says her name is.'

Pete experienced an immediate rush of relief, followed by bemusement, and then a lesser dread, a minor-key dread. Bobby Ranger, what in hell did she want? Better find out. 'I'll be right down.'

She was waiting in reception, a stocky woman in a big black jacket emblazoned with the name of some American sports team, staring at nothing. Then she saw him and smiled. A gold tooth caught the light, but the smile was oddly shy, nervous.

'Thanks,' she said, 'thanks for seeing me.'

'It's all right,' said Pete. 'You want to come up or . . .' he felt oddly bashful '. . . we could get a coffee round the corner.'

'Coffee sounds good,' she said.

Pete led the way over the road and into an empty

brasserie/café/bar-type place. Pete ordered a coffee. Bobby had a hot chocolate.

'So,' Pete said, 'you wanted to talk to me about something.'

'Yeah,' she said. 'Well, quite a lot of things really.' There was that shy smile again. 'Expect you do and all.'

'Yeah,' said Pete awkwardly, trying to improvise his way through a wholly unfamiliar situation. 'Well, I dunno. I suppose in the end it's not between you and me, it's up to Kim . . .'

'Yeah, no, actually, I mean you're right I suppose, but that's not why I'm here. What it is is the Leslie St Clair story.'

'Oh,' said Pete, 'right.'

'Yeah, well, I don't know how much Kim has told you . . .'

'Well,' said Pete, 'I know it was you who brought her the story in the first place and everything.'

'Yeah, she tell you he's my dad?'

'Who?'

'Leslie St Clair.'

'No,' said Pete, 'she didn't tell me that. Christ, when did you find that out?'

'Just the other day.' She shook her head, again the nervous smile. 'Well, you can imagine.'

'God,' said Pete, 'don't know if I can.'

'No, you're probably right. Anyway, thing is I know I've got no right to ask you this, really, but is there any chance you can keep the story back till the day after tomorrow?'

Pete frowned. 'Why?'

Then he listened as Bobby explained that St Clair would be completely ruined if the story came out before the deal was signed. She was just starting to go on about job losses, clearly laying it on a bit, when Pete cut her off.

'S'all right,' he said. 'I've already agreed not to run it till next week. Someone else been on to me about it already.'

'Who?'

'One of your dad's business partners, Malcolm Hopkin.'

'Mal? Should have bloody guessed.' He watched Bobby shake her head like she too only had part of the whole story.

Finally she looked at Pete and said, 'So why did Kim tell me you were going to be running the story first?'

'I dunno,' said Pete, wondering the same thing. 'I tell you what, why don't I ask her?'

He got out his mobile, called Kim's number. Voicemail. Called her flat, got the answering machine, thought about it for a moment and called the main BBC number. Got put through to her department and finally spoke to some woman with a North Walian accent said she thought Kim was out filming something for tonight's news, the big hush-hush story.

'Oh yeah?' said Pete. 'I'm Pete from the *Post*, yeah, I've been working on the story with her, yeah? You wouldn't know whereabouts she is?'

'Oh, hi Pete,' said the North Walian. 'Yeah, she's mentioned you. But I've no idea where she is; all very secretive, it is. She said something about going back to the scene of the crime, that's any help.'

'So?' said Bobby, as he clicked off the phone.

'She said she was going to the scene of the crime – that mean anything to you?'

Bobby thought about it, then grinned. 'She's at the Prince of Wales.'

39

Bobby led the way into the building. They'd parked the car round the back, next to the car park, blatant double yellow and the Pete feller was worried about it, but she told him not to be stupid. He was a funny bloke, the Pete feller, but all right; she could see why Kim liked him. He had the dependable sensible thing going. Good-looking too, though he dressed like a bit of a bank manager and listened to Radio 2 but then so did she, now and again when Maria wasn't looking. Maria! Christ, she hadn't even thought about her the last day or so, there had been so much going on. Been no calls or anything, though; no 'Oh Bob I'm so sorry I made such a mistake', so she supposed that was well and truly over. She took a deep breath as they entered the lobby. Well, if a part of her life looked like it was coming to an end, this was where it had all started.

They checked inside the pub first; no sign of any TV crew.

'Let's have a look upstairs,' said Bobby and they went back to the entrance and up the stairs. No sign of anyone in what used to be the circle either. They walked slowly back out to the first-floor foyer by the toilets.

'Must be somewhere else,' said Pete.

'I dunno,' said Bobby and looked around her, trying to figure out what was new and what was old. There was a door over by the wall, said No Admittance on it. Was that the one? She walked over and opened it. It gave on to a narrow staircase going up. That was the one, all right.

They walked up to the top of the stairs, faced another door. A chill passed through Bobby as she opened it.

Christ, it was like time had stood still. The room was exactly the same, apart from being half full of boxes. For an instant she was sixteen again, stood on the edge of adventure, of knowledge; Eve about to eat the apple of desire.

Her eyes automatically tracked left to the bar area, half expecting Leslie St Clair to be sat at his table with a bottle of wine open, his serpent's smile in place.

He wasn't there, of course. But Kim was. She didn't see Bobby at first; there was a cameraman filming her as she talked earnestly into camera. Bobby couldn't make the words out from where she was standing, just the hushed tone of TV concern.

Then Kim must have fluffed her lines because she stopped, swore loudly, turned and saw Bobby frozen there in the doorway.

'Well bloody hell,' she said. 'Give me a shock, why don't you?' She walked over, a smile – a slightly puzzled smile but still a smile – firmly in place. 'How the hell did you find me here? I thought you were looking for Pete.'

'Well, I found him, didn't I?' said Bobby, moving forward into the room as, right on cue, Pete stepped through the doorway.

'Jesus,' said Kim, giggling nervously. 'Don't tell me it's *This Is Your Life*.'

'Hardly,' said Bobby. 'More like this is my life, isn't it? Thought you said you would wait on the story.'

Kim looked at her, gave this bright brittle liar's smile, same smile Bobby had seen on a thousand lawyers and a million hustlers and on everyone who'd ever let her down. 'Oh c'mon, Bobby, it's my job, you got to understand that. I don't do the story now, someone else will do it, someone who doesn't understand you the way I do.'

Bobby felt like kicking her, couldn't find the words to express her disgust. Kim turned to Pete. 'Pete, tell her that's how it is.'

Bobby looked at Pete, wondering which way he would jump.

Hell, what was she wondering about? It was obvious. Kim and him, they were two of a kind – media people, liked a bit of a walk on the wild side maybe, but knew which side their bread was buttered on all right. Why did she ever think an ambitious girl like Kim would be seriously interested in her; what was she on? She was just a bit of rough, wasn't she? Well, they wanted a bit of rough, they could have one; least she could do was smack Kim one on her smug little Rhiwbina face. She was just winding herself up ready to throw the punch when Pete spoke.

'Christ sake, Kim, it's only a fucking story. It doesn't matter if you run it today or tomorrow. Doesn't matter if HTV get it the same time as you at the end of the day, does it? We're not God here.'

Bobby watched Kim stare at Pete in disbelief. 'Might not matter to you, Pete. That's why you've been stuck in the same shit job for twenty years. It matters to me cause I am getting the fuck out of here.'

Pete's turn then to stare at Kim like he was ready to smack her one. For a few seconds no one said anything, then all four of them jumped as the cameraman spoke up.

'Kim,' he said, 'are we shooting this or not? Cause if we're not I've got work to do.'

Kim turned round. 'We're shooting it,' she said, 'just as soon as . . .'

Suddenly there was the sound of the door below being opened and then the clumping of four large men hurrying up the stairs.

Seconds later they emerged into the room, Kenny Ibadulla in the lead.

One thing about Kenny, Bobby thought, was once he was in the room everyone knew who was in charge, especially when, like now, he was carrying his trusty baseball bat.

'Bob,' he said first, 'you a part of this?'

'Part of what, Ken?'

'Digging up a load of old shit for the TV.' He nodded towards Kim.

'Well, no, Ken, not really, like. I've been trying to get her to lay off.'

'No good telling them,' said Kenny. 'You got to show them.'

Kenny walked towards Kim who was backing away fast, staring at him in wide-eyed terror. Bobby didn't reckon he would hit her; Kenny, bastard that he was, was still a bit of an old-fashioned gangster type, didn't hold with beating up women. But obviously Pete didn't realise that cause all of a sudden he's like running at Kenny from behind and Bobby doesn't know whether to laugh or cry cause Kenny's going to lick him down in a second but it makes her think that maybe the poor sucker's really in love with Kim and – state that she's in – it brings a tear to her eye as Kenny swings the bat behind him and it goes thud into Pete's thigh and then he's down on the floor groaning and Kim's screaming bloody murder and the camera-man's looking like he's going to weigh in and the situation is just ripe to get out of hand when a voice calls out, 'Ken! That's enough of that,' and the whole room freezes and there, standing behind the bar, a door flapping open behind him, is the Prince of Wales himself, Leslie St Clair.

'Les,' says Kenny. 'Just sorting things out.'

'Yeah, I can see that,' says Les, a little bit sarcastic, which is still the most sarcastic Bobby's ever heard anyone try on Kenny Ibadulla. 'Thing is, Ken, you know how they say no publicity is bad publicity; well I've got to say I'm not sure that goes for hospitalising TV reporters. So, you don't mind Ken, I think it might be best you leaves this to me.'

Kenny stared at Les then looked round the rest of the assembled crew. 'You sure, Les, cause if this deal goes arse up tomorrow I am not going to be very fucking pleased.' He fixed

Kim then Pete with a particularly hard glare. Pete didn't seem to notice, but Bobby could see Kim flinch.

'Yes, Ken,' said Les, and Bobby could hear the tiredness in his voice, 'and nor will the rest of us.'

Kenny nodded, then did a bit of huffing and puffing to show that no one ordered Kenny Ibadulla around, but soon he was out of there and Bobby watched in reluctant admiration as her father turned his charm on to Kim. Would she like an interview? Of course she would and all of a sudden Kim was interviewing Leslie St Clair right in his old position next to the bar of the Prince of Wales. And for the next ten minutes Bobby watched, experiencing a bewildering mixture of emotions, as Leslie St Clair lied his heart out, swore black was white and rivers flow uphill. His accusers were troubled individuals with long histories of drug abuse and psychiatric illness who had sadly focused their inadequacies on the successful figure of Leslie St Clair – just an unfortunate part of the fame game, he called it, and Bobby could see Kim half believing it. Christ, she half believed it herself and she knew it was all false.

And then Kim was done and the cameraman was packing up and there were the four of them stood in the middle of the room, her and her dad and Pete and Kim and all of them awkward now.

'Right,' said Kim finally, as the cameraman made for the door, and she turned and looked Bobby in the eyes and Bobby was just fixing her face into a scowl when Kim leaned forward towards her and then they were hugging, a hug that was definitely a goodbye but a decent one, a let's-remember-the-good-times one, and, as they parted, Kim breathed a single word in Bobby's ear. 'Sorry,' she said, and Bobby breathed back, 'It's OK,' because in the end she understood her; the girl was only trying to get on, and if there was one thing Bobby had learned it was that if you wanted to get on you did what you had to.

Then Kim turned to Pete and something went on between their eyes too, and it ended with Kim smiling and saying, 'You coming then?' and Pete saying, 'Yeah, I guess,' then he turned and hugged Bobby too, awkward like she'd have expected, but nice too and real and then they were gone and she was left alone in the Prince of Wales, with her father.

'Well, Les,' she said once the others' footsteps had faded away, 'what d'you reckon?'

'Oh,' said Les (she thought she'd stick with Les from now on; he wasn't Dad – he had never held her as a child – he was Les, always had been), 'I thought it went pretty well. Plausible old bastard when I want to be, aren't I?' and he looked at her like he was expecting a pat on the back.

'Yeah,' she said, 'you always were that.'

'That's right,' said Les. 'Now, as long as Kenny gets your old friend Frog to change his mind about what he remembers, we should be all right. And he's a persuasive fellow, Kenny, as I'm sure you know.' This time the grin he gave Bobby was pure evil and Bobby couldn't bear the complicity of it, the blood-is-thicker-than-water sharing of it.

Gone suddenly was the St Clair she'd walked the Castle with; here instead was a shifty dangerous bastard: the Leslie St Clair she remembered, in fact. Not the one she'd met at first when he was drawing her in, but the one she'd met later, when she'd tried to get out.

The strange thing was that suddenly she had an overwhelming sense of relief. All the time she'd spent with him, she'd felt like it was nice but it wasn't real. This felt real.

'You fucking bastard,' she said suddenly. 'You fucking blackmailing bastard.'

St Clair looked shocked for an instant, then his eyes went reptilian. 'Don't give me your airs and graces, girl. You and me, we're the same; we do what's got to be done. You've said worse things to your girls a hundred times.'

'You what?' Bobby looked at him in horror: what did he know about her business?

'Oh,' said St Clair, 'you forgetting you're a pimp?' He dug in his pocket. 'Or isn't this your card?'

He held out a card. Bobby grabbed it: it was one of hers all right.

'Where did you get this?'

St Clair smiled. 'The Hilton. You must congratulate the lad does your distribution, gets them in all the right places. So it's a good service, is it? Been tempted to call it up myself. Like father, like daughter, you know what I mean?'

Bobby rocked at that. God knows it was true; he may not have known it at the time but he'd been a true father to her, all right. He'd shown her the ways of the world. And now at last she had her chance to throw it all back in his lying face. She'd give Kim that interview after all.

'Fuck you,' she said and waited a beat before adding 'Dad' and heading fast away from him, her fingers closing on the mobile phone in her pocket.

40

'Did you know he was ill?' Pete asked Bobby as they stood outside the crem up in Thornhill two months later.

'Well,' she said, 'not really. I mean, he had a terrible cough and you know, now you think of it he smoked a hell of a lot and he looked a bit red round the eyes, but no, I didn't have a clue.'

'You think you'd have done anything different if you'd known?'

'What? You mean the interview with Kim?' Bobby thought about it. 'Nah,' she said finally. 'Anyway, he'd told me he was dying, I wouldn't have believed him. Didn't believe he was dead now, till I went round the funeral parlour and looked in the coffin.'

'You didn't?'

'Yeah.' She smiled at him then, the shy smile he'd come to see as the real Bobby Ranger, the one lived inside the tough girl. 'I suppose I wanted to say goodbye to him by myself, like. I hate these things.'

'You been to a lot of funerals then?'

'One or two, you know. First time it's ever been a family one, obviously.' Bobby tried a weak smile but her mind was going back to the last funeral she'd attended. Debbie's. Nearly fifteen years ago now but the thought of it still freaked her out. Well, it had freaked everyone out, of course, what happened to her — carved up by some psycho punter in a derelict house over by Tindall Street. Bobby shivered, watching a couple more motors pulling into the car park, flash ones again; amazing how many friends old Les had now he was dead.

She felt responsible of course, when Debbie died. Wasn't pimping her herself or anything – Debbie always found some right charmer to do that for her – but she'd played her part in turning Debbie out there, she knew that. Her and Les St Clair both. No, that wasn't fair on her; she could see that now. She'd only been sixteen herself; it was St Clair was at the root of it. It wasn't even like there was any malice or whatever in it, thinking about it now, waiting for his body to be turned to ash; she couldn't see him as evil exactly, just without any moral sense at all. And there was something so charming about that, that it corrupted practically everyone he ever came in contact with. And that was why she was glad he was dead.

She hadn't been glad when she heard. 'Cancer?' she'd said to Bernie when he'd called her up and given her the news. 'He didn't have bloody cancer. He didn't tell me.' And then she'd cried buckets partly cause he was dead, partly cause he hadn't told her. And partly, yeah, partly cause she'd felt guilty. There wasn't any big reason to be guilty on one level; he'd been diagnosed six months before. But still the speed it had taken him at the end there, she couldn't believe there was no connection with what had happened. First the scandal fuelled by Bobby's testimony. The Welsh Development Authority had put the Castle Market deal on ice right away, and the day after that Les's associates, Malcolm Hopkin and the rest, had cut him loose. Week later the magazines went into liquidation. The whole house of cards had come tumbling down.

She saw a familiar car pull into the car park, a black Saab. She touched Pete on the arm, pointed. They watched as Kenny Ibadulla emerged from the driver's side, then the passenger's side door opened and out got Malcolm Hopkin.

'Jesus Christ,' said Bobby, 'don't know how they've got the nerve, the way they dropped him.'

Pete looked at her and gave an apologetic sort of smile. 'Well,' he said, 'I suppose some people might say the same about you.'

'No,' said Bobby, 'no way. First, he was my bastard father so I got a right to be here whatever. Second thing, it's not the same . . .' She tailed off. How wasn't it the same? What the hell made her any better than Kenny Ibadulla or Malcolm Hopkin, these fellers who knew how the world worked and how to make a profit out of it?

'Tell you why it's not the same,' she said. 'You see me, right, you take one look at me and you know who I am, always been that way. All the time I've been a pimp – and yeah, yeah, don't worry, that's all finished with more or less – but all that time anyone asked I told them, I'm a pimp. But you see Mal over there, you see Kenny – thing about people like that, they want to have it both ways. And in the end you ask me, that's the thing you've got to learn in life; you got to make choices sooner or later – no such thing as having it both ways.'

Pete thought about this. He knew she was right, could feel the truth of it in his own life. The only problem was knowing what to give up – the cake or the eating. Kim had got what she wanted. Her documentary unmasking Leslie St Clair had been – well, not a huge success or an artistic triumph or anything, but it had got her noticed. Got her a job offer from a company up in London, did those *Ayia Napa Uncovered*-type documentaries, one step from porn movies themselves far as Pete could see but still. Anyway it paid lots more money than she'd been making at the Beeb and she'd taken it. Moved up to London within a month.

He was still seeing her, though. In fact the funny thing was, since she'd been in London she seemed to need him more, like she was a bit scared of the pace and the ambition, needed Pete's stability to stop her from going under. So they'd seen each other most weekends and it was good and everything but . . . but what? Well, seeing the hard time Kim was having, adjusting to the pace, just confirmed what he really already knew – no way was he, Pete Duke, moving up to London. The St Clair story had given him plenty of Brownie points with Graham, his job was about as secure as any job in journalism ever was and frankly he couldn't see himself leaving. And maybe in turn that was why he'd been seeing more of Viv. He wasn't sure really which one of them had initiated it but gradually they'd got into the pattern of him taking the kids out for the afternoon or whatever then afterwards him and Viv would go for a drink and a bit of a chat and catch up on how things were going and, well, the other day they'd got on so well that he'd suggested going back to the house after and Viv had said God no, what about the kids, but he'd given her a lift back anyway and they'd ended up parking up on Caerphilly mountain and doing it in the back of the car like a couple of kids. And now really he didn't know what to think and he was going to see Kim at the weekend and he was really going to have to make his mind up, but deep down he had a feeling that his mind was made up already.

'Yeah,' he said to Bobby, 'you're right there,' and then he looked up, saw another car pulling in, a four- or five-year-old Lexus. Bernie Walters climbed out.

'How's the job going?' Pete asked her then.

'Good,' she said. Bobby was enjoying working for Bernie. He'd taken her on three days a week at first, setting up his website, sticking the details of all his acts online, then administering it. Wasn't that much of a culture shock, specially when it came to booking the lap-dancers who were probably the steadiest-working section of Bernie's talent roster. But it wasn't all strippers; there were plenty of singers and dancers, even a couple of magicians. 'Got a couple of cruise-ship bookings this week via the site, so that was good.'

'Oh right,' said Pete, 'good.'

'Yeah,' said Bobby, feeling a definite sense of pride. It was amazing how her skills had translated to the showbiz world. Bernie noticed her then and came over, his face creasing into a sympathetic smile.

Bobby hugged him. She felt easy around Bernie these days and now they walked for a little while in silence, Bernie looking at her, gauging her mood before starting to talk.

'You know,' said Bernie, 'and maybe this is just the kind of bullshit that people talk at funerals cause they're trying to be nice, I was thinking about old Les today and all this trouble, and it made me think about the city as a whole and the way things are changing. Specially I was thinking about the place it all happened; you know, the Prince of Wales.

'Now, you remember how people used to say it was an eyesore. Well, I don't know about you and maybe I'm biased, but I kind of liked it being there. You close down all the dark and seedy places, what you're left with is a fake. It isn't real any more, it doesn't sweat and bleed like it used to. I suppose what I'm saying, Bob, is the thing about the Prince of Wales, places like that, you only ever miss them when they're gone. And that's kind of what I think about old Les too. Does that mean anything to you or am I just burbling on like an old fool?'

'No,' said Bobby, 'I kind of know what you mean . . . You got a fag, Bernie?'

He frowned at her. 'Thought you quit, young lady?'

'Yeah well, give me a break all right, not today.'

'Your funeral,' said Bernie, then clapped his hand over his mouth and Bobby couldn't help laughing and then, before she could light up, the funeral director started ushering everyone in, so Bobby stuck the fag in her pocket and went inside to bury her father.

Afterwards a few people came up, the few who knew about her and Les, said how sorry they were, but really she couldn't wait for them all to go. She'd held firm all the way through the service but now she wanted to be alone.

Last to go was Pete. He asked her if she wanted a lift and she said no thanks she'd walk and he said you sure and went off with Mikey Thompson in tow, and she smiled cause any time you saw Mikey you ended up smiling, but then they were all gone and she was left in peace to mourn.

She went round the side of the crem to where the wreaths and flowers were laid out. She looked at the labels – couldn't help but be struck by how none of them seemed to be from anyone really close to Les. You never really noticed it in life because he was always surrounded by people, but now you could see he was a loner at heart. Even when he was making those films he was never really involved; he certainly never took part. She'd read his obituary in the *Post* that morning. Amazing how much she hadn't known about him. She sat down overcome by self-pity for a moment. Truly fatherless now; motherless and childless too. Lord, it wasn't St Clair she was mourning; it was herself.

And then it was gone. She was watching a big black crow fly over the cemetery and she had that song that goes I'm like a bird I want to fly away in her head, but then it passed and instead she felt like the bird was carrying St Clair's soul off and with it the dark part of herself. And she knew these moments are never for ever, that the darkness once touched always returns, but for now as she turned and walked down the hill, the city of Cardiff once more laid out before her, she felt as light as she ever had.

A Note on the Author

John Williams lives and works in his hometown of Cardiff. The author of five previous books, most recently *Cardiff Dead*, he also writes screenplays and journalism.